Jane Lane was born Elaine K Dakers and her first novel was published when she was just seventeen. She adopted the pen-name of Jane Lane to reflect the historical nature of her books, Lane being the maiden name of her grandmother, a descendant of the Herefordshire branch of Lanes who sheltered King Charles II after his defeat at Worcester. A versatile and dynamic author, Jane Lane has written over forty works of fiction, biography, history and children's books.

BY THE SAME AUTHOR
ALL PUBLISHED BY HOUSE OF STRATUS

Bridge of Sighs
A Call of Trumpets
Cat Among the Pigeons
Command Performance
Countess at War
The Crown for a Lie
Dark Conspiracy
Ember in the Ashes
Farewell to the White Cockade
Fortress in the Forth
Heirs of Squire Harry
His Fight Is Ours
The Phoenix and the Laurel
Prelude to Kingship
Queen of the Castle
The Sealed Knot
A Secret Chronicle
The Severed Crown
Sir Devil-May-Care
Sow the Tempest
A State of Mind
A Summer Storm
Thunder on St Paul's Day
A Wind Through the Heather
The Young and Lonely King

JANE LANE

Conies in the Hay

HOUSE OF STRATUS

This edition published in 2001 by House of Stratus, an imprint of Stratus Books Ltd., 21 Beeching Park, Kelly Bray, Cornwall, PL17 8QS, UK.

www.houseofstratus.com

Typeset, printed and bound by House of Stratus.

A catalogue record for this book is available from the British Library and The Library of Congress

ISBN 0-7551-0835-3

To Joyce Dibble
Whose unfailing friendship has meant so much to me

'And as for this Action of *Babington*, it was in truth rather a snare to entrap them, than any device of their owne, sith it was both plotted, furthered, and finished by Sir *Francis Walsingham* and his other Complices, who layd and hatched all the particulars thereof, as they thought it would best fall out to the discredit of Catholiques, and cutting off the *Queene of Scotts*.'

An Humble Supplication to Her Majestie. 1595.

Prologue

England late in the month of October in the year fifteen hundred and eighty-five.

Enclosed within the mellow brick of Greenwich Palace, enshrouded by the damask curtains of her bed, Elizabeth of England lay staring up at the royal beasts embroidered in the tester. The watch-light burning in its silver basin, upon a shelf contrived in the elaborate carving of the bed, shed a flickering radiance, but no longer, as during the past ten days, did that radiance make the lions and leopards stretch their claws at her, and nod and wink and snarl.

She was better. The fever was passed. The dreaded presences which had kept her company had withdrawn: the gross, corrupting mass of flesh which had been her father, the cancer-racked body of her sister Mary, the headless shape of her mother, and that most frightening Presence of them all, a black and bony thing whose name was Death. Her thin lips smiled; her fingers touched the talisman she wore, given her by a woman of a hundred-and-twenty to ensure long life; her narrow eyes stared up at the Crown of England embroidered in gold in the midst of the beasts. Her personal possession, for which she had schemed and plotted and risked her immortal soul, and which she was going to enjoy to the last

So she lay there; not the Gloriana her subjects worshipped, a stiff figure in jewel-encrusted stomacher and monstrous verdingale, scented hands loaded with rings, lips and cheeks encarmined with rouge, red wig combed and frizzed and wired into the latest mode; but an ageing, lonely bitter woman, savouring the triumph of cheating once again the last enemy, the only enemy she feared.

In a room below, Lord Treasurer Burghley played chess with an unfortunate courier whom he had kept up for the purpose all night. With his soft white beard, slightly forked, sunk into his ruff, and his furred gown enwrapping his upright little figure, my lord moved his queen, raised his pale and somewhat furtive eyes, and looked with contempt at his haggard-faced opponent. He's supposed to be the best chess player at Court, my lord reflected, and yet I have won every game since we sat down to play. He lacks that attention to detail, that retentive memory and that foresight, which are as necessary to the chess player as to the statesman.

Complacent, Burghley leaned back in his cushioned elbow-chair, forgot the tired man opposite, stared down at the red queen he had just moved so skilfully, and allowed his thoughts to return to that other red queen whom he had played even more skilfully for nearly thirty years.

He had carved a devious but brilliant career for himself since that day when, as young William Cecil, the son of a nobody who had become suddenly rich on the spoils of the monasteries, he had entered public life. He had observed consistently two favourite precepts of the Italian philosopher, Machiavelli, his guide and mentor: 'Take care always to have some Great Man to your friend', and 'A man's first duty is to himself'. At the outset of his career he had attracted himself to the Great Man of the day, Lord Protector Somerset; he had foreseen the ruin of Somerset in 1552, had deserted him, and entered the service of the rising Great Man, Northumberland. He had been careful to be unwell to avoid being present at the wedding of Northumberland's son with Lady Jane Grey, whom Northumberland was determined to foist upon the realm as a puppet queen; and as soon as he had discovered that the rising for the rightful Successor, the Princess Mary, was formidable, he had made haste to join with those who proclaimed her. Thus had he saved his head in a very awkward situation; but though he had made the most abject personal submission, ostentatiously fingered his beads in public, made generous offerings to the Catholic charities, gone to Mass with the best, no public office had come his way.

But he had been patient. Mary was sickly like the rest of the Tudors, and already middle-aged. She would die anon, and, always looking to the future, he had entered into secret correspondence with her half-sister, the vigorous, scheming Elizabeth who, though she had invited the earth to open and swallow her if she was not a true Catholic, possessed a passionate desire to rule absolutely, both in Church and State, and therefore must rely for support upon the new rich men who had risen on the destruction of the monasteries.

Well, thought Burghley, stroking his venerable beard, his patience had been rewarded, and with the accession of Elizabeth it was he himself who had become the Great Man. And had remained so ever since, despite many a storm, many a crisis. But for several years now he had known that there was one storm which would sink him. If Elizabeth should die without taking advantage of the unprecedented right he had given her, of setting aside the Statutes of the Realm and naming her own Successor, he was doomed, he and his life's work, 'The Device for the Alteration of Religion'. For there was only one lawful Successor, the woman who, indeed, on strictly legitimist grounds, had an incontestably better right to the throne than Elizabeth: Mary, Queen of Scots.

And if Mary Stuart were allowed to succeed, it would not be for Burghley as it had been for him with Mary Tudor. Naturally tolerant though she was, the Queen of Scots could not overlook the fact that it was he who had persuaded Elizabeth to send armed assistance to the rebels against her mother, the Queen Regent, he who had ordered English ships to lie in wait for her when, as the young widow of the King of France, she had sailed to claim her Scottish crown, he who had prevented Elizabeth from honouring her promise to her cousin Mary to assist her against her rebellious nobles, he who had kept her, an independent Sovereign, immured in an English prison for the past seventeen years.

He sighed gently, and his thoughts reverted to the sick woman in the bedchamber above. Whether or not she is better this morning, he thought, I shall have to broach the forbidden subject of the Succession. I shall have the same old abuse; I shall be called as welcome as a death's head; I shall be accused of sounding her knell. And she will remind me, of course, of the Statute of Silence which I myself insisted on making law four years ago; she will even quote it: 'Anyone who shall set forth by express words, deeds, or writings, who shall reign as King or Queen after her Highness' decease, every such offence shall be a felony, and every offender shall suffer the pains of death and forfeiture without benefit of clergy.'

It was a convenient pretence that the Highest One (as he termed her) was immortal and did not need heirs. Convenient to Burghley because it silenced the very large majority in the realm who hoped for a return of the Old Religion under the rightful Successor, Mary of Scots; convenient to the Highest One because of her morbid terror of death. They formed a partnership for mutual advantages, did the Highest One and her Lord Treasurer; only he could keep the Crown securely on her head in this strong Catholic revival which had been running in England since 1580; only she could keep his head upon his shoulders by refusing to name Mary as her Successor. But unfortunately she refused also to name Mary's son, the pliable and Protestant James.

Since I am so indispensable to your New Order, she said in effect, we will keep to the letter of your Statute of Silence, we will play perpetually the game of 'Let's pretend'. The question of the Succession shall be taboo for you as well as for my enemies. I am not called upon to disturb myself about what may happen to your upstart class after I am gone. If, when I go, there is to be a settling of old scores, that is your affair. Thanks to you, I am safe enough for my lease of life, and like me you must live in the present...

"Did I ever tell you the story," said Burghley suddenly, to the wretched courtier who, during the past ten minutes, had been striving to hit upon a way of saving his king, "of the device I used to retrieve my youthful indiscretion of gambling away all my goods, even to my bedding, when I was studying law?"

His haggard-faced opponent twisted his features into an expression of interest, and inwardly groaned. Had he ever told it? A thousand times at least! Light-headed with fatigue, the courtier had the fancy that the venerable head sunk upon the tubular-pleated ruff resembled a picture of John the Baptist's upon a charger.

"I contrived a hole in the wall near my companion's bed that night, and muttered through it ghostly admonitions. 'Oh, mortal man,' I groaned, 'repent of thy horrible sin, play, cosenage, and such-like lewdness, or else thou art damned and cast into Hell.' And in the morning my companion was in a sweat of fear, vowed he would never gamble thereafter, and returned the whole of his winnings."

Burghley did not hear the forced compliments of the courtier. A device, he thought, always in emergencies have I been able to contrive a device. And this is an emergency which calls for the greatest device of all. Before Philip of Spain declares war against us (as inevitably he will), Mary's head must fall. I must try that which never yet has failed; I must insinuate into the mind of the Highest One a fear of her life and her Crown; and with the help of Mr Secretary, I must incriminate the Queen of Scots.

In his rural retreat at Barn Elms, Mr Secretary Walsingham awoke punctually at five o'clock and began his day. He said an extempore prayer (for he was a Calvinist by conviction, though he had to conform to my Lord Burghley's Establishment); he stretched a hand beneath the coverlet to make sure that Dear-love his favourite cat and Knave his spaniel were curled peacefully together there; and then, to the accompaniment of his wife's gentle snores, he collected his thoughts.

For the past fortnight they had been very uncomfortable thoughts, and for these few moments of privacy he gave them full rein. If her Majesty should die! It was not so much his head he feared for as his work. That patient woof woven day by day with such skill over seventeen years (a dangerous work, too, because he could have no warrant save the favour of his Sovereign for many of his actions), to be torn in pieces in a moment – it would be intolerable! And all because the Highest One shrank from the obvious remedy for all their troubles, the putting to death of the Popish Successor, the Queen of Scots.

It could have been done many times during her long imprisonment in England. She could have been sent back to Scotland, where her rebels would have put an end to her – at a price; but the Highest One would not pay that price. Or it could have been done secretly in one or other of her prisons, and everyone would have accepted it as natural death. Mary of Scots had been ailing for years. And then the Successor would have been James, who had been managed from infancy by a rabble of semi-barbaric Scots nobles, and who would be as wax in the hands of civilized English statesmen.

'Everyone would accept it as natural death.' But that, he thought with painful honesty, was not quite true. The Catholics, secret or open, a formidable majority, would not so accept it; neither would the foreign Powers. And moreover, for the saving of her reputation of which she was so tender, the Highest One would repudiate the assassin and his instigators. She had a nasty habit of finding scapegoats if what was done with her secret approval was seen to be unpopular. To her subjects she must remain Gloriana, accorded a worship almost oriental, goddess as well as queen.

Mr Secretary rose, drew aside the bed-curtain, and put on his nightgown. Softly he padded to the window, opened a casement, and began placing on the outside sill the pieces of bread set ready overnight. And here they came for their breakfast, his dear birds; first a sparrow, sober-coated, then the blackbird with the white feather in its wing, then a plump pigeon, slate-grey, with neat white ruff. But Mr Secretary did not think of them by their species. Since the day when, at thirty-eight, he had entered the then Mr Secretary Cecil's service as an agent (some crude persons would have used the term 'spy'), and, having quickly proved his worth, had got the whole of the Secret Service into his capable hands, he had even thought in the language of espionage, referring to everything under names other than their own.

The sparrow, then, was 'Arthur', dear little Arthur Gregory, whose puckish face was always creased into lines of good humour, whose expert hands could unseal and reseal an intercepted letter so skilfully that no one in the world could guess it had been tampered with. The blackbird was Thomas Phelippes, most valuable member of an army of agents. Phelippes, Mr Secretary reflected, would just be going to bed; it was his habit, when he had some important task, such as discovering the key to a secret alphabet or writing in a counterfeit hand, to work all night. And the plump pigeon was no less a person than my Lord Treasurer Burghley.

Walsingham was meticulously faithful to Burghley; he had never forgotten that he had been Burghley's find, and owed his post of Principal Secretary of State to his lordship. He admired his lordship as a master of statecraft; as a man he disapproved of him. For his lordship had no real religion; his Establishment had a political foundation; he was anti-Catholic only because he had risen to power and wealth on the loot of the Old Church, whereas he, Walsingham, was anti-Catholic from sincere conviction.

There was personal and less worthy reason for Walsingham's secret dislike of his chief. Everyone knew (though of course no one, except the Highest when she was in a temper, ever mentioned the fact) that Burghley's grandfather had been an innkeeper; yet my lord insisted on pretending that he was of the old nobility. He had engrafted his pedigree upon the ancient Sitsilts of Herefordshire, taking their coat of arms and having it engraved upon all his possessions. (The Sitsilts, being Catholics, dared not protest.) And he went out of his way to remind Mr Secretary that the latter's forebears had been cordwainers, vintners, and exporters of fish. It was perfectly true, and Mr Secretary was not in the least ashamed of it; though dearly would he have liked the courage to retort that on the occasion of the Field of the Cloth of Gold in King Henry's reign, his own father had represented the County of Kent, whereas Burghley's father had been present in the capacity of a humble page.

The dark brows drew together in a frown, the black-bearded face took on its grimmest expression. For there she was as usual, the female thrush, her little body outlined against the dawn sky as she sat in the topmost twigs of her favourite oak tree, ignoring the feast upon the window sill, oblivious of the kindness and condescension of Mr Secretary, Sir Francis Walsingham, the second most powerful man in England.

Ridiculous to think of this free wild-bird as the close-incarcerated prisoner, Mary of Scots; and yet he did. Identifying the two in his mind, it would have given him satisfaction, fond though he was of creatures, to have got his bow and shot the thrush; but it would have been a sign of weakness. Mary of Scots was not to be brought down simply and swiftly and in the open. She must be hunted craftily, entrapped in a web which he alone was clever enough to weave.

But so far, not clever enough. Oh, for how many years had he tried to ensnare her; how many plots, real and faked, had he used to persuade the Highest One that while Mary lived neither her Crown nor her life could be secure. The plotters and the dupes had paid the price of their treason or their gullibility, but Mary lived on in her prison.

It was not his fault. In the years he had spent abroad during Mary Tudor's reign, he, like Burghley, had read, marked, learned, and inwardly digested the precepts of Machiavelli; he knew, none better, how to thrust at the weakest point in his enemy's armour, to trick him by fair promises, to betray him with false hopes, to catch him unawares. Again and again he had tried to convert the Highest One to the Machiavellian precept that information could not be bought too dear, that the employment of highly paid agents was necessary to the prince who would conquer by his wits and not by his sword. But always he had come up against the Highest One's parsimony.

His agents must work for a pittance, or for paper promises, or like dear little Arthur and good Mr Phelippes, for sheer love of their art. And for the incriminating of Mary of Scots in a plot against her jailer, the Queen of England, Mr Secretary needed an agent who could command a very high price indeed. He needed that rare character, a man high in credit with the Catholics, a good linguist, of sufficient standing to gain the confidence of the royal prisoner, reckless enough to undertake a task for which, naturally, he could not be protected by an official warrant, cunning enough to play his part on all occasions, and with all men.

In short, what Mr Secretary needed for something which might turn out to be the greatest 'practice' of his career, was an *agent provocateur.*

In the apple-loft in the old house called Dethick, remote among the Derbyshire hills, young Anthony Babington gabbled the Paters and Aves of his rosary while waiting for Mass. He was in one of his most emotional moods, wherein real devotion to the Faith mingled indistinguishably with his keen sense of the dramatic.

He could not remember the time when those of his religion had not been ill-treated, but during his boyhood persecution had been mild. The fine of a shilling per month for each member of the household not attending the new Protestant service, one hundred marks for assisting at Mass. And even such fines could be evaded; the old Marian priests would say Mass secretly before reading Morning Prayer in their parish church; Catholics who were locally popular or powerful were left undisturbed; and some of them had even contrived to hold the office of justice of the peace without taking the Oath of Supremacy.

But in 1570, when Anthony was nine, the saintly recluse, Pope Pius V, had pronounced against Queen Elizabeth, who had violated her Coronation Oath, deposed her bishops, and persecuted her Catholic subjects, a sentence of excommunication, thus providing Sir William Cecil (who was about to become Lord Burghley) with the excuse he wanted for stamping out the Old Faith by persecution. Henceforth it was treason to reconcile any of the Queen's subjects to the faith of their fathers, or to be reconciled, to say or assist at Mass, and to harbour priests. The Oath of Supremacy could be tendered to anyone over sixteen years of age, and the penalty for a second refusal of it was death.

Anthony shifted his knees on the rush-strewn floor of the apple-loft. Had he been born in pre-Reformation days, he would have grumbled at the length of a sermon, and during Mass would have had to conceal his impatience to be off on a hawking-match; but persecution had pricked him to devoted loyalty to his religion. Moreover there was very strongly present the element of romance; Mass seemed a different thing when it had to be said in secret, and when each member of the congregation assisted at it at their peril.

He thought of the servants posted in the park and upon the roof, ready to give warning of the approach of strangers, of the recesses contrived behind the panelling, some mere cubby-holes for the concealment of altar vessels and vestments, others large enough to secrete, at a pinch, three men. He remembered the two-day journey from London, from which he had just arrived home, with a young priest fresh from one of the seminaries overseas, riding among his train of servants, rather inexpertly carrying a hawk on his fist, the thin portable altar-stone, the books of devotion and holy medals, conveyed in the lining of the valises strapped to his pack-horses.

The priest, Mr Simpson (an alias, of course), had been nervous. It was his first mission, and though ready enough to face death for his priesthood, he was distressed by the knowledge that those who harboured him could share his fate. But Anthony had laughed away his fears; the penalties were enforced capriciously, he had asserted; in a county like Derbyshire, where the Faith was strong and even the Protestant magistrates sympathetic, Catholics were still left more or less undisturbed, if they were discreet. There was always the danger, of course, of a visit from the professional pursuivants, whose ranks had been swelled by rogues on the look-out for pickings; but twice during the past year there had been a search of Dethick, and not so much as an Agnus Dei had been found.

Often, in his more irresponsible moods, he had imagined the scene which had been enacted in so many other Catholic houses taking place here: the sudden hammering on the outer door, the feet thundering up the stair, the women crying in terror, and he, the young master of Dethick, calming them all by the force of his personality, issuing crisp orders, whisking priest and vestments and altar-vessels into the hiding-holes, refusing to think of his own safety. It was a dramatic scene which he dwelt upon with pleasure, for drama was as the breath of life of this youth...

" '*Sicut-erat-in-principio-et-nunc-et-semper-et-in-saecula-saeculorum-Amen,*' " gabbled Anthony, and found that he had told his beads without a moment's meditation on the Glorious Mysteries. Such distractions were disgraceful, but the hour was so early, and he had been kneeling here for over an hour while the priest heard the confessions of the friends and tenants who had come from a distance.

He heard his wife sigh softly beside him, and turned his head to look at her. So delicately pretty she was, in her old-fashioned gable headdress with the lappets framing her oval face; she knelt with hands clasped loosely on her breast, her eyes closed, the dark lashes lying on her cheeks. Beyond her he could see little Meg, their daughter, face still flushed from sleep, wide eyes gazing at the crucifix and the candles on the old chest which had been turned into an altar. Tenderness overwhelmed him, and his mood changed abruptly.

It was intolerable that women and children should be threatened with destitution, imprisonment, and even death, only for worshipping as their ancestors had worshipped ever since Christianity had come to Britain. Was it not, after all, his duty to take Margaret and little Meg overseas? And immediately he was off in another dream of his, of a life of study and security somewhere in France or Spain, indulging his own passion for travel and for reading, yet nobly, at the price of voluntary exile, safeguarding his wife and child, until such time as it pleased God to remove the bastard tyrant who sat upon the Throne of England, and Mary of Scots, Queen of a United Kingdom, restored the Faith.

Mary of Scots, the hope of persecuted Catholics, the woman of legendary beauty, the wronged and betrayed princess. And he, Anthony Babington, had seen her, even had had a smile from her. It was when she had been in my Lord Shrewsbury's keeping at Sheffield, and he was finishing his education by learning courtly manners as my lord's page. The two households, the royal prisoner's and her jailer's, were entirely separate, but often the boy Anthony had had glimpses of her as she rode out to take the air, to distribute alms to the poor, to hawk or hunt.

Once he had been sent with some trifling message to her steward, and had been taken into an apartment hung with faded blue velvet embroidered with *fleurs-de-lis*. His quick eyes had registered impressions, the cage of turtle-doves at the window, the gentlewoman reading from the Book of Hours, the little dog which fell a-barking at him, a whiff of French perfume, the chair of estate with its canopy, surmounted by a royal crown. And then he had fallen on his knee, dropping his glance before that of the lady who lay upon a couch before the fire; but not before he had seen her smile at him, a smile so heavenly that it had made him understand for the first time what men meant when they spoke of her beauty.

From that day onwards there had grown up in Anthony Babington the most vivid and the most precious dream in all his world of make-believe. He would rescue the Queen of Scots from her prison. The details varied, but one essential remained fixed: his own figure kneeling to receive her enraptured thanks when his courage and his quick wits had sprung the trap...

The shuffling of the close-packed congregation, which overflowed on to the stairs, brought him back to the present, and he saw emerging from behind the screens which served as sacristy the young priest he was harbouring at risk of his life. The red vestments gleamed in the candlelight like blood; he had forgotten that it was the feast of a martyr.

Part One

Chapter One

On a morning early in the December of that same year, a man stood watching a gallease approach the little port of Rye. Through his spy-glass he observer her drop anchor; then, as a boat was lowered from her side, he stuck his glass under his arm and went purposefully down to the quay. His name was Richard Daniel; he was a searcher in the employ of the Government; and he had his orders concerning the solitary passenger who was being rowed ashore.

A mere boy this passenger appeared, beardless, slim, flaxen of hair, with a pair of wide-open candid grey eyes. He burst into almost tearful protests when Mr Daniel informed him that he must accompany the latter to my Lord Cobham, Warden of the Cinque Ports; he was a Frenchman, cried the youth (speaking in that tongue); his name was Pietro; he was come to England on his lawful concerns; his papers were all in order.

But once they were in the coach which Mr Daniel had waiting, Monsieur Pietro appeared to reconcile himself to his arrest. He drew from his pouch a comfit-box, popped a sugared violet into his mouth, snuggled into his furred surcoat, and hummed a little tune.

Mr Daniel for his part cast a surreptitious glance or two at his captive but said nothing. In such cases, he had learned, it was always safest to keep one's speculations to oneself. He was paid for making these arrests, and this one was going to be unusually profitable. For his orders were to take this Pietro up to London and deliver him safely into the hands of Mr Secretary Walsingham after a formal call upon Lord Cobham. He would be able to present quite a large expense account, and with any luck would see the sights of London before returning to Rye tomorrow.

Mr Secretary sat in his office in his town house in Cheapside, busy as usual, despite the fact that he had a boil on the back of his neck and his starched ruff tortured him. The roar of London intruded through the closed casements, the ring of hammers from a workshop, the bawling of 'prentices at their masters' doors, the rumble of drays, the hollow ring of hooves, raucous laughter from a group about a side show, the undercurrent of footsteps, and a voice intoning, '*Sweep* chimney *sweep*, mistress! With a hey derry sweep from the bottom to the top! *Sweep* chimney *sweep*!'

He loved that cacophony; he loved this plain merchant's house of his; he loved the view from his window of Cheap Cross, with the statues of saints and apostles hacked down, and, rather strangely, a figure of the goddess Diana crowning it. (He was not sure that he approved of Diana, but at least she was better than the Virgin Mary, whom she had replaced.) Here, he was at the heart of things, snug as a spider in its web, listening to the hum of foolish insects, selecting those whom he wished to entice into its silken threads.

But his complacency vanished when one of his clerks announced that Mr Topcliffe had called, and begged the honour of a few words with him.

"Take the dogs into the next room and shut them up," said Mr Secretary shortly.

Curious, he thought for the hundredth time, how his dogs hated Topcliffe; it was as though they could smell that horrible dungeon under the White Tower where the man performed his grisly work. He himself shared his dogs' distaste, but while they, if left in the room, would have flown at the man's throat, their master must humour him, amicably confer with him, conceal the shuddering revulsion with which he received his reports. In the elaborate system which Walsingham controlled, Topcliffe was as necessary as Bull the hangman; but fortunately Mr Secretary did not have to receive Bull into his presence.

He was a very brisk, very spruce gentleman who now entered the room, lifted his hat with its high stuffed crown, replaced it on his head and took the seat indicated. From his dress and manner no one would have guessed his trade; he affected the airs of the courtier; he wore rich stuffs, for he had made a nice little fortune in recent years; his bright red lips smiled perpetually between well-brushed moustaches and dagger-pointed beard. Does he jest, wondered Mr Secretary, when he fits on the Iron Glove or wrenches out teeth with the Brakes? Is that hatefully merry laugh of his the last sound some wretches hear before they faint upon the rack, the first when, bathed in sweat, they are revived for more torture? Mr Secretary mentally shook himself; the man was the greatest rack-master in Europe, and torture was necessary to the safety of Her Majesty and religion.

"At last I can report success in the case of Simpson, the priest," began Topcliffe happily, crossing one shapely leg in a carnation-coloured nether-stock over the other. "Upon my soul, sir, I have seldom had a harder subject. From his manner when the pursuivants took him at Derby you would have sworn that the mere sight of my instruments would have loosened his tongue. But no. I tried the Duke of Exeter's Daughter, I tried the Scavenger's Daughter, I tried the Prickers; and all we got out of him was an admission of his priesthood. Upon the other matter he would say not a word."

Walsingham understood what that 'other matter' was: a list of Mr Simpson's penitents. For among these there might be some as yet undiscovered Catholics who had contrived to avoid paying the twenty pounds a month per head (thirteen months being reckoned to a year) which was now the fine for recusancy.

"Then I did bethink me of a trick I have known to work before," went on Topcliffe, with the enthusiasm of the craftsman. "Oh, a very simple one, you will say; even those ignorant of my art might stumble on the fact that a man who will endure great pangs may succumb to a lesser one. But it is the precise moment when to catch him in that trap, Mr Secretary; you must watch him like a hawk; you must have made yourself thoroughly acquainted with his temperament; you must spend tedious hours at the peep-hole into his cell, and survey him when he is private; and then – "

The hateful laugh jangled Mr Secretary's nerves.

"It was my little Pilliwinks which broke Master Simpson, my simple little Pilliwinks," said Topcliffe roguishly. "One turn of those upon his fingers, and we had the whole story from him. A tiresome young man was Master Simpson," added the rack-master, cocking one foot, and regarding with complacence the coloured lining pulled through the slashes, "but doubtless his fellow Papists will hail him as a martyr."

"*Was* Mr Simpson?" repeated Walsingham sharply.

"Hanged himself in his chamber this morning," replied Topcliffe; and closed one bright eye in a wink.

Again Mr Secretary understood him. It was the custom to give out that those who died under torture had committed suicide; it sounded so much better in the official record, besides attributing a guilty conscience to the victim.

A few minutes later he was absorbed in studying the list of Simpson's penitents which Topcliffe, ere taking his departure, had laid before him. The priest, it seemed, had confined his activities to Derbyshire during the brief time between his coming to England from some foreign seminary (and how in the world, irritably wondered Walsingham, did so many contrive to get past the searchers at the ports?) and his arrest; and that was interesting, because Derbyshire was known to be a hot-bed of Papistry, it contained some wealthy gentlemen, and its remoteness and inaccessibility made the work of the priest-hunters difficult.

Moreover it was one of those counties where the magistrates were still appointed from among the old families, and many of these magistrates, though they went to church, were lamentably lacking in public spirit when it came to informing against their kinsfolk and friends. It had been explained to Mr Secretary by one of the Queen's favourites, the dandified Mr Vice-Chamberlain Hatton, that this was natural enough; when you hawk and hunt and dine with a man you have known all your life, or whose kinswoman you may have married, you are reluctant to prosecute him only because you do not see him at church on Sundays. But to Mr Secretary it was not natural enough; he did not come from that sort of family; and he knew, none better, that Catholicism, still the popular cause, was a menace to this brave new England.

The stubby, capable forefinger came to rest presently upon a name: Anthony Babington. Now why did that name mean something special to him? He went to his book-shelves, and from among the neat files, the records of strangers and denizens, the books of maps with the shires divided into hundreds, he took one from a score of volumes which contained lists of recusants with blank pages left for comments. Returning to his desk he opened the file, found the place he wanted, and read carefully the brief facts noted there:

'Anthony Babington, esquire. Born 1561. Inherited estates on death of father 1571. Mother a grand-daughter of that Lord D'Arcy who perished for Catholic religion in the Pilgrimage of Grace. Educated at home, and for a short while page to my Lord Shrewsbury at Sheffield during time Queen of Scots in my lord's keeping. Married at eighteen Margaret, daughter and heiress of Philip Draycot, esquire, of Paynsley, Staffordshire. In year of marriage made a six months' tour of France. On returning to England entered a common pensioner of Lincoln's Inn, with a house in Barbican and lodgings in Hern's Rents, Holborn. Between 1580 and 1583 – ' (ah, this was it!) – 'suspected of smuggling packets of letters to Queen of Scots, but certainly discontinued this service when Sir Amias Paulet became her keeper. Open recusant; pays his fines; Dethick, his country seat, raided twice during past year, but nothing found.'

That was all, but Mr Secretary found it interesting. He sat for a long while apparently idle, actually turning over in his mind the possibility of using Anthony Babington, esquire, in connection with a 'practice' which, since the Highest One's illness last October, and her continued refusal to enter into any discussion regarding her Successor, had been taking shape in that most acute brain of his.

"Signor Cornedin," announced the clerk a few hours later, ushering into Mr Secretary's office the identical slim young man with the wide-open, innocent, grey eyes who, as

Monsieur Pietro, had been arrested by the searcher at Rye the day before.

The slim young man jabbered in fluent Italian until the door was shut behind the clerk; then, bowing with just a touch of insolence, he said in perfect English:

"Gilbert Gifford, at your Honour's service, come from France in obedience to your Honour's command."

Without offering his visitor a seat, Mr Secretary regarded him for some moments with a frown. He must be in his middle twenties, thought Walsingham, yet he looks no more than eighteen. He had a slight air of effeminacy, a feline elegance, a most artless manner, almost naïve.

" 'Gilbert Gifford,' " said Mr Secretary, quoting by heart from another of his files. " 'Son of John Gifford, at present in the Clink for his recusancy, of Chillington in the county of Staffordshire. Educated abroad, contrary to the laws of this realm, and in April, 1579, entered as a student in the English College at Rome. Failed to comply with the Statutes of 1584, whereby all English priests and students overseas were commanded, under pain of treason, to return home within six months, recant, and take the Oath of Supremacy.' "

He paused to let the lesson sink home. His shrewd eyes had noted that faint suggestion of insolence, and it was as well to let the young man know from the outset who held the whip hand.

"You were approached by an agent of mine, Solomon Aldred, tailor of the said College, as a possible candidate for my service. But shortly afterwards, for certain moral crimes, you were dismissed the College, and for near upon three years you led a vagabond life roaming over Europe – "

"But making such useful contacts here and there," murmured Gilbert, with an ingenuous smile.

"In March, 1583," went on Walsingham, frowning at the interruption, "you appeared at the College at Rheims, in rags, without money, professing great repentance for your sins, and a desire to renew your studies for the priesthood. Dr Allen, the President, admitted you, and there you remained till October last when, upon receipt of a message from me, you left the College to perform a certain task. You see, Mr Gifford," concluded Walsingham, bending his grim, black-bearded face towards the other, "I know all about you, so pray do not waste my time with untruths."

"I am too well acquainted with Mr Secretary's all-seeing eye to attempt it," said the youth, tossing back his flaxen hair in a curiously girlish gesture. "Yet I can lie well enough at my masters' bidding, else would not your Honour have enlisted me in your service."

Yes, I believe you can, thought Walsingham, beginning to change his mind about his visitor. At first sight he had been disappointing, but really such artlessness of manner, such a youthful, delicate air, combined with Gilbert's background, might prove invaluable. He was the son of a recusant in prison for his faith; he had a cousin who was a priest; his family had never wavered, and were of ancient stock. So long as his peccadilloes abroad could be concealed, his credit with the English Catholics would remain high, and his credit with someone else, the all-important someone else, might be established.

"Well, sir," said Walsingham, undoing his ruff-strings, taking off the torturing accessory, and exposing a neck with a vivid red line about it as though he had been recently executed and his head stuck on again, "and now let me hear from you."

Gilbert sat up straight, and with downcast eyes, like a good little boy repeating his lesson, he began:

"Since I received your Honour's message last October, I have employed my time in cultivating the acquaintance of the Queen of Scot's agents in Paris, sitting at the feet of the Archbishop of Glasgow when he lectured me upon theology, playing endless games of primero with Charles Paget, and earnestly discussing politics with Thomas Morgan. (It was simple enough to gain access to the latter, by the way, for though the French King, wishing to stand well with Queen Elizabeth, has put him into the Bastille, he holds a sort of court there, and is treated more as guest than as prisoner.)"

"What opinion did you form of Morgan?"

"Very Welsh, rash, pugnacious, indiscreet, and quarrelsome. The control given him by the Queen of Scots over her French income has been a fruitful source of discord among the Scots and English Catholics abroad, for he distributes pensions or withholds them as he pleases."

Walsingham nodded, watching the young man closely. His sharp eyes had marked the change in Gilbert directly that young man had come down to business; there was no ingenuousness now.

"I presented myself to Morgan, who already knew my name. I said I had heard it whispered that in times past he had accomplished, by his skill and courage, the seemingly impossible, namely the finding of a secret way of communicating with the Queen of Scots. I laid the flattery on thick, for I judged my man. He opened his heart to me. It was true, he said that when she was in my Lord Shrewsbury's keeping, and afterwards in that of Sir Ralph Sadler, he had contrived it, but alack, now that the Puritan Sir Amias Paulet had charge of her, it was impossible, so strict he is."

Gilbert paused, smoothed the flaxen hair which he wore a little longer than was the fashion, smiled, and continued:

"I told him that was why I had come to him. For my family seat being no great distance from Chartley, whither, so I had heard, the Queen of Scots was shortly to be moved, surely I could hit upon some means to smuggle letters in and out. He almost wept for joy. She must be starved for news, he cried, and for contact with her kinsfolk and her friends. But I can do nothing, said I, without a letter from you recommending me to her Majesty of Scots, for otherwise she will not trust me. He wrote it on the spot," concluded Gilbert, "and here it is."

Walsingham took the slim packet, glanced at the blank outside, and said briskly:

"She is not the only whose confidence you must gain. The clearing-house for her letters to and from England, during the time when she was not so closely warded, was the French Embassy here in London. They were taken to and fro across the Channel in the diplomatic bags, which could not be searched, and by various means the Ambassador contrived to convey them to their destination. He must have many lying there now, lacking the means to forward them to her. It is necessary for the 'practice' I have in mind that you convince the Ambassador that henceforth you can be that means."

Gilbert reached again into the full German breeches he wore, and from among the horsehair and the rags which formed their stuffing, pulled out another packet.

"I guessed," said he modestly, "that some such thing would be required, and therefore did I obtain from all three of the Queen of Scots' agents in Paris letters recommending me to the Ambassador as one who might safely be employed in the Queen of Scots' service."

Mr Secretary did not often praise his agents; he did so now.

"You have done excellently, excellently, Mr Gifford; I begin to have great hopes of you."

He rang a silver hand-bell on his table, and when a clerk appeared bade him send hither Mr Gregory. In a few moments a little puck of a man, with a face lined as a peach-stone, and long, pointed ears, entered the room, soft-footed, smiling. He did not need to be told what to do with the packets handed to him by his master; Mr Secretary kept Arthur (as he always affectionately called him) specially for his skill in unsealing and resealing letters.

Arthur took the packets, and without a word bore them away, like a dog with choice bones, to his own little sanctum. It was his one idiosyncrasy that he would never let anyone, not even his master, into the secret of his art; no one in the world knew what those clever fingers did behind the always locked door. Walsingham humoured the quirk, though sometimes it worried him to think that if anything were to happen to Arthur his secret would die with him.

Cleopatra, the gross sandy cat, which lay about all day in Mr Secretary's office, rose from before the fire, delicately stretched herself, and leapt on to Gilbert's knee. Her master regarded her with astonishment as, settling herself with her paws tucked under her chest, she began to purr. He had never known her behave so before, for she was indifferent to humankind; and foolish though he knew it was, the honour she had accorded Gilbert Gifford completed her master's approval of the youth.

Then he frowned. Only last week he had taken the liberty of informing the Highest One that he believed he was on the track of a really effective *agent provocateur*, and that such a man could demand a high salary. He had waxed eloquent; money so spent, he had urged, might save the fitting out of fleets and armies; it was a true saying that 'That pound is well laid out that saveth the spending of many pounds'. The Highest One had told him tartly that those who had the honour of working for herself should work for love; and having no great liking for Mr Secretary (whose Puritanism she suspected and detested), she had added for good measure one of her more outrageous witticisms.

"You are aware, of course, of the dangers of the task you undertake, Mr Gifford," said Walsingham shortly. "No official warrant can cover your consorting with the Queen's enemies. And as for reward, why, you will have your expenses, and for the rest you must rely upon her Majesty's generosity."

To his infinite relief the youth smiled at him; though, when he came to think of it, it was not a very pleasant smile.

"I shall enjoy my work, your Honour," said he softly, looking at Walsingham from under his long lashes. "It will prove its own reward."

When Gilbert had gone, with instructions to take the two packets, unsealed by Arthur, for decipherment and copying by Mr Phelippes at the latter's house in Leadenhall Street, Mr Secretary permitted a few moments of self-congratulation.

He was almost certain that he had found a first-class *agent provocateur*, and one, moreover, who did not demand high pay. He had marked the effeminate manner, the hidden spite when Gilbert had spoken of the squabbles among his fellow Catholics abroad, the malice which lay beneath the ingenuous surface; and he knew the nature of those moral crimes for which Gilbert had been dismissed from the English College at Rome. He had had no difficulty in interpreting that soft remark 'I shall enjoy my work' as 'I shall enjoy indulging some private grudges'.

Mr Secretary had forgotten all about his boil as he took up his quill again. The Queen of Scots made desperate by her isolation; the perfect *agent provocateur* engaged; the time was ripe for the inauguration of that 'practice' which should put an end to all their troubles.

Chapter Two

It was on Christmas Eve that the Queen of Scots was moved from Tutbury to her new prison of Chartley, an ancient moated house belonging to the Earl of Essex, close to the Derbyshire border.

Having given her keeper, Sir Amias Paulet, a week to settle in, Walsingham sent thither his most trusted henchman, Thomas Phelippes, who, on a January afternoon of the new year, 1586, came riding up to the gatehouse beyond the moat, was challenged by the men-at-arms on duty, was made to wait a full ten minutes while a senior officer was fetched, was examined closely by this officer, was escorted across the drawbridge, was forced to wait again, was re-examined by a still more senior officer, and at long last was convoyed by two soldiers to the side of the house occupied by Sir Amias and his staff.

Phelippes bore these delays with admirable patience. His calling had made him a patient man; and besides he admired the elaborate precautions taken by Paulet for the keeping of the Woman (so Phelippes always thought and spoke of the Queen of Scots) a close prisoner.

He found Sir Amias in a large room, unceiled, with draughts blowing down from the bare rafters and making the fire smoke and the arras billow out from the stone walls. There were filthy rushes on the floor, a stand of pikes leaning against the mullion of the window, and the portrait of a gentleman, in the dress of twenty years ago, hanging in a dark corner as though in disgrace; as indeed he was. He had been Sir Amias Paulet's father-in-law, and had persisted in his Catholicism until his death in 1564.

Sir Amias himself sat upon a joint-stool before a table strewn untidily with papers, an immensely tall, spare man in his fifties, with a grim, lined face, suspicious eyes, grizzled hair which he cut very short, and whiskers so coarse that they rasped when he scratched them. He wore always a steel corselet and cap, and thigh boots with spurs, as though at any moment he was about to take horse. His linen was dirty, his manner rough, his mind slow-moving and not a little stupid.

Mr Phelippes, his visitor, was a very different person. He was no more than thirty, though he looked older; he was slender and short; his hair was a dark yellow and his beard almost flaxen; his cheeks and forehead were deeply pitted with the smallpox; his eyes peered myopically through steel-rimmed spectacles. Within certain limits he was immensely intelligent, had a flair for grasping a situation however complex, the indefatigable energy of a man really in love with his work, and so great a skill as a cryptographer and as a master of 'counterfeit writing' (the polite term for forgery) that from 1576 to '79, when Paulet had been Ambassador to France, Mr Phelippes had been lent to him by his master, Walsingham, though Mr Secretary could ill spare his services at home.

The two men had found a bond which had linked them in friendship. Unlike a majority of their co-religionists in England, they were not political Protestants, swimming with the tide; neither had the least sentimental hankering after the old forms of worship, the old unity of Christendom. On the contrary, they shared a burning hatred of Catholicism, and a sincere conviction that the one true faith had been discovered in their own day.

They really believed that the Pope was Antichrist, that all Papists (the contemptuous new term) were damned, that Rome was the Whore of Babylon. Intelligent though he was, Phelippes accepted without question the most sensational ale-house stories of Jesuits carrying poisoned daggers under their gowns, of men being canonized for attempting to assassinate the Highest One, of troops of armed monks being drilled for the invasion of England. It was this unadulterated hatred of the Old Religion which made Phelippes formidable as an agent of the Government; and it was this hatred of her religion, which made him so bitter against the Queen of Scots, with whom he had had no personal contact whatsoever.

Sir Amias, on the other hand, had a more personal antagonism towards her. It had been a surprise to everyone, including himself, when he had been appointed the Queen of Scots' new jailer, for he was a Somerset man and his appointment would be sure to create jealousy among the northern magnates. What he had not been told was that he owed his appointment to Mr Secretary. As far-sighted as Burghley, Walsingham had had in his mind for a long time the rough outlines of the 'practice' he was now inaugurating for the destruction of the Queen of Scots, and it was essential for its success that she should be starved of news and kept in the strictest confinement. He had guessed rightly that this grim Puritan, Sir Amias Paulet, was the very man for the job.

"Lord bless me, I believe this house will be my death, sir," groaned Sir Amias, when compliments had been exchanged between the two old friends on this January afternoon. "The naughty airs arising from the moat and the unhealthy situation torture my gout. But I must endure it as long as the Lord and her Majesty require it of me, though for her Majesty's sake, sir, I trust it will not be for long. The expense, sir, the vast expense of this Queen's household! Look at these accounts."

He waved his hand towards the papers on the table.

"Five gentlemen, fourteen servitors, three cooks, four boys, three gentlemen's gentlemen, six gentlewomen, two wives, ten wenches and children. The two secretaries and the steward and the physician must have a mess of eight dishes, and the gentlewomen and the children two messes of no less than nine. My own table is furnished with plenty of good meat (the Lord and her Majesty be thanked), but without fiddle-faddles of spices and kickshaws such as this Queen's table must have, not to speak of Popish fast days when there must be fish provided."

"Who is this 'Sir John' who must have a mess to himself?" asked Phelippes, peering short-sightedly at an item.

Paulet laughed darkly.

"Aha, you may well ask, sir, you may well ask who is this Sir John. Thus did I nickname him when first I was appointed this Queen's keeper, being unable to pronounce his heathenish foreign name, and he giving himself such airs, wearing a court-like suit, with a brooch in his hat and silver buttons on his doublet. This Queen's reader, he called himself; but I can smell out a massing-priest, let him dress how he will. And sure enough did I discover that the Scottish secretary, Curle, and the gentlewoman, Mowbray, who, having refused my offer of a minister to wed them, I supposed to be living in sin, had been wed by this Sir John. I was shocked, sir, I was very deeply shocked," concluded Sir Amias solemnly.

Phelippes made a sympathetic murmur.

"In my simple opinion," continued the knight, "he should be dismissed, and I have written several times to my Lord Burghley to the purpose. And then," he went on, well launched upon his grievances, "this Queen applied to me but the last week (you will scarce credit it, sir) that she might send for woollen and linen cloth to prepare her Maundy. Ever since she was a prisoner, said she, she had been permitted to distribute this charity to the poor of the neighbourhood where she was. Not while you are in my charge, madam, said I. She was pleased to be sharp with me, reminding me that she was a queen. So likewise was Jezebel, madam, said I; and since Papists are not permitted to read the Scriptures, I recounted to her the story of that harlot."

It being Sir Amias' favourite Bible story, he could not resist the temptation to recount it all over again to his friend.

"Then must she have her humours and her sicknesses; she cannot eat her meat like an honest woman (and at that I do not wonder, for an honest woman she is not); and she must keep to her bed for weeks together with the rheumatics. In my simple opinion it is the mighty hand of God which has struck you with these pains, madam, said I, and I took leave to remind her of her sins. But so hard is her heart that she would not hear me. If you would but let me take the air a little, says she, as I was used to do. Ay, and have half the traitors in the neighbourhood flocking to kiss your hand, says I. Open your window, madam, if you would have air."

Paulet glanced at his friend to make sure that he appreciated the wittiness of this remark, opening his own mouth to expose large square yellow teeth like a horse's.

"I am very precise and painful to have warrant for all I do, sir," he went on, becoming solemn again. "Look you here, these are the orders I received from Mr Secretary when first I was appointed this Queen's keeper: 'You shall order that she shall not, as heretofore, ride abroad for hawking or other pastime, for that, under colour of giving of alms, she hath seduced the hearts of the people that dwell about those places where she hath lain.' She has begged me, even with tears, that 'Sir John' may be permitted to distribute her alms if she cannot do it in person, but the laws of this realm, I told her, have provided so carefully for the relief of the poor that none can want, save by their own lewdness, and therefore, madam, they have no need of your charity."

"You have done admirably, my dear friend," said Mr Phelippes. "And now I must make known to you the reason for my visit – "

But Paulet had not quite finished yet.

"I would have you report to Mr Secretary how closely I have confined her now we are come to Chartley. I have forbidden Sharp, her coachman, to exercise his horses without my men-at-arms accompany him; none of her people may take the air upon the walls; there are sentinels stationed beneath every window on her side of the house, and no provision of any kind is conveyed thither without I have well searched it. And I have, as she is pleased to complain, overcrowded her apartments by bringing the very laundry-maids into the house who, at Tutbury, were lodged in the village. It is impossible, sir," concluded Sir Amias triumphantly, "for any friend of hers to convey to her a piece of paper as big as my finger."

"Yet now is the time come when papers must be conveyed to her," said Phelippes softly, "and that is the reason for my visit."

There was a silence, during which Sir Amias sat goggling at his friend, his mouth fallen open, an expression of blank bewilderment on his face. At last he repeated stupidly:

"Papers must be conveyed?"

"It is Mr Secretary's desire that a channel of communication be opened between the Woman and her friends – "

"After all my precautions, all my painful arrangements to prevent it – "

" – which she shall believe to be secret, but which in fact will be controlled by Mr Secretary himself."

Mr Phelippes waited for a few moments for his friend's slow mind to grasp the idea. He waited in vain. Realizing this he began a little dissertation.

"My dear Sir Amias, permit me to remind you of the situation generally. For the past few years Spain has been becoming more and more the accepted champion of the Old Religion, and our country the champion of the New. A clash, therefore, must come, hastened, I am afraid, by the rather unfortunate – er – attacks made by some of our adventurers upon Spanish treasure ships."

It was a delicate subject. Burghley was known to be opposed to the provocation given to Spain by men like Drake and Hawkins, but was unable to prevent it because the Highest One Herself was doing very well out of their piracies, and indeed had lent them one of her ships, the *Jesus*, for their slave-trade.

"Because of his difficulties in the Low Countries, and the ancient jealousy of France, Philip will continue to do his best to avoid open war with us. But if he does decide to invade, the release of the Woman will be placed first upon his programme, whereby he will hope to gain the support of the English Papists. Therefore, while the Woman lives she is a link between her Majesty's enemies at home and abroad; and therefore," he added softly, "she must be allowed to live no longer."

According to his lights, Paulet was an honest and an honourable man, and at that last sentence he jibbed like a horse. For it had been suggested to him more than once, since he had become the Queen of Scots' keeper, that he should rescue her Majesty and her government from their dilemma by poisoning his prisoner's food. But Phelippes, realizing what was in his mind, hastened to reassure him.

"Don't mistake me, my dear friend," said he soothingly. "What is aimed at is judicial execution."

"Her Majesty would never permit it," said Paulet with regret. "That a crowned sovereign be brought to the block – it is without precedent! Moreover, as her Majesty rightly fears, it might well encourage the Papists to lift violent hands against herself – "

"Her Majesty would permit it if the Woman were incriminated in a treasonable plot against the realm."

Paulet licked his lips. His slow brain was moving at last.

"Why," he mused, "there is the Band of Association of '84 might give you what you desire. Did it not authorize all who joined it to pursue to the death every such wicked person who encouraged or consented to rebellion at home or invasion from abroad? And, moreover, did it not lay down that 'every such person by or for whom any such act shall be executed, being anywise consenting or privy to the same, shall be judged partaker of the treason'? Privity is enough, sir; if there is a plot, and this Queen but knows of it – "

He broke off, and a great light seemed to dawn on him. He slapped his thigh, making his spurs ring, and cried:

"I see now what you would be at! Mr Secretary desires to let this Queen communicate with her friends in the hope that one or other of them will confide in her a plot against the realm."

Mr Phelippes smiled in approval.

"Just so. But alack, my dear friend, it is not quite as simple as you imagine. For one thing, for practical purposes privity would not be sufficient. To take the life of an independent sovereign only because she was made privy to a plot against a sister queen who has been detaining her against her will, would set the Papists, both at home and abroad, by the ears. And for another, there has been of late a lull in the Papists' plotting at home; Mr Secretary has his agents everywhere, as you know; yet he can hear of no conspiracy worthy of notice. And I need not remind you that the Woman, being exceedingly cunning, would be shy of conniving with anyone save those thoroughly vouched for by her agents, in high credit with the Catholics, of good social standing, and with a practical scheme to suggest."

He sighed. Heaven knew the Catholics had been given provocation enough in recent years, ruined by fines, imprisoned, tortured, hanged. It was really too bad of them not to plot just at the moment when their plotting was required by the Government.

"But with the blessing of God," added Phelippes devoutly, "a suitable plotter or plotters will appear; and in the meantime we must set the trap for the Woman."

A bell, harsh and severe, interrupted the conversation. Paulet rose at once; it was the hour for changing the guard, he said, and it was his invariable custom to preside over the ceremony.

After supper, when the conserves and muscadine had been set out in Sir Amias' chamber, the two men resumed their talk; and it was now for the first time that Phelippes mentioned the name of Gilbert Gifford. He was, said Phelippes, to be a key-man in Mr Secretary's great 'practice'; he had lived in Phelippes' own house in Leadenhall Street since his arrival in England; his fidelity had been tested in various ways devised by Mr Secretary; and already he had been set to work.

"After I had deciphered and copied the letters of recommendation brought over by Mr Gifford from the Woman's agents in France," said Phelippes, "and Arthur had resealed them, they were taken by Mr Gifford to the French Embassy, where he obtained an interview with

Cordaillot, the Ambassador's secretary. Cordaillot was wary and somewhat cold when Mr Gifford told him he believed he might be able to convey correspondence between the Woman and her friends; but we must be patient. Once the Woman accepts him, the Ambassador will do so likewise."

"And think you she will?" growled Paulet. "She has the cunning of a vixen, and is not easily to be hoodwinked."

"I think she will after we have contrived to convey to her the letter of warm recommendation Mr Gifford brought from her agent, Morgan, in whom she has implicit trust."

Phelippes drew from the old-fashioned cod-piece he wore his own decipherment of this letter.

"There is a long description of Mr Gifford's family, their sufferings for their religion and so forth, Mr Gifford's education beyond seas, and his studying for the priesthood. Then Morgan goes on as follows:

'Knowing the honesty and faith of this gentleman, and considering his habitation and credit in his county, and as far as I can conceive, your Majesty's intelligence discontinued, I thought it my duty to deal with the said Gilbert to practise with his kinsfolk and friends for the furtherance of your Majesty's service. This he promised to put into execution with care, and required my letters to your Majesty, thereby to give him credit, and a means to enter into intelligence with you. For this purpose I gave him these few lines, assuring myself of his faith and honesty, and as such I heartily recommend him to your Majesty's favour.' "

Paulet merely grunted. He was back upon his former grievance.

"After all my precautions against the conveying of letters to this Queen, after all my pains, now must my work be undone. It is hard, Mr Phelippes, it is hard."

"My dear friend," said Phelippes earnestly, "had you not kept her fasting as you have done, had you not so closely confined her, she would not leap, as now I hope she will do, at the chance of communication offered her. But how to contrive it so that she will be convinced that it is the work of some skilful and daring friend, while we on our side may be sure of scrutinizing every paper which passes – that is the question."

"Ay, and that you must unriddle for yourself," said Paulet in sombre triumph. "And with my precautions (which cannot be laid aside, or she will suspect somewhat), I'll warrant you'll find it hard."

The room was hot, the night was mild, and going to the window, Phelippes opened one of the horn-paned casements and stood looking out into the courtyard.

Lights burned sparsely here and there in the old house, a tribute to Paulet's respect for his mistress' parsimony; the only sounds which broke the silence were the tramp of a sentry's feet, the clink of his mail as he turned, and rough voices from a guardhouse. For how many years, thought Phelippes gloatingly, has the Woman listened to such sounds, reminding her that she is a captive. He dwelt upon the image of her he carried in his mind, growing older, losing her beauty and her health, seeing no visitors, receiving no letters, her rheumatism increased by lack of exercise, draughty prisons, and now the foul airs from this moat. If it were not that she constituted such a danger to the realm, he reflected, such close imprisonment would be a fitter punishment than death for this vivacious creature, with her passion for dancing and hunting, her strong affections for family and friends, her active, intelligent mind...

He raised his head sharply as he heard, from the direction of the gatehouse, a sentry's voice challenging, clear in the silence of the night. There followed a confusion of sounds in which he thought he could distinguish the rattle of bolts, the creaking of a chain, and a heavy thump as the drawbridge, always raised at sunset, was lowered. Another challenge, nearer this time, and then, to his astonishment, the rumble of iron-shod wheels over paving-stones and the clump of horses' hooves.

"What visitor comes to Chartley at this hour?" he exclaimed.

"Eh?" said Paulet, who had been dozing in front of the fire. His hand went instinctively to his sword-hilt, he made to rise, uttered a most unpuritanical oath as his gout caught him, and sank back again. "The brewer from Burton. It is his day for delivering the beer for our two households."

"From Burton? Why, that must be twenty miles distant."

"It is eighteen," said Sir Amias shortly. All unwittingly, Phelippes had reminded his friend of another grievance. "I represented to her Majesty, when first Chartley was suggested as this Queen's new prison, that there was no brewhouse within it great enough to supply our needs, and furthermore that there was no public brewery within the whole county. But her Majesty made no reply, doubtless having greater matters to trouble her, and therefore have I been constrained to buy my beer from the same brewer of Burton who supplied us at Tutbury. It is a most troublesome arrangement," grumbled the knight, "for when the roads are foul we know not when to expect our drink, the men-at-arms grow surly for lack of ale, and – "

"What kind of man is this brewer?" interrupted his friend, with a sort of soft alertness.

Paulet stared at him in affront.

"What kind of a man, quotha? Why, how should I know? His ale is good, his bills are in order, his prices are reasonable and that is all that it concerns me to know about a rude peasant."

Phelippes came quickly and stood by the other's chair, bending his myopic glance upon his friend.

"Nay, pray think, Sir Amias, for I believe this may prove of the first importance. Is the man a blabber with his tongue, does he favour the Woman's cause, has he an itching palm? I'll tell you anon why I ask these questions."

"Then I will answer you," said Paulet crossly, "that every peasant has an itching palm, that every rascal hereabouts favours this Queen's cause, because, forsooth, they have heard tales of her giving of alms, and have a rustic pity for her imprisoned state. But as for a blabbing tongue, this brewer is the stupidest, dumbest creature ever I encountered; marry, sir, he is an animal walking upon two legs. Come, since you are so concerned in him, you shall see him for yourself."

The dray stood in the midst of the great courtyard, with servants busy about it unloading the heavy barrels and casks by the light of torches flaring in rings in the wall. The four huge horses had their heads down in buckets of oats, jingling their bits as they munched; and perched upon a piece of sacking on the front of the dray, with the reins lying slack in one hand and a hunk of bread and cheese in the other, sat a lump of a man, as placid as his steeds, and as absorbed in the business of taking nourishment.

Standing with Paulet in the shadows, Phelippes closely scrutinized this brewer of Burton, rather as a stage-manager might appraise an actor whom he is thinking of casting for some important role. The brewer wore a vast apron, stained black with ale, which covered his cloth hose and reached to his clogs, a kersey doublet, with an old cloak thrown over for warmth, and a red cap on his tousled hair. His face was like a block of masonry on which some sculptor had begun to carve a device and then abandoned it; rudimentary features could be distinguished, and that was all.

Phelippes' attention was diverted by a peculiar ritual which was taking place among the barrels unloaded from the dray. Two of them, together with a cask, had been set aside from the rest; the stoppers being removed from the bunk-holes, an officer stepped forward, and thrust into the interiors a long iron rod. Catching his friend's eye, Paulet smiled grimly.

"Those two barrels and the cask of strong-ale are for this Queen's side of the house," said he. "Never are they conveyed to her without I have them searched."

He was surprised and puzzled by his friend's response.

"I believe," said Mr Phelippes, "that I have found the answer to our problem."

The brewhouse stood on the outskirts of the little town of Burton, convenient to the river, with a ramshackle dwelling-house arm-in-arm with it and open country behind. Tying his horse to a ring in the wall next morning. Mr Phelippes picked his way daintily between the puddles of ale in the yard, and entered the brewery. In the steamy air he identified the figure of the brewer, perched on the top of a short ladder, busy inspecting the copper in which the liquor was being heated.

The brewer of Burton was, as Paulet had said, an extraordinarily dumb personage. His speech was almost entirely confined to 'Ah', with an occasional 'Mubbe so-a, mubbe no-a', which was not helpful in carrying on a conversation, and his ordinary method of communicating with his fellow men was by winks, leers, nudgings of the elbow, and other elementary gestures. When it became absolutely necessary for him to enunciate a sentence, he did so with his teeth tightly shut, running all his words together, so that what he said was entirely unintelligible to any stranger.

These facts Mr Phelippes quickly discovered for himself this morning. Having informed the brewer that he must have some private speech with him where there was no possibility of their being overheard, Mr Phelippes understood the man to say that they would adjourn to the cow-shed; it transpired that what he had really said was that they would go and get the cows in, and a few minutes later Sir Francis Walsingham's right-hand man found himself stumbling over rough moorland, now and again sinking ankle-deep in bog, and, being London born and bred, losing his breath and very nearly his temper.

"What is your name, friend?" panted Mr Phelippes.

"Ah," said the brewer.

"It does not signify. In the business in which I hope to employ you, names are best kept close. I shall call you 'the Honest Man', for I am sure you merit that title, and if you have occasion to refer to me, you will do so simply as 'the Gentleman'. Can you remember that?"

"Ah," said the Honest Man.

"Very well, then; now pray listen carefully. I am one of those who much desire to serve a certain noble lady who is held prisoner in these parts, and whose name I am sure you can guess. I and my friends have hit upon a device whereby we may communicate secretly with her, which is to enclose a corked metal tube within a specially constructed cask which shall have a false bottom; within this tube letters in cipher will be placed, and when they search with their rods they will find nothing but ale in the cask – "

"Gitupgitupoldbitch," said the brewer.

Mr Phelippes wasted several moments in endeavouring to interpret this remark, until it was borne in upon him that the Honest Man had been addressing one of his cows.

"Tomorrow, at a certain secluded spot near here, I shall meet you, bringing the cask with the tube inside it. In due course another gentleman, whom we shall refer to in future as 'the Secret Party', and whose appearance I shall describe to you anon, will bring you letters in cipher. These you will put into the tube, the tube you will push through the bung-hole of the cask, and this cask you will deliver on the next occasion of your taking supplies to Chartley, taking care that it is placed with the two barrels which are for the lady's side of the house. In the same way, when you collect your empties, you will meet the Secret Party at the rendezvous, and he will – "

Phelippes broke off; for, from the total lack of expression upon that lump of face beside him, it appeared to him that the Honest Man was not taking in a single word.

Sighing a little, he began all over again, very patiently, for indeed he was a patient person. It was the simplest thing in the world he was asking; so long as the Honest Man obeyed his instructions, kept his mouth shut, asked no questions, and dealt with none henceforward but the Secret Party or those the Secret Party might have occasion to employ, he would be risking nothing, he would be doing great service to a distressed lady, and he would earn a handsome fee.

At that word 'fee' the Honest Man came suddenly to life. His granite face twisted into a whole series of winks and leers, he nudged Mr Phelippes so hard in the ribs that Mr Phelippes exclaimed aloud; he even indulged in speech which, though the words were mere gibberish to his auditor, by its tone suggested a willingness to co-operate. Mr Phelippes smiled ruefully. He ought to have mentioned money in the first place; he ought to have remembered that even the rudest peasant understands that language. He drew from his cod-piece a knitted purse, untied the string from about its neck, and counted out five silver angels into the large and horny palm which had been suddenly thrust towards him.

He was feeling very pleased with himself when, having duly delivered the cask and the tube, constructed by his own clever fingers, he rode towards London next day. There remained much to be done; the Honest Man's honesty, as well as his ability to carry out his simple instructions, must be tested; some way must be found of suggesting to the Woman or a member of her household that the cask of strong-ale always delivered with the two barrels of beer would be worth a close investigation when next it came to Chartley; time must elapse before it was seen whether she would swallow the bait.

But a start had been made; Mr Secretary's great 'practice' had been inaugurated; the trap was set. The next step was the sending to the neighbourhood of Chartley the 'Secret Party', Mr Gilbert Gifford.

Chapter Three

Old Mr Bourgoign, the physician of the Queen of Scots, was surprised and somewhat dismayed to receive, on the morning of Saturday, January 15th, a message from Sir Amias, summoning him to that gentleman's apartments immediately. He was dismayed because he feared it might mean dismissal, and perhaps the introduction of some strange physician into his mistress' household. He shuddered at the thought and its implications. She was delicate and ailing; what simpler than to replace him by a doctor in government pay who, by neglect or wrong physic, would cause her to die a 'natural' death?

It was an enormous relief to him when, having come into Paulet's presence, he learned the real reason for the summons.

"There is a stranger, who by his dress is a man of quality," said Paulet, "has had a fall from his horse outside the house of Mr Newport, steward of this estate, early this morning. I have sent my own physician to him, but he is unable to understand a word the stranger says. You being a man well versed in languages, it is my pleasure that you call upon him, attend to his injuries, and enquire who he is."

The physician's heart leapt with sudden hope. Could it be, he wondered, some friend of his mistress', who was seeking to convey to her that communication from the outside world for which she starved? Sir Amias' next words stifled the new-born hope.

"But in case this accident has been staged, sir," growled Paulet, "by some traitor to her Majesty and religion, you will examine this stranger in the presence of Mr Newport, to whom I have sent instructions for the purpose, and you will be searched upon your return to Chartley. So pray don't imagine that you may be the bearer of any little secret notes."

"His name appears to be Señor Murato," said Mr Newport, as he ushered old Bourgoign into the chamber where the patient lay. "And that is all I can understand of what he says."

The curtains had been drawn across the windows, those of the bed drawn back; candles, burning in a branched stick on a table near by, illumined a face very appealing in its youth and pallor, with thick flaxen hair, worn somewhat longer that was customary, spread upon the pillows. As Bourgoign approached the bed, long lashes fluttered, two grey eyes opened, and a little moan came from the lips, followed by a whisper. The physician bent his head to catch the words.

"Do you speak Spanish, Sir?"

"I do. A Spanish gentleman," he added over his shoulder to the jealously watchful Mr Newport.

"I have a message to convey," came the whisper again. "Make a great show of examining me while I give it you, but say at the end that I am but bruised. You must not come hither again, or they will suspect."

The physician's hands trembled as he opened the stranger's shirt to listen to his heart, but he was an old, frail man, and it seemed that Newport suspected nothing. The whispering continued, with now and then a realistic groan or two, as Bourgoign set up his pendulum to ascertain the rate of the patient's pulse, and carefully felt the limbs for signs of fracture.

"You must say that I am travelling to Derby, but missed my way because of my ignorance of the roads. That my servant, who speaks English, was taken sick at Lichfield, and that I was obliged to leave him behind. That he has my valises with my papers in them, and my passport signed by my Lord Leicester whom I visited in the Low Countries. That my business in Derby is with Mr Manners, who is a magistrate and my mother's uncle. Have you this aright?"

Bourgoign nodded, his heart beating sickeningly.

"So much for what you shall say to those who shall question you. And this is what you shall say to your mistress: That next time the brewer of Burton visits Chartley, she must search well the cask of strong-ale, wherein she will find that which will pleasure her. I dare talk no more, or this man who is with us may grow suspicious."

Then, as though utterly exhausted, 'Señor Murato', alias Gilbert Gifford, turned his fair head on the pillow and gave a great sigh.

Sunday, January 16th, passed as usual at Chartley.

The drawbridge remained lowered, since no couriers were sent out, and none expected; the guards were changed at regular intervals; in the chapel Sir Amias and his household attended the severe form of worship to which he was attached. The funereal bell tolled for dinner; in the little hamlet which had sprung up outside the gates to accommodate those men-at-arms for whom there was no room in Chartley, the soldiers, away from Sir Amias' puritanical eye, threw the dice, or regaled one another with bawdy tales. And when dusk had fallen there sounded as usual the familiar rumble of wheels, the clump of heavy hooves, and the lowering of the drawbridge. To the scandal of Sir Amias, it was the invariable custom of the brewer of Burton, who was a law unto himself, to call at Chartley every Sunday evening for his empties, even though he might have delivered his beer on the previous day.

But it was remembered afterwards that on this particular Sabbath evening, Sir Amias had seemed extraordinarily pleased to hear the rumble of the dray. He hastened out into the courtyard; with his own hands he performed the ceremony of thrusting a rod into the empty ale-cask which came from the prisoner's side of the house; he even went so far as to make a jocular remark to the effect that 'this Queen's' household must have been celebrating some Popish feast, so quickly had they consumed their ration of strong-ale. Certain of his own household, taking advantage of such unusual good humour, absented themselves from evening prayers, and were soundly rebuked for it by their master next morning.

In the prisoner's quarters, a strange atmosphere of excitement had prevailed ever since the previous evening, beginning at the moment when the new supply of beer had been delivered by the brewer. No sooner had some of Sir Amias' servants brought it over and departed, than Mr Melville, the steward, and old Bourgoign, the physician, had come bustling down to the cellar, called for flagons for running off the ale, locked themselves in, and remained there for some time. A scullion who happened to be passing when they emerged, reported to his fellows that both gentlemen looked as though they had been left a fortune.

The atmosphere had grown as the evening progressed, and though the servants knew nothing of its cause, the excitement communicated itself to them. As close prisoners as their mistress, they felt as it were a fresh breeze blowing in from the outside world, whispering of hope, even of liberty.

Above stairs, in the Queen's apartments, there were hurried footsteps which seemed to have a new lilt to them; sad faces smiled; for the first time for weeks the supper dishes, which ordinarily came down scarcely touched, gave evidence of appetites suddenly renewed. One of the gentlewomen was heard singing; Melville who, in his shabby velvet and tarnished chain of office, usually looked like a mute at a funeral as, white rod in hand, he led the little procession of servants carrying the royal supper, actually joked with a clumsy fellow who split some gravy. Even Bijou, the Queen's little dog, was heard to bark in a lively fashion, as though he too was infected with this mysterious excitement.

In the Queen's little Presence Chamber, with its chair of estate upon a dais, its sweaty stone walls behind the arras, and the much mended French carpet on the floor, Mistress Kennedy, the Queen's favourite gentlewoman, murmured anxiously to old Mr Bourgoign:

"Her Majesty will not go to bed, sir. She is yonder with her secretaries, and you know how sick she has been."

But the old man, with happy tears running down into his beard, shook his head at her.

"If you had known her Majesty as long as I have, mistress, you would not fear for her now. All her life she has suffered frequent distempers, but that delicate frame contains a spirit so dauntless that in times of need it triumphs easily over the frail flesh. Remember you how, when she was far gone with child, and her rebellious nobles thought to slay her by murdering her secretary in her presence, the need of her child gave her the wit and the strength to ride twenty miles through the night to safety. And now it is joy that has proved more efficacious than all my potions. After near upon a year of being starved of all communication with the outside world, she has the inexpressible happiness of receiving some letters from her friends."

All through that night tapers burned in the Queen's Closet; all through the dark hours the murmur of voices and the scratching of a quill was heard from behind the closed door. And on the next day, Sunday, when the household assembled at dawn as usual to assist at the mass said by Camille de Preau, the 'Sir John', whom Sir Amias rightly had suspected of being her almoner, for the first time since the move to Chartley the Queen of Scots was kneeling there at her prie-dieu; and some said afterwards that at last they understood why the poets of France had praised in such extravagant terms her beauty when she was young, for there was a kind of radiance about her, and her eyes were full of a blinding fire.

By that Sunday evening the mysterious atmosphere of gaiety seemed to have spread itself throughout the whole of that grim, bleak house, even extending to the brewer who called for his empties. He was seen to indulge in such a series of winks and chuckles directed at no one in particular, that the general opinion was that he had been imbibing freely his own ale.

Never having known normal happiness himself, it was the chief delight of Gilbert Gifford to destroy it in others. So he too was cheerful when, having met the Honest Man at the appointed rendezvous, a wood near Burton, early on Monday morning, he set off on his long ride to London, with a packet of letters, faintly redolent of ale, tucked inside his doublet. Even the tedious journey did not unduly trouble him; he had a licence to ride post, and therefore had a fresh horse every ten miles; he arrived, splashed from head to foot with mud, at supper-time on Tuesday evening at Mr Phelippes' house in Leadenhall Street, looking extremely self-satisfied.

Mr Phelippes had a hot supper awaiting him, fussed and fumed while Arthur Gregory (lent him by Mr Secretary for the occasion) must needs withdraw into another room to open, in his secret manner, the packet which Gilbert had brought from Chartley; then, bent nearly double over the table, got down to the long business of decipherment. It was not so arduous as it might have been, for with each of these, her first letters for so long to her friends, the Queen of Scots obligingly had enclosed new cipher-keys.

There was a reply to Morgan, thanking him for his recommendation of the young Catholic gentleman, Gilbert Gifford; there was a letter to Mary's brother-in-law, King Henry of France; and lastly a note to another of her agents in Paris, Charles Paget. All were in the neatly formed characters of the Scots secretary, Curle. Gilbert was still a-bed next morning when Mr Phelippes, a little haggard from his all-night labours, but exceedingly cheerful, almost pranced into the bedchamber, waving the packet which had just been resealed by clever Arthur Gregory.

"The Woman is not entirely convinced that this secret post is safe," said he. "She writes to Morgan that 'My keeper having settled such an exact and rigorous order in all places where any of my people can go, it is very strange if they receive or deliver anything which he is not able to know very soon after.' She is concerned for the safety of 'the brave bearer' of the letter to her from Morgan, who, she fears, may fall a victim to his own loyalty and daring, as so many others have done. She has enclosed, she writes, a little reward for him in the tube with these letters. Did she so?"

"She did not," replied Gilbert, stopping abruptly in the middle of a yawn.

"Never mind," soothed Phelippes. (He did not believe Gilbert, and it was a delicious thought that the Queen of Scots was paying for her own betrayal.) "Doubtless she will do so with the next packet. There is nothing of importance in this, but if we are patient and discreet, all her present misgivings will be dispelled, and then will it be time to find some suitable plotters to communicate with her."

He gave a little giggle. He was almost light-headed with fatigue and excitement.

"Meanwhile you must carry this packet to the French Embassy. It should serve to convince the Ambassador of your good faith, so that he will readily give you any letters he has lying by him for the Woman from her friends abroad." He hugged himself with glee. "Our secret post is working; a little testing of the machinery, and then to find, with the blessing of God, some treasonably minded dupes."

Miles away in Burton the Honest Man was snoring in contented slumber. Hidden away in an old stocking under a loose brick in the chimney piece was a money-bill for ten pounds. He had found it when, at a lonely spot on his road home from Chartley on Sunday night, he had stopped his horses, withdrawn the tube from the empty cask, and looked inside. It was wrapped round a packet of letters; the letters he had duly delivered to the Secret Party next day, but the money-bill he had kept for himself.

The Honest Man might be only a rude peasant; but he went to church every Sunday, and there was one text he had by heart: 'The labourer is worthy of his hire.'

Part Two

Chapter One

Anthony Babington was awakened by his chamber-boy opening the shutters, bringing the wooden bathtub to set before the new-lit fire, and placing his shirt and ruff, the latter freshly pleated with the poke-sticks, to warm. Anthony sighed deeply with homesickness as he heard the sounds from without which reminded him that he was in London once more.

Yet it was a very pleasant part of London in which he lodged, and a very pleasant lodging. He had his own things about him, all brought up from Dethick, his feather bed, his court-cupboards and joint-stools and a solitary elbow-chair; his table-mirror of crystal; his precious little collection of books, the *Colloquies* of Erasmus, Cicero's *Epistles*, Turberville's *Booke* of *Hunting*, and even (very daringly) *The Ordinarye of Chrysten Men*, an old Catholic book of devotion translated from the French.

In the parlour which opened out of his bedchamber there was his long-bow on the wall, a pair of fencing-swords, a leather lure and jesses with silver varvels which had his name and crest engraved on them, a lute with coloured strings. Across the little courtyard there was a stable for his horse, with room for those of his servants, and a mews where he kept his favourite hawk. And outside this old house, now know as Hern's Rents and turned into lodgings for gentlemen, there were the gardens of the Inns of Court and of Ely and Southampton Houses, with a view from his parlour window of the windmill lazily turning in Gray's Inn Fields, and only a distant hum from the London eastwards beyond Holborn Bars.

Yet in this early morning mood he hated it all, consumed with nostalgia for Dethick, thinking of his wife making her ritual visits to brewhouse, pastry, dairy, stillroom, the ploughmen fastening the yokes on their oxen, the falconers and huntsmen starting heron or hare. Petulantly he thrust from him his 'morning', a cup of ale and a manchet, and glancing at the March sunlight streaming through the casement, called to his boy to lay out his new *mandilion* with hanging sleeves, his sage-coloured doublet, and the rather absurd little trunk-hose which he wore in town.

He would not go to the lecture this morning; his reading law was only a farce. Like most young country gentlemen of great estate, he had joined one of the Inns of Court in order to be able to administer justice to his tenants, but the authorities of Lincoln's Inn, from the Master to the Steward, were indulgent to his frequent absences from lecture or moot, for he took care to have regular supplies of country delicacies sent up to them from Dethick, a brace of pheasants, a barrel of trout, a potted goose.

He might play a game of tennis; but no, he was not in the mood for sport. He would walk in Lincoln's Inn Fields; he would clear the fumes of last night's wine from his head by brisk and solitary exercise in the spring sunshine; he would dine dutifully with his aunt, Lady D'Arcy, he would spend the long afternoon with Virgil, Ovid, or Horace, those safe and unfailing companions; and this evening –

Oh Lord, he thought, rubbing his teeth with a cloth dipped in honey and vinegar, this evening he had an appointment with some of his fellow Conductor Companions at the Plough outside Temple Bar, and it was going to be difficult to tell them that he had made up his mind, absolutely made up his mind once and for all, that he was going into voluntary exile overseas. But surely they would understand that his first duty was to his wife and child; Margaret had been really frightened when Mr Simpson, the priest whom he had harboured at Dethick in October, had been caught by the pursuivants no farther away than Derby.

Thrusting his case of picktooths of scented wood into his pocket, and his sword into its velvet sheath, he called briskly to his foot-boy to follow him, and ran down the outside stair of his lodging. A few steps across the unpaved road, and he was through Great Turnstile into Lincoln's Inn Fields, where once the Knights Templars had held their jousts. At this early morning hour the fields were deserted except for the cattle which were prevented from straying into Holborn by the turning-stiles; to the north was an uninterrupted view of the heights of Hampstead and Highgate; to the south was the Strand, with the old episcopal inns now occupied by the new upstart nobility.

The day was fair indeed; his new *mandilion*, as a glance in his mirror had shown him, was becoming; he was still boy enough to relish smart clothes and the admiring glances of chance passers-by; and in this happy atmosphere his spirits rose. After all, it was not a question of running away, this going overseas; it entailed enormous self-sacrifice, the leaving of many kinsfolk and friends, of Dethick, the beloved house of his ancestors, of the native country so dear to him. And as for the underground organization, which had been blessed by the present Pope, Gregory XIII, and was known as the Conductor Companions – why, it had been intended for young unmarried men without ties.

Chidge Tichborne, his best friend, whom he had met when each was making a tour of France, most certainly would understand. Chidge was a leading Conductor

Companion, and had thrown himself heart and soul into the dangerous work of meeting priests on their landing in England, getting them past the searchers at the ports or arranging for their being met at some lonely spot on the coast, equipping them with suitable disguises, and conducting them to some Catholic house. But several times already Chidge had told Anthony that, valuable though the latter was to the organization, since he was rich enough to bribe the pursuivants and searchers, it had never been intended for married men, and that his first duty was to his wife and child.

Yet how they would miss him, Chidge and the others! They all regarded him as their natural leader, and so it had always been with youths of his own age. He had so much natural charm, was so cultured that he actually possessed a private library, and possessed also that quality of the self-dramatist which convinces others, besides himself, of his ability to perform daring and brilliant exploits. He was intelligent enough to be slightly ashamed of this side of his character; his mother had tried to impress on him that a dream world robs the real one of its proper worth; but it had become a secret vice, and he was too young to realize its perils.

Yes, he thought, with pleasant melancholy, exile was the only sensible course. Apart from the perils attached to his recusancy, the foolish talk in which he was wont to indulge when the wine got into him might bring Margaret and little Meg into trouble one day. He blushed with shame as he remembered last night's brags to his friends in their private supper-room at the Plough; he had been full of that favourite old dream of his, the rescue of the Queen of Scots from her prison, and he had made it sound as though he were quite capable of accomplishing it. And exile, hard though it would be, was only for a time, until the ageing Elizabeth died, and Mary reigned, and the Faith was restored. He was young, and he would still have many years, please God, in which to dwell in his native land.

But, he reflected, turning as he heard the church bells chime eleven o'clock, the hour at which his old-fashioned aunt still dined, to go abroad was impossible without a licence, and though he had approached certain Schismatics (as the recusants termed those Catholics who went to the Protestant service in order to save their estates or to obtain offices) whom he knew at Court, all had told him that they could not contrive to get him such a thing.

He sighed. He would have to raise the price. As the head of a wealthy house, and the husband of an heiress, he had found hitherto that almost anything could be got for money. On the other hand, if he remained much longer in England he would become a poor man. No one, not even of his fortune, could continue indefinitely to pay twenty pounds a month to the Government for each member of his household not attending the Protestant service. Meanwhile, until he obtained the necessary licence to travel, there must be no more of that stupid dangerous talk in which he had indulged last night.

They were eagerly awaiting him, these intimate friends of his, in the private room called the Fleur de Luce, when, about five o'clock that evening, he arrived at the Plough outside Temple Bar. He liked to arrive just a little late for such appointments in order to give himself the pleasure of their welcome; like all those who are aware of their own weaknesses and are secretly ashamed of them, Anthony needed the assurance of his own popularity.

"Thank the Lord you are come," cried the Irishman, Robert Barnwell, tall, rugged, fair-bearded, "or the mutton would have been ruined. We have sent it back to the kitchen once already, and I have eaten your oysters as well as my own."

"These peascod-bellied doublets must be mighty convenient to you, Robin," mocked Anthony, flinging his *mandilion* upon a chair, "for they make that girth of yours look modish. And is hunger responsible for your glum looks, my gossip?" he added, addressing Tom Salisbury who, sitting beside the fire, had his cheek on his hand.

"I am not glum but thoughtful," replied Salisbury. "We have finished reprinting Campion's *Ten Reasons* on our secret press, but cannot hit upon a way of distributing it safely. The searchers of the Stationers' Company are becoming hotter than ever in their inspection of the booksellers, and only last week they impounded the stock of Jameson at the sign of the Cannon over against St Dunstan's, because they found the *Litanies to Our Lady* there.

"We'll contrive something," said Chidiock Tichborne quietly. "We can hand them out as play-bills as we did with More's *Dialogue of Comfort*."

"Jesuit literature is the most dangerous of all," objected Salisbury, "for it's not only the Protestants who are hostile to that Society. Even though it was the Jesuits who started the Catholic revival here in '80, they have no place in Catholic tradition like the monks and the friars; their founder was a Spaniard, and there's persistent rumour that they are sworn to Spanish allegiance. Besides they are so absolutely uncompromising that they alienate many."

"We'll contrive something," said Tichborne again; and he smiled across the hearth at his best friend.

From their first meeting in France when they were in their 'teens, Anthony and Chidiock had felt the attraction of opposites. Anthony was tall with flamboyant good looks, restless and picturesque, slapdash, unreliable, extravagantly generous, impatient of criticism, easily gulled, the victim of perpetually changing moods. Chidiock was slight; though good-looking would pass unnoticed, though charming was not immediately popular. There lay in him a deep core of quietness and of constancy; and he possessed to a remarkable degree the virtue of compassion, which made him seem older than his twenty-five years. He was the younger son of a Hampshire recusant of good fortune, though not nearly as wealthy as the Babingtons, and like Anthony he was supposed to be studying law.

"I have had ill news from home," said Tichborne, changing the subject. "Sir James Paton has declared that he will go to church at Easter, and that his family and tenants must do so likewise."

A melancholy silence fell. Another old Catholic house fallen, another gap in the gallant ranks of recusants – where would it end? Babington began a hot denunciation of Sir James, but Tichborne intervened.

"It is well enough for you, Anthony, living in a part of the realm where the Faith is still strong. But in Hampshire we are harried in all classes; the justices are of the new men and keep to the letter of the law in their persecution of us. The poor who cannot pay these crushing fines have their goods and two-thirds of their lands seized; I have known a husbandman who had his only cow taken, and another who, having no livestock, lost his blankets and even his winter stores."

They sat down to supper at last, becoming more cheerful over a leg of mutton with gallandine sauce, a hen stuffed with leeks, and a quince pie. As the wine was passed about they drifted into the talk proper to their years. Barnwell had seen a new play by Peele at The Theatre in Shoreditch that afternoon, and had sat next to a lady in a verdingale so huge that it had nearly pushed him off his stool; Salisbury had played a venue with a friend at the fencing-school and had won spectacularly.

"And what have you been at, Chidge?" asked Anthony, making a long arm for the wine-jug.

"I've spent most of the day with Harry Dunn," replied his friend. "And by the way, he is coming to see us here this evening."

"Oh *no*!" exclaimed Anthony in disgust.

He knew perfectly well that his dislike of Dunn was unreasonable. Dunn was a most enthusiastic Conductor Companion; he was actually in the employ of Mr Vice-Chamberlain Hatton, and at Ely House (which Queen Elizabeth's foppish favourite had wrested from the unfortunate Bishop of Ely, paying to the Crown the modest rent of one red rose and ten bushels of hay), Dunn gleaned all kinds of useful information. Moreover he, like most of Babington's acquaintances, had fallen to that youth's native charm.

"Converts are so tedious," said Anthony in self-defence. "They have the wrong kind of piety, they lower their voices in awe when they mention holy matters, they think every priest is a saint. And they think we're being irreverent when we, who have the Faith in our blood and bones, jest about our religion. They're so solemn – "

"In other words, you don't like Harry Dunn," interrupted Tichborne, with his quiet, dry humour. "Well, I'm afraid I've invited him hither this evening, or rather he invited himself. For he is most anxious that we should make the acquaintance of a new friend of his, a man we've all seen about the town, one who calls himself Captain Foscue."

"Black Foscue – isn't that what some name him?" asked Barnwell. "A loud-voiced fellow, gaudy in his dress. I've seen him; he was at a bear-bait in Paris Gardens when I was there last week, and I heard him say he was recruiting for the Earl of Leicester's forces in the Low Countries."

"That's the legend he has put about," said Tichborne, "but it seems that he is a priest, and from what Dunn says there has been no one like him since Campion."

They were astonished and excited. The Jesuit, Edmund Campion, had become a legend since his coming to England in 1580 and his martyrdom a year later; endless stories were told of his skill and daring in eluding the priest-hunters, his gaiety, his wit, his holiness. They were deep in speculations about this mysterious 'Captain Foscue' who might be another Campion when there was a discreet tap on the door, and the insignificant figure of Henry Dunn insinuated itself into the room.

He was not an attractive little man. He was much older than the others, had a manner which was alternately prim and conspiratorial, and wore a very obvious wig, for he was completely bald (a state which, since he shared it with Queen Elizabeth, intensely mortified him). He affected the pointed beard and small upturned moustaches which had been fashionable in the days of Mary Tudor, with the long, grotesquely padded breeches of that time. He was always shabby, but old-maidishly neat; though he had the right to call himself 'gentleman', he gave an impression of being slightly ill-bred. These deficiencies outweighed with the not very charitable Anthony the sacrifice the little man had made of his modest inheritance on his conversion to the Catholic church, his absolute sincerity, and the fact that he had devoted his life to the service of his new faith.

"His Reverence is below in the common-room," breathed Dunn, tiptoeing up to the group around the table, and radiating a hen-like excitement, "regaling the customers with his stories of foreign wars. Hark!" he added, as a great rumble of laughter sounded from the room below. "You would think he had not a care in the world. I thought I would come hither before him to prepare you to meet his Reverence – "

"I've told you, Hal, a dozen times" interrupted Babington, "not to use that mode of address. Oh, I know the landlord here is our friend and the tapsters well tipped, but it's agreed amongst us that we forbear 'fathers' and 'reverences' and all terms of that nature, lest they slip out in undesirable company. Have some wine," he added, for though impatient and intolerant, he was at heart a kindly boy, and Dunn's fallen face had made him ashamed of his sharpness.

Carefully blessing himself, Dunn took bird-like sips at the Rhenish.

"There has been none like him since Campion, Mr Babington," said he earnestly. "His real name is John Ballard, by the way. He passes backwards and forwards across the Channel – "

"Then how is it he has not made use of the services of the Conductor Companions?" broke in Salisbury, a little suspicious.

"He vows he will imperil none besides himself if he can help it. And such daring! Why, he has reconciled men to the Faith even in our London taverns, and says Mass there, too, ordering that a tankard and mugs be set out in the chamber, so that if the pursuivants should come it should seem to be merely a convivial gathering. The tales he has to tell of his adventures! And yet he is the soul of caution; he knows you all by name, and the nature of the services you perform, but unless he thinks fit he will not let fall a word in your company to betray the fact of his sacred calling. Hush!" he whispered, in a fever of excitement, "here he comes."

John Ballard, alias Captain Foscue, was a stout man in his middle thirties, and certainly his looks and manner made him the last man in the world to have been suspected of being a priest.

He had the military air to the life; he wore the full breeches favoured by soldiers, who found them convenient for storing of loot, a gold-laced cape swathed about his body in what was known as the Venetian style, garishly embroidered boot-hose, a ruff of extravagant proportions with wire under-proppers, and a hat stuck at a rakish angle, with a bunch of quills drawn through the slot. His walk was an insolent swagger; his voice, as he greeted the company, was loud and assertive; he puffed at a long pipe, surrounding himself with a little cloud of smoke, making much of this novelty of tobacco which had only just appeared on the Continent and had not yet reached England. His eyes were merry yet shrewd, and his whole manner infinitely self-assured.

Behind him, as he entered the upstairs supper-room, came a gaunt man, whom Ballard introduced by the name of Montalto, whose eyes scarcely ever left the figure of his companion, and who treated him with a deference which had more than a touch of servility. A confidential servant, the young men took him to be, and for a while at least, Mr Ballard showed no inclination to make Montalto's position clearer.

Indeed, as they sat down round the fire, and a refilled flagon of wine was passed about, Mr Ballard seemed deliberately evasive. He faintly patronized these young gallants, impressing them with the ease with which he acted his chosen part, talking in the jargon of the soldier, of culverins and serpentines, of harquebusiers who could fire as many as forty shots an hour, of forlorn hopes and charges in flank, of siege batteries behind their protecting ramparts of fascines. Yet all the while, under cover of this, he was drawing them out, encouraging them to a greater and greater indiscretion as the wine loosened their tongues; until, by ten o'clock, Babington was enlarging upon his favourite dream, the rescue of the Queen of Scots. It was in the midst of this that Salisbury said suddenly to the priest:

"Ever since you came in, sir, it has stuck in my mind that I have seen you before, and I do not mean in London. It would be about a year ago, at the post-house near Llewenny, of which I am a native. And yet it cannot have been you, for this man was fair, and moreover he was hiring post-horses, which is not to be done without a government licence."

Ballard looked at him a moment, then threw back his head, with its crow-black hair and beard, and burst into a hearty laugh.

"A rope on it!" said he. "I've heard enough this evening to convince me that it's safe to lay aside the mask. It was myself you saw, Mr Salisbury, fair hair, post-horses, and all. Hair can be dyed, my friend, and let me tell you that I have made a thorough job of it." He pulled up his sleeve, exposing an arm covered with black hairs. "When a man of my calling puts on a disguise, by cock! he must wear it like his own skin, especially if he has broke prison once, and is proclaimed."

"Broke prison – " began Anthony in astonishment.

"But the post-horses!" chimed in Barnwell, his eyes dancing.

Ballard lifted a hand for silence, and looked round the circle with an indulgent smile.

"Nay," he laughed, "I see I must make a full confession." He crossed one strong leg over the other and sat nursing his knee, staring into the dying fire, and now and again throwing a merry glance round his companions to make sure that they were appreciating his tale.

"I was ordained at Châlons in '81, and came straight over to England. I was not then well acquainted with the rules of the game, and so it was that nine months later they caught me and threw me into the Gatehouse at Westminster. I was busy preparing my soul for death, when a friend contrived to smuggle in to me some *aqua fortis*, with which

I burned out a bar in my window and got clean away. Then did I perceive that the way to keep clear of the pursuivants was not to skulk by day and travel by night, but rather to create a character under which I could show myself openly, ay, go into the kennels of the hounds and pass unsuspected by them."

"That was blessed Edmund Campion's way," breathed Dunn, nodding his head.

"Maybe," said Ballard shortly, not seeming very much to like the comparison. "Well, thus was 'Black Foscue' born, Captain Foscue who has become such a familiar figure in London and Westminster and many another town, who spends his money freely, is full of good round oaths and stirring tales, has servants to attend him, the mysteries of war at his fingers' ends, talks familiarly of this action and of that, and has persuaded more than one hopeful young gentleman that it's his duty to enlist in the forces of our Sovereign Lady, Queen Elizabeth, God bless her!"

"God damn her for a bloody persecutor and heretic!" muttered Babington, tipsily fierce.

Ballard shot him a quick, searching glance, seemed about to speak to him, evidently thought better of it, and went on to the company in general:

"It ill becomes me to cry up my own excellence as a stage-player, yet I will say this: that since I broke prison, which was in the spring of '82, I have come and gone throughout the North of England, I have been overseas and returned a dozen times, and not once has my disguise been penetrated, nor have I been fain to lie in hiding-holes like the rest of my brethren, nor have I been suspected by any man."

"But the post-horses!" insisted Barnwell, eager as a child to hear the details of some adventure story.

Ballard winked genially.

"Why there," said he, "is where my friend Montalto comes in". He turned to the gaunt man, and then laughed softly, for Montalto was fast asleep. "O'erthrown by Sir John Barleycorn," chuckled Ballard. "He can never carry his drink. But it's as well, for I can speak the more freely. His real name is Bernard Mawde, and before I met him he was a Protestant and in the household of him whom they call the Archbishop of York. One fine day Mawde haps upon his Grace in the arms of a local alewife, which sight so filled our honest Mawde with disgust that he begins to wonder concerning the truth of the religion professed by his Grace. Thus was he brought into that fold which has so many ways whereby a man may enter into it."

He paused, and looked at the sleeping man with real affection.

"He left the Archbishop's service, but concealed the fact of his conversion, hoping that by so doing he might be of assistance to those who had become his brethren in religion. And by cock! so he has. For Mawde has a cousin in the employ of Mr Secretary, and from this cousin he is always able to obtain passports and licences to ride post. I cannot help but laugh sometimes when I think what Mr Secretary would say, he who so congratulates himself upon his marvellous spy system, did he but know that one of his own clerks was making it as simple for a poor priest to go whithersoever he pleases as it is for a gentleman of the Court."

Ballard rose briskly. Though he had taken his share of the wine, it appeared to have had no effect upon him, save that his laugh was a trifle louder and his eyes glittered with a hint of fanaticism. He tapped out his pipe upon the hearth, then put the precious instrument into its case.

"It must be near midnight," said he, "and while you young gallants may snore in your beds till noon, I must be on my road to Dover–" again he winked at Barnwell "–riding post"

"You are going to France, father?" asked Dunn in hushed accents.

"To France," replied the priest, swinging his gold-laced cape on to his shoulders, "and am but new returned from Scotland. A man must be active nowadays if he should serve his religion – and his rightful Queen."

He had looked directly at Babington while speaking those last four words, and the young man, fuddled though he was with wine, was instantly alert. He paused in the act of flinging money upon the table in payment of the night's score, glanced sharply at the priest, and met his eyes.

"From all I have heard since I came among you tonight," said Ballard, addressing the company in general, "I believe that it is in you young men that there lies the hope of bringing England back to the Faith. Nay, I will say no more at present, but only this: Lift up your hearts, my gallants; this trial of persecution may prove shorter than you think."

They went downstairs with him and out into the deserted street, with the stench of the Fleet ditch wafted on an east wind towards them, the candles in the lanthorns over the doors of householders guttering in their sockets, and London a-bed long ago. They were all, save Ballard, a little drunk; they were excited by the priest's talk, intrigued by his mysterious hints, fascinated by his romantic personality, flattered by his confidences. In the shadows cast by the links held by yawning servants, who waited to escort their respective masters home, Ballard looked larger than life-size. In the bustle of saying goodnight, he contrived to draw Babington aside, and when he spoke his voice was low and impressive.

"I think we are well met tonight, Mr Babington. And to you alone I will say this, for it is clear from what I have seen that you are the accepted leader of these young men: my sacred duties do not occupy all my time when I travel about England as 'Captain Foscue'. It was Lord Claud Hamilton whom I went to Scotland to see, the principal supporter of the Queen of Scots in her native country, and tomorrow I go to France on purpose to consult with her agents there. In two months' time I shall be back in London and then you shall hear further."

Then, without giving the young man time for comments, Captain Foscue went swaggering off into the darkness, with the gaunt 'Montalto', the convert Bernard Mawde, keeping close as his shadow to his patron and friend.

It was not until he reached his own lodging that Babington remembered his resolve of the morning, and that after all he had not mentioned to Chidge and the others his firm and fixed intention of going into voluntary exile overseas.

Chapter Two

Mr Secretary rose for the third time to replenish the dish of milk for the yowling Cleopatra, and cast a fond eye upon his favourite as the sound of lapping filled his office. Crossing to the window, he opened the casement, and stood for a while smiling benignly down upon Cheapside, where the street-sellers and the side-show, the clumsy drays and the pack-horses, the porters with their loads and the 'prentices at their masters' doors, were all bathed in the sunlight of this fair April morning.

Mr Secretary was felling happy, but not because the sun was shining. His great 'practice' was going very well indeed. The machinery of the secret post had been thoroughly tested during the past months; GG, as Mr Secretary always referred to Gilbert Gifford, had proved a real find; the confidence of the Queen of Scots, and that of the French Ambassador, had been won.

Clever Mr Phelippes (who wrote all the letters supposed to be from Gilbert) had taken infinite pains to encourage the Queen of Scots to write freely in her replies, inserting little scraps of gossip from home and abroad to please her, so attentive to detail that he dated his own letters according to the New Style used in Catholic countries, and which, from her intercepted letters, he knew she adopted. Drawing freely upon his imagination, the no less clever GG had satisfied the French Ambassador about the rather suspicious length of time which elapsed between the writing of Mary's letters and their delivery to him (a delay actually necessary for their decipherment and copying by Mr Phelippes). For additional security in transit, he had explained, he had contrived an elaborate arrangement whereby they were taken from one Catholic house to another on the road from Chartley to London.

But one essential character in the great 'practice' was still lacking: a suitable plotter; though there had been one of whom Mr Secretary had had great hopes, the man who called himself 'Captain Foscue'.

Mr Secretary had known all about John Ballard, alias Captain Foscue, for some years past, and had left him at liberty with the idea of making use of him in just such a 'practice' as this. He had seemed ideal for the role, for he was fanatical, rash, and reckless and of so strong a personality that it was likely he would draw others into his plots. Mr Secretary had seen to it, of course, that he was at the same time harmless; ever since Ballard had broken prison, Walsingham had attached to him an agent of his own, Bernard Mawde. But Mawde's recent reports had been disappointing. Ballard, it seemed, was not a *persona grata* among the older and wiser English Catholics, and was being held at arm's length by the Queen of Scots' agents in France, whither, attended by Mawde, he had gone in the middle of March.

Or could it be, wondered Mr Secretary, staring down unseeingly upon busy Cheapside, that Ballard had had the sense to become a little suspicious of the ease with which 'Montalto' obtained passports and licences, and had ceased to give the spy his full confidence? For the matter of that, was Mawde himself wholly to be trusted by those who employed him? He owed Mr Secretary his release from prison, it was true, and he was well aware that Mr Secretary could put him back there at any time he chose. But human nature was very ungrateful, and the worst of having to employ rascals like Mawde was that inevitably they got to know too much about official secrets. Of course some capital charge could always be faked against them, when they had served their turn or proved troublesome, but Mr Secretary's conscience would never permit him to resort to such extreme measures unless the safety of the Highest One and religion absolutely demanded it.

Well, while keeping Ballard in reserve, he had already begun to explore another avenue. He had sent for GG to London, ordering him to find a thoroughly trustworthy substitute to stay in the neighbourhood of Chartley to deal with the Honest Man and the secret post at that end, and in London he was to set about acting the *agent provocateur* among his many Catholic acquaintances. Surely there must be *someone* who, provoked beyond bearing by persecution, was meditating a conspiracy, or could be induced to do so by the clever GG.

Mr Secretary had returned to his table and had been running his eye down the lists of London Catholics while he meditated, and at one name he smiled in indulgent contempt. Poor John Savage! Now there was a genuine conspirator who would stop at nothing; it was most unfortunate that he was low-born, without credit, and in fact the last person in the world whose childish plots would be likely to win the approval of the Scottish Queen.

While in London Mr Secretary was feeling complacent, even though temporarily frustrated, at Chartley, Sir Amias Paulet was suffering agonies of doubt.

Since it was his old friend Mr Phelippes who had contrived the secret post, Sir Amias had acquiesced in it; but as soon as Phelippes had returned to London in January, Paulet had become uneasy. He had taken an instant dislike to the 'Secret Party', Gilbert Gifford, who appeared to him frivolous, sly, and entirely devoid of true Protestant zeal. Moreover, having brooded over the matter for a long while, Sir Amias' suspicious mind had suggested to him an obvious and terrifying flaw in the arrangements; what was there to prevent letters being smuggled in and out through the secret post, other than those which passed through the hands of the Government?

His fears increased tenfold when, in this month of April, Gilbert was recalled to London, having appointed a substitute of his own choosing to stay at Mr Newport's house in the woods of Chartley. Paulet knew nothing of this substitute, whose name was Barnes, except that he was an old friend of Gilbert's, a fact which merely increased Sir Amias' suspicions of his honesty.

Having wrestled and prayed for some days with these fears, Sir Amias decided to take certain elaborate precautions. They would make a complicated arrangement still more cumbersome, but anything was better than the risk that the Substitute was smuggling in something besides the letters either written or copied by Mr Phelippes.

He wrote to Phelippes. In his simple opinion it was absolutely necessary that in future all letters sent from London should be given by the post-boy direct into his own hands. He would note the size of the packets; he would then convey them to the Substitute at Mr Newport's. And after the Substitute had given them to the Honest Man, the latter should bring them back to him, Sir Amias, before they were sent in to 'this Queen' in the ale-cask. Thus would he be able to test the Substitute's honesty; if the packets were thicker than when they had from London, or showed any signs of having been tampered with, the Substitute would have been proved a rogue.

The next step was to summon the Honest Man. Hitherto he had been left to believe that he was genuinely serving the Queen of Scots, for whom, like most of the ignorant countryfolk in these parts, he appeared to have a sentimental devotion. Now he would have to be disillusioned, and this might be dangerous. For even if his conscience (always supposing that he had one) did not compel him to refuse outright to continue the service under such conditions, he might talk among his neighbours, and somehow or other such talk might reach the unsuspecting Queen of Scots.

But really, reflected Sir Amias, regarding the Honest Man when that person appeared at Chartley in answer to the summons, I believe he is so nearly an animal that he will do what he is told without question. Self-preservation being the one thing that even animals understand, Sir Amias decided on a frontal attack.

"So you have been smuggling letters to this Queen, you rogue!" he snarled. "It is useless to deny it, for I have proof. And let me tell you I have a mind to call up my men-at-arms and have you hanged for your horrid treason."

"Ah," said the Honest Man, his little piggy eyes expressionless.

"There was a fellow at Tutbury was hanged upon a wall opposite this Queen's windows for attempting the like," insisted Sir Amias, determined to make his threats penetrate.

Whether they did so or not it was impossible to tell. The Honest Man just stood there like some immovable rock, exuding a powerful odour of ale, and muttering at intervals, 'Mubbe so-a, mubbe no-a', like a parrot. Sir Amias sighed sharply with exasperation, hoped for the best, and without more ado disclosed the real reason for which he had summoned the Honest Man to Chartley.

For the next twenty minutes he explained and repeated in words of one syllable what the Honest Man must do in order to prove that he was a loyal subject of her Majesty, and that he repented him of his treasonable practices, into which, said Paulet, he was willing to believe that so simple a fellow had been tricked.

When next he received a packet of letters from the gentleman he knew as 'the Substitute' at the rendezvous near his home, he must keep it safely until the following day. Then he must return to the rendezvous at dusk, where he would be met by Sir Amias. Sir Amias would inspect the packet which the Honest Man had received from the Substitute; if satisfied, Sir Amias would give it back to the Honest Man, who must then insert it into the ale-cask in the former way. Paulet was sweating when he had repeated these simple instructions for the dozenth time; how in the world, he wondered despairingly, was he to know whether the brutish creature had taken in a word he had said?

The answer came in a most unexpected and distasteful form; a large and horny hand was thrust, palm upwards, towards him. Sir Amias stared at the palm in furious affront, indignation swamping any satisfaction he might otherwise have felt in this proof that the brutish creature had understood very well indeed that he was being asked a favour. When he had controlled himself sufficiently as to be able to speak, Sir Amias informed the Honest Man, very succinctly, that far from receiving a reward for doing what he was told, undoubtedly he would be hanged if he did not, and so dismissed him.

The packet which arrived from Mr Phelippes a week later, and which, according to Sir Amias' request, was delivered straight into his own hands by the post-boy, had a brief covering note from Mr Phelippes himself. This packet, wrote Phelippes, contained something which might prove of the very first importance, 'and therefore I beseech you to hasten it into the hands of the Woman, and to return her answer, when it comes forth, with the like expedition'.

Sir Amias was cheered by this cryptic message. Evidently Mr Secretary's pet 'practice' was on the eve of bearing fruit, which would mean his own release from this uncomfortable house, besides, of course, the destruction of that prime menace to his religion, the Queen of Scots. He thrust the important packet into his doublet, called for his horse, and galloped the short distance to Mr Newport's house in the woods. He gave the packet into the hands of the Substitute with orders to carry it immediately to the place of rendezvous with the Honest Man. And here he met his first check.

The Honest Man, said the Substitute, came to the rendezvous once a week only, upon a Wednesday; sometimes, if there were no letters in the empty ale-cask, he would not come even then, though it had been pointed out to him that there might be letters arrived from London for him to send in with his next delivery of beer. It was unlikely, however, added the Substitute, that he would break the appointment this week, since he had done so last, and the Substitute had never known him to absent himself for two weeks running.

Sir Amias cursed the Honest Man, the Substitute, and the entire secret post, but there was nothing for it but to wait patiently till Wednesday, for caution prevented him from seeking the Honest Man at his home. But his doubts of the Substitute had been so increased by this interview that he decided, especially considering the importance of this particular packet, that he himself would deliver it to the Honest Man at the rendezvous. He waited, though not with patience; he clanked about the draughty corridors of Chartley like some uneasy ghost, making the lives of his household a misery. On Wednesday he started out a good hour earlier than he need have done for the woods near Burton.

It was raining when he arrived; in this harsh northern climate the trees were only just breaking into leaf, and there was no shelter. The sun set, and it rained harder, becoming a downpour. He heard the bells of Burton church strike seven o'clock, and eight. He got into a panic lest he had mistaken the place of rendezvous. He imagined accidents, treasons, the collapse of Mr Secretary's entire elaborate 'practice'. At half past eight, drenched to the skin and in despair, he threw caution to the winds and rode into Burton.

The Honest Man's wife, dressed in a new gown, opened the door of the brewer's house; from within came the cheerful ring of ale-mugs and an unmistakable odour of roasting poultry. There was, indeed, now Sir Amias came to think of it, an air of new prosperity about the Honest Man's dwelling; he noticed that the roof had been rethatched; also that the Honest Man's wife was wearing a gaudy brooch in her cap.

Her husband, the woman told him, was not at home. He was at the Swan in the High Street, playing skittles with some friends. If the gentleman would care to leave a message... Sir Amias left a very curt message. The Honest Man was to call upon him first thing next morning at Chartley, without fail.

The Honest Man's idea of first thing in the morning was noon. To the furious upbraidings of Sir Amias on his insolence for keeping him waiting, the Honest Man replied with certain grimaces and mumbles which appeared to indicate that he had his work to do. Sweeping aside these excuses, Paulet thrust into the horny hands the precious packet from London, treated the Honest Man to a very detailed account of what would befall him and his family if the packet was not safely conveyed through the ale-cask in the course of the next twenty-four hours, and, waving his hand in dismissal, sank back exhausted.

But the Honest Man, it seemed, was not ready to be dismissed. With maddening slowness he fumbled under his leather apron, and from the depths of some receptacle at last drew forth a paper. Sir Amias sat up abruptly. Could it be a letter which the rogue, either through carelessness or treachery, had kept back until alarmed by the threats just uttered? Paulet fairly snatched the paper; it was unsealed; he stared at its contents for several moments, unable to believe the evidence of his eyes, his bewilderment turning to stark fury.

"You whoreson knave!" muttered Sir Amias in a shaking voice. "What is this?"

"Monthlyaccount," replied the Honest Man simply.

"What is *this*, I say?" repeated the Knight, stabbing with his forefinger an item on the paper. "Sixty shillings a tun for beer – *sixty*?"

"Barleysup," explained the Honest Man.

"What did you say?" thundered Sir Amias, fearing that he had heard only too well.

"Badharvestlastyearpriceobarleysrisenttwoshillins," said the Honest Man, goaded into eloquence.

Sir Amias rose in majesty, and advanced upon the brewer.

"Pox take you, you rogue, if you think to play the harlot with me you are sadly mistaken. I'll have you whipped at the cart's tail; I'll find another brewer: I'll – "

Something in those little piggy eyes cut him short; for the first time the horrible realization that they were cunning dawned upon him. I cannot find another brewer, he thought, trembling with rage, and the villain knows I can't. He tried a last attack.

"If you betray the secret," he snarled, thrusting his face close to that massive one, "that these packets, which are smuggled in and out in the ale-cask, are conveyed with my connivance, I take God for my witness that I will have you hanged without trial."

The Honest Man shook his head solemnly, giving Sir Amias to understand that he had no intention of betraying the secret. After which dumb-show he lifted his monthly account from the table and set it down again, thus drawing Sir Amias' attention to it, and repeating the sublimely simple statement that the price of barley had risen. Not until the wretched Paulet had counted out to the last farthing a sum in settlement of these new and exorbitant charges, did the Honest Man, grinning cheerfully, promise to make a special delivery of beer the very next morning, in which should be included this packet for the Queen of Scots.

"Pricebarleysup," observed the Honest Man to his horses, as he drove upon his homeward way. "Goupaginnextmonthshouldntwonder."

He would buy a new copper; the old 'un was getting worn. And he might engage two more apprentices. The Queen of Scots, poor lady, was generous; every time she sent out a packet there was a handsome tip with it; and now he had hit upon a simple way of compelling the Queen of England to pay him likewise, whether she would or no. At intervals during the rest of that day, and for many days to come, the Honest Man was heard to mutter the cryptic words, 'Barleysup', and each time he did so, he broke into loud guffaws.

It was a pity that poor Sir Amias did not know how invaluable to the great 'practice' this packet was to prove, the packet which had cost him such pains, not to speak of personal expense (for he would have to pay the Honest Man's blackmail out of his own pocket, the Highest One having bound him to a rigid economy). For had he known, he would have found some comfort.

It was a letter to the Queen of Scots from her agent, Thomas Morgan. The secret post, and the good faith of Mr Gifford, wrote Morgan, had been so well treated that the time had arrived when it would be safe for her to get in touch by this means with some of her English adherents, whose desire had always been to work for her release. A start could be made by reopening communication with a young gentleman who had arrived to smuggle letters to her in former years, who was an influential recusant, whose family seat was not very far from Chartley, and who was known to be devoted to her service.

The name of this young gentleman was Anthony Babington.

Chapter Three

Riding along Watling Street, turning into the Tyburn Road, passing through the hamlet of St Giles, the reluctance with which Anthony Babington had left his Derbyshire home the day before grew upon him with every yard. The triangular gallows at Tyburn, to which he lifted his cap in salute to the many Catholic martyrs who had perished there, seemed more sinister than ever; the stump of St Paul's spire (struck by lightning in the year of his birth), which he had seen dominating the City from the northern heights, was like a warning finger; as he passed the manor of St Giles, with the ruins of the lazar-house beside it, his imagination painted a poignant picture of the monastic life now destroyed.

Why, in God's name, had he returned to London? When he had gone home in April, he had vowed stay there, and for a while it had seemed easy to keep his vow. It was the busy season of the year in the country, and the most delightful; the hay harvest would be early; his orchards were a-froth with blossom; and with the roads, knee-deep in mud during the long winter, become passable again, there was a constant visiting between kinsfolk and friends. Oh, there was so much fullness of life at Dethick, and he, as a great landowner, the centre of it. There was the old large hospitality, the army of beggars fed daily at his gates, his tenants coming to consult him on every matter, great or small. The old religious feasts were kept up, though, for caution's sake, under a secular name, there was healthy work, and healthy pastime, the life of his ancestors for which Nature had fitted him.

And he had left it all, not to speak of the company of his wife and child, his sisters and his younger brothers, for this, he thought distastefully, as he saw the back of Lord Treasurer Burghley's pretentious Italianate palace southward in the Strand, as he smelt, even from this distance, the odour of London, refuse-littered streets, lay-stalls, and the Fleet ditch into which the butchers threw their offal. He could find no answer to the question as to why he had left Dethick in this merry month of May, and after vowing that he never would again, except that there had come a return of the old restlessness, an intensification of the old daydreaming, which not all the husbandry and country sports could dispel.

One of the servants who had ridden on before him to prepare his lodging in Hern's Rents came running down the outside stair as Anthony dismounted from his horse in the little courtyard.

"There is a gentleman called upon you, master," said the servant. "He would not give his name, but when I told him you were expected he said that he would wait."

Anthony's thoughts marked time as, having seen his horse stabled and his falcon mewed, he went slowly up the stairs; it was as though he had found the answer to his self-questioning, yet shied away from it. But as soon as he opened the door of his parlour and saw the picturesque figure of John Ballard standing there, he could not longer disguise from himself the reason why he had returned to London. When they had met for the first time in March, Ballard had hinted mysteriously of some service he hoped to do the Queen of Scots; and he had promised that in two months' time he would return from France and would disclose to Anthony a weighty secret.

"I am but new arrived in London myself," said the priest, taking the young man's hand, "and the first thing I have done is to seek you out. I knew I should find you here, Mr Babington; I knew you would keep tryst with me."

There was an undercurrent of fierce excitement in Ballard's manner, and Anthony, sensing it, was half curious, half resentful. He had been exceedingly impressed by the man at their former meeting, but, Ballard's strong personality once withdrawn, he had smelt danger in a further acquaintanceship. He did not know the nature of that danger, and he did not want to know; yet here he was, come up to London on purpose to meet Ballard; and here was Ballard, still playing the swaggering Captain Foscue while the servants brought in supper, becoming John Ballard again when the trenchers were cleared away and the two men were left alone with their wine.

"Is that man Mawde still with you?" asked Babington, less because he wanted to know than because still, for some reason he could not explain, he wanted to delay hearing the reason for the priest's visit.

"Indeed he is, and more necessary than ever, as you shall hear. By cock! I shall have need of post-horses these next few weeks." He gave a short, fierce laugh. "I have left him at my lodging this evening, for you know the old saying, two's company, and what I have say to you, my friend, is very private indeed."

"You know nothing of me, Sir," said the youth uneasily. He poured a cup of sweet Canarian, so carelessly that he overfilled it.

Ballard took the cup, his glance fixed on the other. Then he did a strange thing. He rose, swept off his hat with its bunch of quills, raised the cup, and said deliberately:

"I think I know this much, Mr Babington: That you will not refuse to drink with me to the health and happiness of her who is the centre of all our hopes, our rightful Sovereign, Mary, Queen of Scots."

Anthony stared at him. Then, with a hand which was not quite steady, he raised his own cup, sipped at it, defiantly tossed it off, and set it down with a ring upon the table.

"I make no secret of the fact that I am a recusant, Mr Ballard," said he shortly, "and as such I willingly pledge Queen Mary, the Catholic Heir Presumptive of this realm. But I do not understand, by your leave, why you should take it for granted that I, a comparative stranger, should join you in drinking a health which, as you worded it, would be counted treason."

"Sit down, Mr Babington," said the priest, with that touch of authority which Anthony remembered from their previous meeting. "It seems you have forgotten, as I have not, how you spoke in my presence of the brave plans you cherished for effecting the deliverance of the Queen of Scots, how you damned Elizabeth as a bloody persecutor and heretic."

Anthony was silent, biting his lip. What could he answer? That he lived largely in a world of make-believe? That he had been drunk that night at the Plough?

"I heard much of you in France," went on the priest, pulling out his precious pipe and beginning to fill it. "Thomas Morgan mentioned your name as one who in times past showed devoted loyalty to Queen Mary."

Anthony glanced at him and down again.

"It is true," he said, still rather uneasily, "that several years since I contrived to forward to her some letters which Morgan sent over. But when this Puritan, Paulet, became her keeper, I laid aside the service, for indeed it was impossible to convey anything to her, so strictly does he ward her. As a matter of fact, I have two letters still by me, which I intended to return to Morgan when – "

He broke off. He had been about to say 'when I contrive to get a licence to go over and live in France', but somehow that old desire of his seemed unworthy in the presence of this vigorous priest.

"Paulet will not ward her long," said Ballard, with that oddly fierce smile of his.

He rose, strode to the door, flung it open, looked up and down the passage, then, bolting the door, returned to the fireplace, and stood there, leaning against the chimney-breast. Holding the young man's glance, he began to speak, rapidly and tersely.

"Elizabeth and her government have made us outlaws. She has in effect declared war against us; the harsh and tyrannical statutes, for which there is no redress by the ordinary course of the law, have given excuse for debtors to refuse payment to a man because he is a Catholic, for needy pamphleteers to make a fortune by writing lies about us, for those with private grudges to denounce us for our recusancy. Every common fire in the City is said to be the work of Papists, as they term us; our ancient families are being ruined by fines, those very families," he cried, crashing his fist upon the chimney shelf, "who have the longest records of loyal service to the Crown, the flower of the English nobility and gentry!"

Anthony stirred restlessly on his stool, his blood beginning to fire with the rehearsal of these injustices.

"Walk about these streets of London, Mr Babington," cried the priest, flinging out a hand towards the window, "and mark on every side the destruction of your faith. Mark the sacred vestments being used as saddle-cloths or fashioned into capes for wealthy merchants, the illuminated manuscripts with which the monks enriched us being sold in bulk to butchers and fish-vendors for wrapping-paper;

go to London Bridge and count as many as thirty heads stuck upon the spikes of the gate there, the heads of men whose only crime was that they adhered to the faith of all Christendom."

"Do you think I have not done so?" cried Anthony, springing to his feet and beginning to pace the room. "Do you think I have not marked this and more? I cannot walk a yard in London without having my eyes outraged by the evidences of vandalism, theft, sacrilege. I tell you I can scarce endure to pass Somerset House and think of what it was built – the stones of the charnel-house and chapel of St Paul's, the masonry of St John of Jerusalem, the rood-beams of a dozen other churches. I go near mad to think of the priceless heritage left us by kings and queens, saints and merchants, trampled and destroyed. But what is to be done? What redress is there? What choice have we but apostacy or endurance? What else?"

"Armed revolt," said Ballard very quietly.

There was a long silence. Babington had sat down again, and was drinking his wine, filling and refilling his cup, thoughts and words whirling in his head but finding no utterance.

"I will tell you the choice, my young friend," went on the other, still quiet, but with a deep incisiveness. "The stamping out (and that within a generation) of the Catholic Faith in England, or to become soldiers of Christ, and to fight for our beliefs. Endurance, quotha? None but saints can endure our present plight. It is not only persecution; we are cut off from the main stream of Catholic life; we are regarded by many as mere eccentrics; a new generation is growing up which knows nothing of the old unity of Christendom. For the sake of our posterity, if not for ourselves, you and I and others like us must fight back" – and again he crashed his hand upon the chimney shelf –

"at whatever the cost. The time for praying and enduring is past; the hour is come when he that hath not, let him sell his coat and buy a sword."

Once again Anthony was silent. He thinking of the one and only Catholic revolt which had taken place in his childhood, the Rising in the North. All through his youth he had heard tales of it; the North had been solidly Catholic then, and had raised an army of fifteen thousand. Under the old standard of the Pilgrimage of Grace, the banner of the Five Wounds of Christ, they had occupied Durham, and, weeping with joy, had brought back the altars and heard Mass once more. But somehow or other the rising had collapsed, and a thousand men of all classes had been put to death by martial law alone.

As though he read his thoughts, Ballard said briskly:

"But there must be aid from abroad."

He came and sat down at the table, put his elbows upon it, and his fists on either side of his face.

"That is why I went to France. All last year I was travelling about the English countryside, sounding recusants upon the taking of forcible resistance against this persecution. I found them cautious, I will not deny it; they are spied upon on every hand, as you very well know, racked with fines, and many of the stoutest of them rot in jail. They would promise nothing and yet I would stake my salvation on their rising if they had succour from overseas."

He drew his stool nearer to the other's. Nothing remained now of the swaggering 'Captain Foscue'; here was a man deadly serious, vigorous, dedicated, resolved.

"So I went to France. I represented to Morgan and to Paget the need for striking soon. For mark the situation, Mr Babington: The Queen of Scots is middle-aged and sickly; there has been an ugly rumour more than once that she is being slowly and deliberately poisoned. We have nothing to hope for if her son James succeeds; Burghley has bought him, and bought him cheap – a present of greyhounds and a trifling pension – so that he is content to stand aside and see his mother kept in perpetual imprisonment, even secretly assassinated."

He paused to gulp some wine.

"The news I got was hopeful. It seems that his Most Catholic Majesty of Spain can no longer sit by and watch the destruction of religion in England, the Island of Saints, the most devoted child of St Peter. Before this year is out he will send an armada, and we must be ready to assist in the greatest religious battle since the Crusades."

Had Anthony been less fuddled by wine and intoxicated by the other's heated talk, his common sense might have questioned King Philip's disinterestedness. But the strength of the priest's personality, his own suppressed longing for some action, self-shame because one side of him still longed to escape from it all, these, together with the wine he had drunk, churned his mind into chaos.

"I know not, I know not," he muttered. "It seems to me that the present government is too well settled, that the reign of terror has cowed so many, and that while Elizabeth lives – "

"Yes," interrupted Ballard, very, very softly, "while Elizabeth lives we can do nothing."

A cold shudder went through Anthony. He had spoken in perfect innocence, but suddenly he knew that Ballard was thinking of something other than natural death.

"What do you mean of that, sir?"

"I mean, Mr Babington," said the priest, setting down his wine-cup and leaning over the table towards the other, "that her life will be no obstacle to our rising and the accession of the rightful Queen. The means are already laid; the life of this bloody persecutor and heretic (I quote your own words) is forfeit."

The young man's face was ashen; again a great shudder tore him; he opened his lips to speak, but no words came. Ballard reached out a muscular hand and laid it on his shoulder, saying in a low tone which had more than a tinge of melancholy in it:

"The instrument is one John Savage. He has taken a vow to perform it, and to perish willingly when he has performed."

A kind of horrible fascination occupied Anthony's mind when, at about eleven o'clock next morning, he followed Ballard into the narrow passage called Hanging Sword Alley, on the south side of Fleet Street. Last night he had utterly refused to meet this sinister unknown, John Savage; he had shuddered away from the thought of coming anywhere near the man whom Ballard had referred to as 'the instrument'. For hours they had argued, or rather Ballard, entirely unaffected by the wine he was drinking, had argued, and Anthony, now doggedly, now feverishly, had rejected the proposal. Yet in the end, chiefly to get rid of Ballard, he had agreed to call upon Savage in these most unsavoury haunts.

The neighbourhood still known as Whitefriars, where the religious houses had suffered the same fate as elsewhere in England, had become a kind of fungus growing up amid the ruins. The old right of sanctuary was claimed by half the rogues in London, highwaymen, pickpockets, bawds, cheats and respectable debtors crowding together in indescribable squalor. It was a district into which the constables dared not venture, a warren full of bolt-holes, the river on the south, a maze of narrow passages east and north, and on the west the Temple where the men of law, zealous to maintain the privileges attaching to the Inns of Court, would stomach no arrest made on their territory.

Sickened by the stench of the place, clutching his hat lest it be snatched from his head by some 'prig', picking his way among the heaps of fly-haunted filth, his ears deafened by voices bawling in their peculiar thieves' cant, Anthony followed Ballard up a broken stair, pushing past the verminous humanity which crowded on every floor, to a garret at the top. The skylight was broken, the walls unplastered, the furniture consisted of a few upturned ale-casks and a heap of dirty straw which served for a bed; on a fire which seemed to consist of old rags a small iron pot was simmering.

"He'll be returning for his dinner anon, poor good lad," said Ballard, sitting down on an ale-cask and drawing his pipe from his pouch. "We shall not have long to wait."

Nor had they. There was a heavy thumping on the rotten stair, as though an elephant was ascending, the door of the garret was flung open, and in came its tenant, Mr John Savage himself.

From Ballard's first mention of this sinister 'instrument', Anthony's imagination had presented him with the conventional picture of an assassin: a ruffian with burning, fanatical eyes, reckless in manner, with a cloak half concealing his face, and a hand clutching a dagger beneath it. The real John Savage bore so little resemblance to this picture that Anthony stared at him in ludicrous affront.

He was a giant, at least six foot four, little more than a boy, with a pleasing, touching puppy awkwardness. He had a trick of looking suddenly at his hands and then putting them behind his back, as though ashamed to find them so large; he walked with a stoop, the result of finding all doorways and ceilings too low for him. A pair of frank blue eyes looked out upon the world with an engaging friendliness; his manners was humble, yet without a trace of servility. Though it was plain that he was of lowly birth, he had a natural refinement, an innate gentleness. His clothes, all of which were much too small for him, looked as though they had been bought at Rag Fair, and on one shoulder he carried a porter's knot.

"Why, father," said he, "I did not look to see you this morning." He kneeling to receive the priest's blessing, and then rising, glanced shyly at Anthony. "You must do me the honour of sharing my dinner; I earned tenpence as a porter this morning, so I can run down to a tavern and buy a pottle of ale. A moment, sirs," and he was lumbering out of the room again when Ballard caught him by the sleeve.

"Now harkee, Jack," said the priest, gently and kindly as to a child, "we will dine anon, the three of us, but first we must have some talk. This is a friend of mine, Mr Babington, before whom you may speak freely. He desires to hear from your own lips of this great matter you have undertaken."

Directly this 'matter' was mentioned, the boy's face grew solemn. He stood before the wretched fire, his hands behind his back, and said, very simply and seriously:

"I was at the College at Rheims, Mr Babington, the good fathers taking me in without payment, because I thought I had a vocation to the priesthood. I heard much talk at the College among the young men concerning the state of my dear native country, and one day Dr William Gifford and his young cousin, Mr Gilbert, were saying in my presence that there was no way so fit to restore the Faith of England as by putting to death the Queen, who indeed, said they, is a mere usurper, besides being an excommunicate."

Babington would have interrupted, but Ballard lifted an authoritative hand.

"Proceed, Jack," said he.

"I told them such a thing must be unlawful, seeing that the College had published a book expressly condemning it, but, said Mr Gilbert, that is but a blind to put the English Government off their guard. And he says to me: 'Since you are unable to master the Latin tongue, Mr Savage, and therefore cannot be a priest, the greatest service you can do Almighty God is by undertaking such an act.' I pondered much upon it, and at length, becoming convinced that the deed was both lawful and necessary, I took a solemn vow to perform it myself, and I returned to England last autumn for the purpose."

He broke off, and turned upon Anthony his disarming smile.

"And I would have kept my vow, Mr Babington, but that Mr Ballard here says the time is not ripe. It must be done, says he, when revolt at home and invasion from abroad are organized. So in the meantime I lodge here in Whitefriars, where I am secure from spies and government agents, who durst not venture hither."

"Gilbert Gifford," mused Ballard, puffing meditatively at his pipe. "Now there is a very remarkable young man. I have never met him, but heard much talk of him among the Queen of Scots' agents in Paris. It seems he is a most busy worker in his service, goes by a dozen different names – "

"Evil," interrupted Anthony sharply, bringing the conversation back to the point, "is not to be done that good may come."

"Why," said Savage reproachfully, "this is not to do evil but good."

"Bah, a mere sophism!" cried Anthony. "It might be good in effect, but not in the manner. It's good to slay a robber, but if done by a private person it is a sin."

"It is lawful, sir, to slay a tyrant."

"Not even a tyrant, without lawful authority."

"The Pope would hold the deed as rightly and kindly done. My friends at the College assured me of that."

"And can you kill," demanded Anthony in contempt, "in the hope of ratification by the Pope? I say you cannot. Though technically Elizabeth is illegitimate, this was considered by the Holy See no bar to her accession; she was crowned and anointed according to the rite of the Roman Pontifical, and she took the Catholic oath."

"And violated it," interposed Ballard, coming to the rescue of his protégé. "You are stuffed with Jesuit casuistry, my friend. The plain fact is this: That in Lent of the year 1570, his late Holiness, Pope Pius V, that most saintly man, having sought counsel from God alone, pronounced against Elizabeth the Bull *Regnans in Excelsis*, excommunicating her, authorizing her deposition, and absolving her subjects from allegiance to her. Since we are absolved from allegiance, we may lawfully make war, and if we may lawfully make war, then we may lawfully kill. Would you set up your opinion, Mr Babington, against that of the Holy Father?"

Such arguments as these, coming from an older man, a priest, and one whose personality was so much stronger than his own, wrought in the youth acute perplexity. All he could bring forward against them was his own shuddering and instinctive revulsion from the idea of assassination. Thus it was that Ballard was able to wring from him the promise that when he himself, accompanied by the useful Mawde, left London next day to begin another tour of the North, Anthony would consult with his young friends upon the situation in general and Savage's vow in particular, extracting, of course, a promise of secrecy.

Anthony went straight from that unsavoury garret to his lodging, stripped, bathed, ordered sweet herbs to be burnt in his chamber, vigorously cleansing his body from the contamination of Whitefriars. But upon his mind a shadow had fallen, a shadow of foreboding, of horror, and perplexity, impossible to dispel.

Chapter Four

Fearing that his resolution would fail him if he did not fulfil his promise to Ballard without loss of time, and burning, also, to unburden himself of so dreadful a secret, Anthony met his friends the very next evening in their upstairs supper room at the Plough, and told them all. To his relief, the idea of assassination was instantly rejected by them, with the exception of Henry Dunn.

"You must admit it is the obvious solution to our troubles," said Dunn earnestly. "And I think it might be a bloody necessity. Why, there was a book I saw this morning at Mr Vice-Chamberlain's, put out by the Queen's printer, maintaining that it is impossible for a Catholic to be a good subject, and urging, therefore, that we should all be treated as traitors, even though we live peaceably and pay our fines. It is better that one woman be slain than all those of our faith in England."

"For my part," said Barnwell hotly, "I think it monstrous that this poor simple fellow Savage should have his simplicity imposed upon by those who would not undertake such a thing themselves, but care not if he throws his life away."

"I agree with you there, Mr Barnwell," said Dunn, hastening to justify himself. "It must not be undertaken by one ignorant man, but by a band of gentlemen of quality like ourselves. It must be a ritual murder, as it were," he went on, warming to the idea, his rather foolish eyes alight with enthusiasm, "a tragical execution undertaken from the highest motives by those who know full well what they are doing, and are ready to sacrifice themselves for their religion and their country, being purgers, not murderers, detesting the necessity yet convinced of it."

"Well, you may count me out of your band for one," said Tichborne quietly, "for I am sure my conscience is not and never could be convinced of this necessity."

There was a chorus of agreement from Salisbury and Barnwell.

Relieved though he was to find that his friends' reaction to Savage's vow was the same as his own, Anthony could not rid himself of the shadow which had fallen upon his spirit.

The excommunication of Elizabeth had posed a vexed question to simple laymen like himself, and he had heard that even theologians were still divided upon its implications. Apart from this, he was flattered by the confidences of Ballard and stirred by his talk of armed revolt; he sincerely hated Elizabeth, both for her persecution of his co-religionists and her treatment of his boyhood heroine, the Queen of Scots; and Dunn's talk of tragical executions and ritual murders inevitably appealed to his sense of the dramatic. Though ordinarily he automatically rejected any proposal of Dunn's his habit of indulging in romantic daydreams presented him, whether he would or no, with a picture of a little band of modern St Georges, captained, of course, by himself, setting forth with dedicated swords to slay a dragon.

Such thoughts as these lay at the back of his mind when, a few days later, he walked down the Strand from Whitehall where he had been watching a cock fight with some friends of his, Charles Tilney and Edward Abingdon, who were of the Band of Gentlemen Pensioners. It was always the way with him since that talk with Ballard; the brooding shadow lifted when he became absorbed in a game of tennis or in some other pastime proper to his years; directly he was alone, back it came again, his mind milling round in weary, aimless circles, battered by weighty questions he was incapable of answering, filled with fleeting fantasies, now yearning only for peace and security, now allured with dreams of action.

As, with averted face, he passed Cecil House, that vast vulgar palace which Burghley had built with the loot of the Old Religion, he heard from the direction of Fleet Street a distant shouting as of a large crowd. He was not particularly interested. It might be a hue and cry after some thief, a mad dog, or two drays competing for the right of the road. But as he approached Butcher Row, the unsavoury crescent which ran round the north side of St Clement Dane's, he noticed that little rivulets of folk were running out from the lanes which led down to the river on one side and up to the old convent garden on the other. A moment later and windows were being flung open and heads poked out; a coachman leapt down from the box of his vehicle which he had just driven through the gateway of Arundel House, and was at his horses' heads, frantically backing them in again, as though to keep the road clear. Two ministers, who had been walking in front of Anthony, stopped, and he heard one say to the other:

"It will be her Majesty returning to Whitehall. She dined with the Fishmongers' Company this morning."

Anthony's first instinct was to dive into the little lane which led beside Bedford House to the convent garden of Westminster, and thus to avoid a sight of the woman who embodied the persecution of everything he held most dear. But he was after all but a boy, a natural boy who loved any sort of spectacle, and in any case the press was growing so great, thickening from the Straits of St Clement's right down to the village of Charing, that it was almost impossible for him to escape. So he stood where he was, in an excellent position in the front ranks on the north side of the Strand, and tall enough to see over the heads of the stavesmen who had appeared as if from nowhere to keep back the crowds.

A brazen cry of trumpets heralded the first of the procession, and he saw, emerging from the narrow way by St Clement Dane's, a company of halberdiers in quilted jacks, the sun twinkling on their steel caps as they marched four abreast. It was unusual, he reflected idly, for Elizabeth to drive through the crowded streets of the City instead of taking the ordinary highway of London, the Thames; and the thought came to him unbidden: how easy it would be for Savage to fulfil in such circumstances his grisly vow. His heart beat painfully; suppose the wretch had done it? But, of course, it was ridiculous, the town would be in an uproar, instead of which there was this orderly and colourful procession, fine ladies and gentlemen on horseback, trumpeters and picturesque Yeomen of the Guard, the Gentlemen Pensioners with their gilded pole-axes.

Then he forgot all else as, half-deafened by the shouts of frenzied loyalty, he saw Elizabeth.

She was in her coach, with the curtains withdrawn, seated all alone upon cushions; bare-headed Officers of State rode at her side. On the panels of the clumsy vehicle the Arms of England were emblazoned, and on the roof was a plaster crown, gilded, and flashing in the sunlight. Though she was not in her full state, she was resplendent enough; a golden diadem was perched upon her monstrous red wig; her sharply pointed stomacher and drum-shaped verdingale were stiff with jewels, as were her bolster-like sleeves; every inch of her, from her cartwheel ruff to the hem of her gown, was loaded with embroidery, precious stones, slashing, frills, and ribbons. A hand in a scented glove, with half a dozen rings worn over it, and holding a diamond-studded fan, was raised occasionally in stiff acknowledgement of the cheers.

While he detested this woman for her persecution of his faith, it was inevitable that Anthony should have been infected, all unconsciously, with the prince worship which Burghley had taken care to foster since the beginning of the reign. She was England, this stiff, fantastic, gaudy figure sitting in the open coach, the new England, no longer part of the old Christendom but defiantly national. Yet, on this afternoon in the Strand, it was not the pomp and majesty which affected Anthony Babington; it was not Elizabeth the Queen but Elizabeth the woman who made him take off his hat and stand there staring at her with a strange, irresistible tide of pity flooding his heart.

He looked at that face which, said the gossipers, took an hour for her ladies to paint each morning, and whose image in a looking-glass she herself had not seen for years. The day was hot; she had spent the morning in the crowded City, listening to speeches, watching crude pageants, and the paint was cracking on that sharply peaked face, betraying most cruelly in the sunlight the crow's feet at the corners of the narrow eye, the lines which ran from nose to mouth, the sagging of the muscles of the jaw. She must have known it, and hated it, this most vain of women who would see herself only in the eyes of her flatterers, who expected courtiers to swoon when she permitted them to kiss her scented fingers. Yet she sat there as upright as a ramrod, lifting that ravelled face to the windows where folk craned to see her, playing her chosen role of Gloriana, queen and goddess, embodying the unity of this new England.

The coach, with its unsprung body slung upon the axles, jolted and lurched over the pot-holes in the road. Her waist was squeezed in by stays of whalebone and steel to make it small enough to be spanned by the hands; the sweat must have been pouring down inside the jewel-heavy gown and the bolstered sleeves. But there she sat, betraying no discomfort, calm and stiff as an effigy, save for that formal raising of a gloved and glittering hand in acknow-ledgement of her subjects' acclamations.

Of what or of whom is she thinking, wondered Anthony, behind that painted mask? Of Leicester, for love of whom, they say, she connived at the murder of his wife, or of Hatton, who danced his way into her heart, or of Monsieur, the French King's brother, he whom she has nicknamed her Little Frog, or of any other in the succession of young fops with whom her vanity and her craving for affection make her play at love-making, she whose sexual deformity men snigger over in their cups? But if she thought of these she betrayed nothing of it, nothing of personal frustration; she had chosen the role of absolute monarch, and she played it with magnificence.

And it is this woman (thought Anthony, with a great inward shudder) who, usurper and tyrant and persecutor and excommunicate though undoubtedly she is, is still a woman, a gallant and a pitiful one, without husband or child, without intimates with whom she can share the secrets of her lonely heart, it is this woman whom the ignorant wretch, John Savage, has vowed to murder in cold blood, whom Dunn has proposed to make the victim of a 'tragical execution'. And though all my instincts rejected such a proposition, I have permitted my thoughts to play with it, seeing myself as a knight of old, ridding my country of a dragon.

He turned suddenly and began to push his way through the crowds towards his lodging; and tears of shame and pity ran down his face.

He was still a-bed next morning, exhausted after a night of evil dreams, when his chamber-boy announced Mr Tichborne. Anthony was not particularly pleased to be called upon at this early hour, and was inclined to be fretful even with his best friend.

"Anthony," said Tichborne abruptly, flinging his hat on to a cabinet, pulling forward a stool and sitting down by the bed, "Tom Salisbury tells me he is become acquainted with an old courtier named Robert Poley, who is in the service of Mr Secretary's daughter, the widow of Sir Phillip Sidney, and who has a house called The Garden in Bishopsgate Without. From what Tom tells me it might be possible for this Mr Poley to get you a licence to go overseas."

Anthony sat up instantly, all his peevishness vanished.

"Poley," went on his friend, without giving him time for comments, "is a Schismatic, but it seems he has a genuine devotion to the Faith, and is known for his generosity to Catholics in distress. As a matter of fact I have heard Mr Weston the Jesuit speak of him, of how he has entertained more than one priest at The Garden, and yet has never been suspected at Court."

Babington sat silent, meditatively biting his knuckle. Eager though he was (and more than ever now) to get away from this puzzling, perilous England, his pride compelled him to make a show of reluctance. After all, he had talked so big of contriving the rescue of the Queen of Scots, he had bragged so recently of the confidence reposed in him by her agents abroad, he had acted among his friends the dashing young hero, he had made them believe, in his more irresponsible moods, that his daydreams were perfectly capable of becoming realities.

"You have spoken to me of this desire to go abroad, Anthony, more than once," his friend reminded him. "And you gave me to understand that it was only the difficulty of obtaining the necessary licence which prevented you."

"That was before my meeting with Ballard. From what he told me (and surely he must know), it is the duty of every Catholic gentleman of spirit to stay here and fight for his religion, if the chance comes."

"With all due respect to Mr Ballard," said Tichborne emphatically, "I think that he is wrong. The Church has always taught the duty of submission to the temporal authority, even if it be *de facto* and not *de jure*; it is the ordinary doctrine of Christian obedience, the rendering unto Cæsar the things which are Cæsar's – "

"She's an excommunicate, you cannot get away from that," interrupted Anthony, arguing for the sake of arguing. "The releasing of subjects from their obedience to a sovereign cannot be interpreted negatively; it tacitly preaches the duty of rebellion."

"I've told you over and over again," said Tichborne patiently, "that the Bull *Regnans in Excelsis* is suspended. When Mr Campion lay one night in my father's house in '80, I heard him preach on the text, 'Resist not evil'; he told us that the present Pope had replied to an enquiry concerning his predecessor's bull that it had been issued in the hope that Elizabeth would recant, but that as long as she remained our Sovereign, it was lawful for Catholics to obey her in all matters temporal. And you remember Campion's *Brag*, how he wrote that the Jesuits had made a league 'cheerfully to carry the cross you shall lay upon us, and never to despair your recovery while we have a man left to enjoy your Tyburn, or to be racked with your torments, or consumed with your prisons'. We are to endure, but not to retaliate."

"Then what about the Conductor Companions?" demanded Anthony; unable to resist scoring a point. "If we are just to sit down and endure, we must not break the law which forbids the harbouring and assisting of priests."

Tichborne sighed humorously.

"Oh Anthony! You know that's completely different. But speaking of them, I have thought for a long while that you ought to lay aside that service; it was never intended for married men."

It was so exactly what Anthony had hoped Chidge would say when, in March, he had resolved to tell his friends he had made up his mind to go into exile (and so he would have told them had not the meeting with Ballard put it out of his head), that he no longer disguised his delight at Chidge's news.

"You really think this Mr Poley can get me a licence?"

"Tom thinks so. It will cost money, of course, for there will be half a dozen greedy underlings at Court to satisfy, but such a sum spent now may save you from ruin later."

"I'll offer four hundred pounds," cried Anthony, naming the first extravagant sum which came into his head.

He leapt out of bed, shouted to his chamber-boy to bring hot water for his bath, and padded naked to the press to select the suit he would wear this fine morning. The shadow was dispelled at last; he was a carefree boy again, in contact with the real world, no longer the idle dreamer. Let Ballard and Savage do what they pleased; his own first duty was to his wife and child. He had always known it, and now Chidge had confirmed it; and here was the one obstacle surmounted (for, as easily optimistic as he was easily cast down, he regarded the licence as good as in his pouch).

Splashing in the wooden bathtub, drawing on his fine silk nether-stocks which were sewn to the absurd little padded rings called trunk-hose, choosing his most dashing doublet, of orange-tawny sarcenet with wings at the shoulders to give it width, he babbled excitedly, at his most vivacious and charming, sketching a picture of a life of travel and study abroad.

This mood was still strong upon him when, a week later, he landed at Greenwich-stairs to keep an appointment with Mr Secretary himself, arranged for him by this obliging unknown, Mr Robert Poley.

Paying off the watermen, he gave his name in a loud confident voice to the guards on duty, and followed one of them across a courtyard, looking about him with detached interest. He made no doubt at all of coming out from the interview with the licence; why else would Mr Secretary have sent for him? Really, how easy the whole thing had been since he had offered so enormous a sum for it! He was not in the least afraid of meeting the dreaded Mr Secretary face to face; his conscience was clear; he had nothing to hide; and he would be doing the Government a favour by removing from the realm a brood of recusants.

All this being so, he thought it strange that he should not be able to greet Mr Poley without instinctive hostility. He was too lacking in self-knowledge to realize that, deep inside himself, a voice whispered that for all his own arguments and even Chidge's he was simply running away.

Mr Robert Poley turned out to be a man old enough to be his father, and of a melancholy air which was somehow attractive. His dress was old-fashioned; he wore a linen frill on the collar of his high-necked doublet, and, despite the warmth of the day, a velvet cap with ear-flaps and a furred mantle reaching to his knees. Though of rich material, his dress was sad-coloured, almost suggesting mourning. He walked with the aid of a stick which had a silver knob, and sometimes he would pause to unscrew the knob and sniff at the aromatic herbs it contained. There was something of the look of a hound about his face, permanently sad; the queer beauty of that sadness touched Anthony against his will.

"I am honoured, Mr Babington," said Poley, taking the young man's hand and holding it for a moment in his cold one. "I consider myself privileged to be able to serve so staunch a son of Holy Church. I am, alas, but a weak brother, yet I do what I can, sir, for those who are more constant than myself. Pray of your charity give me your arm up these stairs; I find them troublesome."

"You have not your health, sir?" asked Anthony, his warm heart touched anew, his vanity flattered by the compliment.

Mr Poley stood coughing painfully for a moment or two.

"It is my lungs, Mr Babington," he panted. "The physicians tell me I should seek a gentler clime, but while I am able to perform some trifling services for those of our faith, I must needs stay here, for I am alone in the world, having none dependent on me. And now to see the gentleman whose web is spun to catch poor Catholics." He pressed Babington's arm affectionately. "I thank God he will not catch you."

It was into a little parlour looking out upon the river that Poley conducted him for the momentous interview. Sensitive to atmosphere, Anthony thought that it had a pervading air of secrecy. His footsteps were muffled by the turkey carpet on the floor; there was another carpet enshrouding a table set beneath the window; two elbow-chairs stood side by side before the empty hearth, suggesting intimate talk, a curtain of dark stuff hung before an inner door. Through the casement came the whispering of the river. A ridiculous thought leapt into his mind: It is like a confessional.

The first few minutes after Walsingham's entrance by that inner door heightened the impression. The hawk eyes were veiled to conceal their sharpness, the black-bearded face was solemn and mask-like; the introductions made by Poley were spoken in low tones; the withdrawal of Poley was so unostentatious that Anthony scarcely noticed it. There was something else he did not notice: that the inner door, concealed behind its curtain, was left ajar.

He found himself seated in one of the elbow-chairs before the hearth, with Mr Secretary close beside him in the other, leaning a little towards him as though prepared for confidences. Suddenly the atmosphere was so distasteful to Anthony that he said more loudly that he had intended:

"Your Honour knows my purpose in seeking this interview. I desire a licence to take my family overseas."

Walsingham inclined his head but said nothing, covertly watching his visitor.

"Doubtless you know of me by reputation," went on Anthony, with the high, careless manner of the gentleman of quality and wealth. "I am a recusant and make no secret of the fact; I have paid my fines ever since I came into my estates. But fines such as these cannot be paid for ever, even by gentlemen of good fortune, and it is for this reason, and also," he added with a touch of defiance, "because I desire to practise my religion in peace, that I sue for a licence to travel."

"You must forgive me, Mr Babington," said Walsingham, leaning his forehead on his hand and still regarding the other obliquely between his thumb and first finger, "if I remind you that many of your religion have proved themselves enemies to her Majesty and the realm, and therefore such licences are not granted save upon certain conditions."

"I am prepared to pay highly for one," said Babington, thinking he understood, "since the Exchequer will be the poorer for lack of my fines."

Mr Secretary dropped his hand and smiled grimly.

"I did not mean that, Mr Babington. It is true that according to custom such a sum will be required, but it will be paid to the gentleman who has furthered your suit, Mr Scudamore of my chamber. No, my meaning was that I must require some proof of your loyalty to her Majesty before I can approach her to grant you this licence."

Babington's answer was startlingly unexpected.

"I desire to serve both God and my Queen," said he definitely, "as, indeed, do all of my religion, if she would but grant us toleration. The duty of obedience to the temporal authority is an essential tenet of our faith, and herein is an essential difference between us and the Puritans."

Walsingham's face hardened; himself a secret Puritan, he did not like that last remark.

"And yet, Mr Babington," said he sternly, "there was a time when you were secretly conveying letters to the Queen of Scots."

Anthony's jaw fell a trifle. How in the world did they know about that? Then he said boldly:

"It is true, sir. Her Majesty of Scots is the rightful Successor to the Throne of this realm; there can be no treason in saying so – "

"By the Statute of Silence it is treason to say so," murmured Mr Secretary. "But let that pass."

"In any case I laid aside the service no less than three years since," went on Anthony, now feeling much less composed than he sounded, "as being like to bring my family into danger. And I will offer you, sir, this proof that I am ready to serve Queen Elizabeth: her Majesty has many enemies abroad, and most willingly will I send you intelligence of their plots against this realm." (And so he would, even if they were the plots of his Most Catholic Majesty of Spain; now he came to think of it, he would rather be drawn to Tyburn by the heels than have his religion restored by foreigners.)

But Mr Secretary did not appear particularly gratified. He remained for several moments staring into the empty hearthplace, so that his visitor could not see his expression. At last he said slowly:

"Her Majesty has many enemies at home likewise, Mr Babington, enemies who would stick at nothing to gain their evil ends. If you could furnish intelligence concerning these – " he dropped his voice almost to a whisper – "I would be able to give you something in return which would be more to your taste than a licence to travel."

Babington made a sharp movement. His face was flushed.

"I desire nothing, sir," he said curtly, "but to go overseas, and I cannot furnish you with such intelligence. And I wonder you should suggest it; if you think I am among these plotters of whom you speak – "

He had half-risen, his manner a little wild. Walsingham, laying a hand upon his arm to restrain him, was apparently much distressed.

"Mr Babington, you mistake me, indeed you do. Do you suppose, sir, that you would still be at liberty if I knew such things of you? But you must understand that my responsibility is a heavy one; I am teased continually with talk of plots, and for all my efforts often cannot discover which is real and which but empty talk. I hoped that you, being as you profess, loyal both to your religion and her Majesty, might be able to give me some assistance. It was an idle thought, and pray forget it. Now as for this licence, it will take time, you understand; such things are issued only by her Majesty herself; but I will do all in my power to further your suit... "

So he talked on, courteously, cordially, stilling the young man's indignation and alarm, and finally dismissed him with a promise to communicate with him about the licence very soon. Anthony came out from that little secret parlour elated, even though he had not the licence actually in his pouch as he had hoped, pleasantly patronized Mr Scudamore, who was presented to him by Mr Poley, and took leave of Mr Poley himself in the confidence of having made a new and valuable friend.

Within that intimate parlour, Walsingham remained for a few moments deep in thought, then went to the inner door which had remained ajar, opened it wider, and jerked his head to someone on the other side. As he returned to his chair before the hearth, the slight figure of Mr Phelippes pushed aside the curtain and entered.

"I gave him his chance, as you heard," said Walsingham abruptly. "I made it plain to him that he could enter my service, and mighty useful he would have been. It is his own fault if I cast him for another role."

"I wonder your Honour let him go," cried Phelippes, considerably agitated. "His protests struck me as those of a man so deeply involved that he is determined to get overseas, and now I fear he will not wait for the licence."

"He will wait for it, and he will wait in vain," said Walsingham grimly.

"But Mr Gifford has told us, sir," insisted Phelippes, "that since he has renewed his acquaintanceship with this rogue John Savage, he has learnt from him that Babington is made cognizant of Ballard's treasonable designs and

Savage's vow. Therefore, when you said what you did to Babington about plots, he may have taken fright – "

Walsingham made an impatient movement.

"Really, Phelippes, you must allow me to know what I am at. I said what I did because I thought it possible that Babington might consent to act as an *agent provocateur*, and being a prominent recusant he would have been of great use in that capacity. As for his attempting to flee, I am satisfied I have soothed away all fears he may have entertained by reason of my hints. And if only the Queen of Scots will act upon Morgan's advice and try to reopen communication with Babington, I can cast him for a role in which he will be even more useful."

He got up and began wandering about the room, missing his dogs and Cleopatra (the Highest, in one of her moods, had railed at him for bringing them to Court).

"He is young, handsome, headstrong, shallow, makes no secret of the fact that he is devoted to the Queen of Scots, he is known to her, and has done her service in the past. Oh yes," he cried with sudden animation, "I believe he is the very man I have been looking for, for the role of chief conspirator in a spectacular plot."

He came and sat down again, waving aside Phelippes' comments; there were times when he seemed inspired, and this was one of them.

"From what Savage told GG, Babington is not altogether approving of Ballard's plots, and rejected outright the suggestion of assassination. (And by the way, remind me to order a special guard to protect her Majesty against Savage whenever she goes abroad; he is the kind of simple fanatic who might really endeavour to fulfil his vow.) Possibly Babington is too tender of his safety to listen to men like Ballard, and yet I cannot but hope that we may use him as a decoy to catch the Queen of Scots. Marry, he would be ideal for the part! The vulgar would easily believe that he fell deep in love with her when he was Shrewsbury's page, and she with him. We could stage the Darnley business all over again, with Babington in the role of Bothwell. Her Majesty must be deposed and slaughtered, so that these two could be Queen and King Consort. And now the young fool wants to run away," concluded Mr Secretary, righteously indignant.

A discreet tap on the door prevented further conversation, and in response to Mr Secretary's curt summons to enter, the thin, melancholy Mr Poley appeared, and stood waiting humbly upon his master's pleasure. The great man frowned. Poley had proved useful enough in the past; by appearing as a devout though secret Catholic, always ready to aid his distressed brethren and to shelter priests, he had been able to supply the Government with valuable information. But Walsingham remained unsure of the man, suspecting him of a double allegiance.

"Well? Did he open himself further to you?"

"He did not, sir," replied Poley with a sigh. "He said only that he had such high hopes of obtaining this licence that he would go immediately into the country to arrange for the letting of his houses in Derbyshire."

Phelippes drew a deep breath of alarm.

"It may be a trick, sir," he whispered to his chief. "It may be a cover to his slipping out of the country."

"Keep in close touch with him, Poley," commanded Walsingham. "Do all you can to insinuate yourself into his confidence. Persuade him to remain in London; you may say that you have understood from me that I shall desire to see him again, even that her Majesty herself desires to see him, that she may hear from his own lips the nature of the services he has offered to perform for her if he is permitted to go overseas. Do you understand?"

Mr Poley bowed without speaking, and was dismissed. They heard his painful little cough retreating down the corridor.

On the evening of the Sunday following, Mr Secretary was watering his rose trees in the seclusion of his garden at Barn Elms.

It was lovely summer's evening, and he was enjoying it to the full, but then he always enjoyed his Sundays. He kept them strictly as days of rest from his arduous employment. As one of her Majesty's Ministers, it was incumbent upon him to feign approval of the Morning Prayer read in his parish church, though his Puritan soul detested something which in his opinion was no better than the Mass in English; he disapproved of the clergyman's surplice, the stained glass windows (in one of which the venerable figure of Abraham, eternally about to sacrifice Isaac, always reminded him of the Lord Treasurer), the organ, and other relics of Popery. But this duty done, he spent the reminder of the day in relaxation, enjoying the uninterrupted company of Dearlove, Knave, his birds, and his wife (in that order; he had married in succession two very wealthy, but not very attractive widows).

Thus it was that he was affronted to observe, on this particular Sunday evening, the slight figure of Mr Phelippes hastening across the garden towards him, bearing in his hand a packet. Mr Secretary heartily sympathized with Knave who, interrupted in a frolic on the grass with Dearlove, barked indignantly at the intruder.

To add insult to injury, Mr Phelippes, though well acquainted with his master's habits, did not even apologize for breaking in upon his Sabbath rest. He came hastening up to Walsingham, his short-sighted eyes alight with excitement, and panted out:

"At last, sir, at last the Woman has taken her agent's advice and written to Babington."

In the seclusion of Mr Secretary's parlour, Phelippe's trembling hands laid upon the table three opened letters; then he stood back, smiling as though he had presented his master with a fortune, watching with unusual impatience as Walsingham picked up the longest of them and read it through.

It was from Sir Amias Paulet, and was even more rambling than most of that gentleman's epistles. The Honest Man was 'playing the harlot', breaking appointments and continually raising the price of his beer. Sir Amias had strong suspicions of the Substitute; he had 'doubled in his speech' one or twice; in his, Sir Amias', simple opinion, 'your friend' (Gilbert Gifford) was needed at Chartley far more than he could be needed in London. Finally the knight got down to business.

> The Honest Man on Saturday last [he wrote] brought unto me this little packet enclosed, which being so little as could contain nothing of importance, and the day of the meeting of the Substitute and the Honest Man approaching so near, I thought good to stay the said packet in my hands for these few days, to the end the Honest Man should not think I had intelligence with the Substitute, and therefore sent the said packet again to the Honest Man the 28th of this patient month, to be delivered to the Substitute the 29th; and so I send it unto you.

Walsingham permitted himself some slight amusement; it was plain that poor Sir Amias had entangled himself most hopelessly in his own elaborate precautions. Mr

Secretary laid aside the letter, and turned to the next. This was a short covering note from Curle, Mary's Scots secretary, to the Substitute, deciphered in Mr Phelippes' beautiful and delicate writing. It prayed the Substitute to deliver 'the enclosed little bill marked -)- to Mr Anthony Babington, dwelling mostly in Derbyshire, at a house of his own within two miles of Winkfield, as I doubt not you know, for in that shire he is of great credit and importance.'

Walsingham turned to the third letter, Phelippes' decipherment of 'little bill marked -)-'. It, too, was short:

> My very good Friend,
>
> Albeit it be long since you heard from me, no more than I have from you, against my will, yet I would not you should think I have in the meanwhile, nor ever will be unmindful of the effectual affection you have shown heretofore towards all that concerneth me.
>
> I have understood that, upon the ceasing of our intelligence, there were packets addressed unto you, both from France and Scotland. I pray you, if any have come to your hands, and be yet in place, to deliver them unto the bearer hereof, who will make them to be safe conveyed to me, and I will pray God for your preservation.
>
> Of June 25th. From my prison at Chartley.
>
> Your assured good Friend,
>
> Marie R.

He sat for a long time, reading and re-reading this short, innocent, rather pathetic little letter, taking no notice of Phelippes' fidgetings. He had forgotten his Sabbath rest, his roses, even Dearlove and Knave. He was Mr Secretary again, sitting in the centre of his cunningly woven web, watching a queen bee approach nearer and nearer, waiting for the moment when she would blunder into that fine-spun gossamer which was so deadly, and lose her sting among its silken threads.

At last he stretched out his hand, at the same time raising a face which had such formidable grim triumph upon it that Phelippes was awed.

"The original to Babington," said he abruptly, and when his underling had placed in his hand the little bill marked -)-, Mr Secretary fingered it for a moment or two as though it were some rare treasure.

"We will not deliver this to Babington immediately," he said. "If we did, in his present mood he would either not answer or send what letters of hers he has by him and express regret that he can serve her no more. We will send GG to call on him this very evening; and GG shall prove to me once and for all the extent of his skill as an *agent provocateur.*"

Chapter Five

Babington, like Mr Secretary, had spent a pleasant Sunday. Usually he hated this day of the week when he was in London, for morning and afternoon he heard the clamour of the bells of innumerable churches, churches all built and consecrated by Catholic hands, but bereft of their altars and of the statues of familiar saints. But today, with the knowledge that he would soon be leaving this heretic town for ever, he had been happy.

Chidge Tichborne had dined with him in Hern's Rents, and all the sunny afternoon they had walked in Lincoln's Inn Fields, Anthony talking vivaciously of his own affairs. This delay, he said, was a nuisance, but Mr Poley, who was in constant touch with him, had assured him that such matters always took time. And next week at the furthest he would be able to go to Dethick with the precious licence in his possession, and make his arrangements. He would sell the Babington house in Derby, he thought; he must find a careful tenant for Dethick; and he would have a tremendous task deciding which of his goods he was going to leave behind.

"If only you would come with us overseas, Chidge," he sighed.

"I wish I could," said Tichborne, smiling. "But having no ties, I must continue to do what I can for the entertaining and conducting of the priests who come from abroad. Without them the Faith would perish here in England."

The day had been hot, the long walk tiring, and Anthony, after parting from Chidge when they had supped at the little tavern ominously named the Last Bowl on the road to Tyburn, decided to go early to bed. He was sleeping peacefully again now, undisturbed by those nightmares which had plagued him after his visit to John Savage in squalid Whitefriars. He had come back full circle to the resolution he had taken in March, to renounce his foolish boyish dream of rescuing the Queen of Scots, and to ensure the security of Margaret and little Meg.

The last of the long summer daylight had lain upon the road as he had parted from Chidge at the top of Drury Lane, where Tichborne had an appointment with some of his fellow Conductor Companions; but as Anthony entered the tunnel-like archway which led into the courtyard of his lodgings, it was dusk. He was halfway through the vaulted passage, walking briskly and humming a tune, when he stopped dead, instinctively clapping a hand to his sword-hilt. For a figure, anonymous in the gloom, had stepped from the shadow of a doorway.

"Mr Babington?" enquired the stranger abruptly. "I have been waiting here for you this hour past. I must speak with you privily and at once, if you please. My name is Gillbert Gifford."

They faced one another in Anthony's parlour, the casements shut, the door bolted, wine upon the table, the servants sent to bed. Each had heard of the other; and for a few minutes each was occupied in gathering first impressions.

So this is the mysterious Gilbert Gifford, thought Anthony, whom Ballard described as one of the most daring and active agents of the Queen of Scots, and who was instrumental in persuading that poor creature Savage of the lawfulness of assassinating the Queen of England. He was astonished by the man's appearance. Secret agents should be either furtive or else swaggeringly confident like Ballard; certainly they should not be so young, have such ingenuous grey eyes, such almost feminine elegance, a physique which looked as though it must crack under the least fatigue.

So this is the man Mr Secretary has chosen for the role of chief conspirator in a bogus plot, thought Gilbert. A shallow fool whom I can twist round my finger. But under his contempt was a spontaneous hate, a hate of all that Babington typified, normality, manliness, simplicity, sunburnt hands which would be expert at training a falcon and controlling a blood-horse, clear, unshrewd eyes giving a glimpse into a soul uninhibited, romantic yet practical, childishly sentimental, prickly of honour, the slave of what he would call his principles.

"Some wine, Mr Gifford?" asked Anthony, proffering a carelessly filled cup.

"I thank you, no." Gilbert's voice was a little shrill, and he saw the other lift his eyebrows. "I must not drink with you until I have said what I have come to say. I must ask you, Mr Babington, to let John Savage alone."

Anthony paused in the act of pouring sack for himself, and stared at his visitor in genuine bewilderment.

"John Savage? Why, I – "

"He is a poor man, a simple man, and he is apt to be influenced by fine gentlemen like yourself. You have confused him, and thereby you have done the Queen of Scots an ill service, Mr Babington."

Anthony set down the wine-cup with a ring.

"Let me make my position plain, Mr Gifford," said he, his eyes narrowed and his face flushed. "Of John Savage's vow I strongly disapprove. I told him so, and would do so again. And I am not accustomed, sir, to account for my actions to strangers."

"Or is it that, being yourself infirm of purpose, talking big and acting little, you dislike those who, like Jack Savage, are prepared to act, ay, and prepared to give their lives for a cause you profess to hold sacred?" He waved a hand about the room, embracing with a gesture the long-bow on the wall, the pile of music books, the hunting horn, the jesses. "Why don't you go home to Derbyshire, Mr Babington, and play with your falcons and your greyhounds?"

"Why, you – " snarled Anthony, half drawing his sword, his face flaming.

"That is scarcely an answer to my question. I did not come here to pick a quarrel; my time is valuable. So is Jack Savage. He is a humble instrument in a great scheme. I arrived from France last week, where I had had audience with the Papal Nuncio, and with Mendoza, his Most Catholic Majesty's Ambassador at the Court of France. From these great men, and from others, I had messages of encouragement to convey to Savage, my old fellow-student at the College of Rheims. I found him perplexed, and half inclined to lay aside his solemn vow because, forsooth, some unknown gentleman, rich, influential, the friend, it seemed, of his father confessor, John Ballard, had called upon him in his wretched lodging and had implanted in his mind grave doubts of the lawfulness of that which he had undertaken."

"And I tell you I would do it again – "

"And again I ask, why don't you go home and play the country squire, the only part you're fitted to play? Why don't you leave the Counter-Reformation, the crusade which may yet restore the Faith to England, to men of action, be they high ecclesiastics or humble instruments like poor Jack Savage?"

Anthony could only stare at him, speechless with fury.

"I heard much of you when I was in France," went on Gilbert bitterly. "Morgan and Paget near sickened me with your praises. There, said they, is a most devout Catholic, active, prepared to sacrifice everything for his ideals, a born leader of men, and a staunch servant of the Queen of Scots. They named you as the man to undertake an essential task in this great enterprise. But I think they were mistaken; I think" – he smiled with deliberate challenge – "I think you are a braggart, Mr Anthony Babington."

Again Anthony's hand leapt to his sword-hilt; then reluctantly uncurled itself from around the steel.

"Permit me, sir," said he, icy cold, "to explain the situation. I am both a devout Catholic and a true servant of the Queen of Scots, and have given ample proofs of thesame. But having no longer any means whereby I may serve the Queen of Scots, I have decided, with the advice of my best friends, to go into voluntary exile overseas."

Gilbert lifted his lip in a contemptuous smile.

"In other words, you are running away. You have tired, it seems, even of playing at secret societies; and as for the Queen of Scots, she may rot in her prison, or more likely die at the hand of an assassin, for all you care."

All this while they had been standing face to face like hostile dogs, but now, suddenly, before Anthony could answer, Gilbert sank down upon a stool, dropped his arms upon the table and his fair head on his arms; his voice, utterly changed, came muffled:

"Mr Babington, forgive me, pray forgive me. The disappointment is so sharp. For they had counted on you, Morgan and Paget, ay, and greater men than they. You could do so much, Mr Babington; your weight in the balance could turn the scale in our favour."

Anthony stood there staring at the bowed figure, whose shoulders shook with sobs; and though he did not know it, in that moment he was doomed.

"Mr Gifford," said he presently, still rather abrupt but more uneasy than furious, "I must explain further. Mr Ballard was good enough to call upon me here in May; he is a priest, and as such I would not speak disrespectfully of him, yet I cannot but tell you that I deemed his talk both wild and vague. He spoke of foreign invasion; I take leave to think it unlikely that his Most Catholic Majesty, having so much domestic trouble on his hands, would fit out an armada for the relief of English Catholics. He spoke likewise of armed revolt at home, but he admitted that the influential men of our faith were cold and disinclined to risk re-enacting the tragedy of the Rising in the North. All this being so – "

"No, sir," interrupted Gilbert quietly, lifting a tear-stained face. "Though you will not come in with us, I cannot permit you to go into exile with so false an impression in your mind. Pray, Mr Babington, listen to me, while I make the situation plain to you."

Ballard, in a similar interview, had fired Anthony's blood with a rehearsal of Catholic wrongs and the duty of fighting back. Gilbert Gifford had a far more deadly effect upon him. For after that opening hostile attack, and the sudden moving emotional collapse, Gilbert was utterly calm. Where Ballard had been vague, Gilbert was definite; where Ballard had sketched the broad outlines of an enterprise which appeared to be completely up in the air, Gilbert filled in the details of a scheme which had every appearance of being real, practical, and far advanced.

"There will be invasion from abroad before the end of September," said Gilbert, sipping his sack (for somehow or other they had got to the stage when they were drinking together like old friends). "This I tell you, not from any flying reports, but from the lips of Mendoza. Of course you were right to suspect Ballard's talk of Philip of Spain's putting himself out only for the sake of our mutual religion; but the piratical attacks upon his treasureships and the encouragement of the rebellion of his subjects in the Low Countries have given him provocation enough to declare war against this country. Nor is he alone in his plans for invasion. There is a Papal League formed for the purpose; the King of France is in it, the Prince of Parma, the Duke of Guise and his brother, the Duke of Maine; and the Pope himself, Mr Babington, is the chief disposer."

He paused to let that sink home.

"You and I, sir, are at one, I think, in our dislike of the idea of the conquest of our country and the implanting of strangers in our chief offices, even though these strangers are our co-religionists. But it will not be a question of conquest if our English Catholics do their part by making an effective rising at home. Without such a rising, no invasion could succeed, and therefore the Papal League will be in our debt if we seize the ports which they will require for their landing, and we shall be on equal terms with them. But rest assured of this: whether we like it or not they will come, and that before September is out."

"I doubt a rising in strength at home," said Anthony, drawing his fine brows together, and striving to match the other's man-of-the-world air. "Mr Ballard – "

"We are agreed that we must not speak disrespectfully of Mr Ballard," interrupted Gilbert, smiling, "but I must tell you, sir, though let it be under the rose, that he is but a minor agent, and not in the counsel of the great ones like Mendoza. Without vanity I may tell you that I am, and that I have assurance that the whole of the North will rise, likewise Wales, and parts of the West. Oh, there are leaders appointed for all these places. But there is no man yet appointed for two essential tasks without which the whole enterprise may fail. And I had hoped – that is the great ones had hoped – " He broke off, and gave a little apologetic laugh. "Pray forget what I was going to say; it does not signify now."

He rose, sighed quietly, and reached for his cloak.

"The hour grows late, and I have kept you overlong in talk. I hope you contrive to get safely overseas, Mr Babington, and to enjoy a long life in security. I am sure we shall have your prayers for our success, we who have dedicated ourselves to that which may prove after all but a lost cause."

He had reached the door when Anthony's voice halted him, abrupt and a trifle breathless.

"A moment, Mr Gifford. These two essential tasks: what are they?"

Gilbert turned; his wide open grey eyes glanced at the other in artless surprise.

"Why, Mr Babington, the gaining of the authority of the Queen of Scots, and her rescue from Chartley," said Gilbert Gifford.

Covertly, from under his long lashes, he watched the effect of those words. He saw the other's eyes grow dreamy, the left hand begin to fidget with the sword-hilt, the breath quicken, the tall, active figure start to wander restlessly about the room.

"You were going to say something just now, Mr Gifford, and broke off. You had hoped, or rather certain great men had hoped – what?"

Gilbert lowered his eyes and feigned embarrassment.

"Why, if you will have it, there is a rumour everywhere abroad that you had spoken of some scheme for rescuing the Queen of Scots. Nay. Mr Babington, we all talk like that when we grow excited, or – er – have had more wine than usual; it should not be held against us."

Anthony threw up his chin.

"So you think I was bragging in my cups, do you?" he bit out, his pride pricked intolerably. "Oh, I had plans," he said, really believing it. "But you might as well talk of rescuing her from the Tower of London as from the keeping of Sir Amias Paulet."

"Nay, I would not go so far as to say that," murmured Gilbert, putting his head on one side and seeming to ponder. "She was close kept at Lochleven, yet the boy, Willie Douglas, contrived her escape, and contrived it single-handed."

"He was on the spot, a member of the garrison. Co-operation on her part would be essential, and how is that to be obtained, seeing that it is impossible to communicate with her? Why, I have had letters lying by me for close upon two years, sent me by her agents to forward; but not even the French Ambassador himself, so it is said, can send her anything secret nowadays."

Gilbert looked at him in silence for a moment with a mysterious smile.

"There is a way of communicating secretly with her, as none should know better than myself, seeing that I contrived it."

Anthony had been sitting on the window-seat, idly plucking a string of his lute. Now he threw the lute aside, and sat tense, staring at the other.

"You don't believe me, Mr Babington?"

"I – I don't know."

"Or is it perhaps that you are so settled in your – your resolve to renounce all further efforts on behalf of your religion and your rightful Queen that you would prefer not to believe me?"

Anthony drew a sharp breath.

"I shall not go into exile if I have proof that it is possible for me to serve the Queen of Scots," he said deliberately.

"Then I think I can convince you. Very shortly, by means of my secret post, you will be receiving a letter from the Queen of Scots, most fortunate Mr Anthony Babington."

"You must not ask me how I know this," said Gilbert, seated once more at the table. "You must trust me, as tonight I have given you ample proof that I trust you. I have come to you, a stranger, and spoken that which could send me to Tyburn tomorrow; I have put myself at your mercy, you who, since you are seeking a licence to travel, must be in touch with Mr Secretary."

"You need have no fear of me, sir," said poor Anthony, very solemn.

"Nor have I. Now, sir, when you receive this letter, it will be by the hands of a trusty messenger of my own. I will not tell you his name, and nor will he, but I will describe him. He will appear as a foot-boy, he wears a dun-coloured livery with a black braid upon it, has a cast in the left eye, and a trifle of stammer in his speech. Have you that pat?"

His heart thumping with excitement, Anthony repeated the simple description.

"Good. I cannot tell you precisely when he will call on you, but it will be soon, within the next few days, and either after dusk or before dawn. And when he comes, you must have ready to give him in return a letter to the Queen of Scots, giving her intelligence of this great enterprise, and asking her authority for it."

"But – "

"It will be perfectly safe. Since you communicated with her secretly in times past, you must have a cipher to which she has the key, and therefore, even were your letter to be intercepted, it could do neither her nor you any harm. But it will not be intercepted. For six months – for *six months*, I say, Mr Babington – letters have been going in and out of Chartley by way of my secret post, and not one has miscarried."

"But would she give her authority to – to me?"

"To whom else? You would suspect me of flattering you, Mr Babington, if I told you half of what her agents have written her concerning you. But from what they told me, there was no need of their recommendations, for she has remembered you ever since you were a boy in the household of my Lord Shrewsbury, and has carried in her heart so high an opinion of you that she would not hesitate to trust you with her innermost secrets."

He paused. He saw the young face swept by a deep flush of pleasure, and tears come into the unshrewd eyes. But his own pleasure was a little diminished by Anthony's next words.

"I shall not ask her authority for the fulfilling of John Savage's vow," said Babington with decision. "She would not give it, and nor can I, or my friends, approve of it in conscience."

"So you have consulted with your friends concerning it?" asked Gilbert softly.

"I have, for I promised Mr Ballard that I would. They rejected it, as I did, upon the first mention of it."

And then, because he was really touched by the trust this young stranger had show in him, he added honestly:

"There was, indeed, a suggestion by one of my friends that it should be performed as a kind of ritual murder, a tragical execution undertaken by, say, six gentlemen, banded together to rid this realm of a tyrant, at certain sacrifice of their lives." He paused a moment. In the mood of high emotion which had fallen on him, Dunn's proposal took on a new light of romance; like noble Romans, they would be liberating their country by slaughtering one whom they reverenced, but whose lust for power was enslaving them. With an effort he shook the image from him, and added briskly: "But for the rest, I am willing to ask the authority of the Queen of Scots."

Gilbert immediately became businesslike. He requested pen, ink, and paper; they would note down some headings, here and now, if Mr Babington was not too tired. Anthony assured him that he was not. Indeed he felt full of a sort of supernormal energy, stimulated to an excitement such as he had never known before.

Hour after hour they sat before the table, the beech-brown head and the flaxen one bent side by side over a sheet of paper, now arguing, now discussing, now jotting down a note. Anthony drank steadily from a new flagon of sack; Gilbert drank not at all. Anthony's bleared eyes were blinking in an effort to keep himself awake when, round about midnight, Gilbert added the two words 'Tragical execution' to his notes of those matters for which the other was to seek the authority of the Queen of Scots. For one never knew. The young fool might include the assassination business after all, or at least he might keep these damning notes.

"You have a heavy task before you, Mr Babington," said Gilbert, rising at last and reaching for his cloak, "in composing and enciphering so long a letter. Yet I envy you every pang of fatigue."

He took the sunburnt hands and held them for a moment in his slim ones. Then, slinging his cloak about his shoulders, he walked to the door.

"I envy you, and I honour you, Mr Babington. Your name will live for all time as that of a hero. Our Lord has chosen you, I verily believe, as a principal instrument in the restoration of the one true faith, and as the liberator of our rightful Sovereign. I must ride tonight into the country on urgent business; those who put their hand to this mighty task can take no rest. But I hope we shall meet again, my honoured friend, even though it be not in this world," breathed Gilbert, making a suitably dramatic exit.

Really, he thought, collecting his servants at Holborn Bars, toiling up the steep hill to the New Gate, showing his pass to the watch there, waiting impatiently for the postern to be opened, and following his link-boy through the deserted streets of the City, really it had been as simple as stealing a baby's pap-bottle. The young ass! Blown out like a frog with his own importance, solemn as an owl, blundering into the trap like some stupid coney. He spat with spiteful contempt.

"The Highest One ought to knight me for this," said he, yawning, as he marched to a court-cupboard in Mr Phelippes' parlour, and helping himself to a cup of wine. He sat down upon the table, carelessly scattering Mr Pelippes' neat pile of papers, and looked insolently over his wine-cup into those short-sighted eyes which were huge with suspense. "Your decoy is upon the wing, my good sir; he is about to write that to the Queen of Scots which will enable you to show all England her head upon a dish."

Chapter Six

Anthony had got his second wind.

Directly Gilbert had left him, he had fallen into a sleep of sheer nervous exhaustion, but the nasal tones of a watchman, crying the hour of three o'clock, aroused him, and, feeling broad awake on the instant, unnaturally refreshed, he seized pen and paper and began his great task. With the reverent ardour of the born hero-worshipper that he was, his pen began to fly across the paper.

> Most mighty, most excellent, my dread Sovereign Lady, and Queen, unto whom only I owe all fidelity and obedience...

He imagined her, or rather the image of her he had created in his mind, reading those words, the languishing spirit reviving, the sad eyes filling with tears of joy. Friendless, she had found a friend; immured for so many years in prison, at last she was receiving the order for her release. The little boy whom she had never forgotten had grown up into an active, determined and chivalrous man, her champion, who through all the years had cherished his resolve to contrive her liberation or die in the attempt.

He had always been able to express himself on paper; he loved the nice turn of phrase, the apt allusion; and never had his pen flowed so fluently as in this all-important letter. The infirmity of purpose, the doubts, the indecision, the homesickness for Dethick, the hankering after a life of study and travel abroad, all had vanished, leaving only an old daydream about to become reality. He wrote as one inspired.

He told her of the definite intention of the 'Papal League' to invade before September was out. He wrote boldly (glancing at Gilbert's notes) that he could answer for risings in the North, in Wales, and in parts of the West. He stated roundly that himself and ten gentlemen, 'all my noble friends', with a hundred followers, would contrive her rescue from Chartley. He mentioned that it would be necessary to assure these friends that 'their heroical attempt may be honourably rewarded in them, if they escape with life, or in their posterity, and that so much I may be able by your Majesty's authority to assure them.' (How practical and realistic he was being!)

He rose and went to the window, unhooked the shutters, and threw them wide. The sky was red behind the crowding house-roofs eastwards, dramatically red as though London were a-fire. So suitable a setting enhanced his mood. He himself scorned the very notion of reward; but certainly Margaret and little Meg must be provided for, the widow and the orphan of a hero. For by this time he could not bear to contemplate a less dramatic end than that of himself fighting single-handed, falling at last riven with a hundred wounds, and, the cause triumphing, his body lying in Westminster Abbey, and Queen Mary attending his Requiem Mass.

> 'I vow and protest before the face of Almighty God,' he wrote, 'Who miraculously hath long preserved your sacred person, no doubt to some universally good end, that what I have said shall be performed, or all our lives happily lost in the execution thereof.'

"Thank God you are come, sir!" cried one of Anthony's servants to Chidiock Tichborne, when the latter called at Hern's Rents some hours later. "For I am sure my master must be sick. His chamber-boy has been there several times to call him, but the door into the parlour, out of which, as you know, the bedchamber leads, is bolted on the inside, and Mr Babington does not answer. We began to fear – "

But Tichborne was already running up the stair. He had to knock and call repeatedly before at last there came a groan from within the parlour, a lurching step, and the door was unbolted, disclosing an Anthony fully dressed save for his ruff, his brown hair tousled, his face pale and haggard.

Once Tichborne had satisfied himself that there was nothing physically the matter with his friend, his alarm died down. He was well accustomed to Anthony's rapid changes of mood, and therefore was not unduly surprised to find the sensible, serene friend from whom he had parted last evening become this feverishly distraught person. He acted quietly and sensibly, sending the foot-boy to a tavern to buy some small beer (for Anthony looked as though he had been drinking hard, and this was the favourite pick-me-up), ordering the cook to bring hot food and the chamber-boy hot water, and persuading his friend to strip, wash, and shave.

His tact was rewarded. Bathed and changed, and with a meal inside him, some of the wildness disappeared from Anthony's manner, and a nervous excitement took its place. When the dishes were cleared, he gave orders to his servants that he was on no account to be disturbed, dramatically bolted the parlour door, sat down, and told his friend everything.

After reading the pages scrawled over in an untidy hand, Tichborne sat silent for a while. Though still unconvinced of the lawfulness of armed revolt, and intensely disliking the idea of foreign invasion, he was impressed against his will by this remarkable letter. Mistaking the reason for his silence, and disappointed by his lack of enthusiasm, Anthony cried challengingly:

"You think I have been misleadingly confident. Had you listened to this Mr Gifford, you would not think so. As for the rescue from Chartley, it will be simplicity itself to raise a hundred men from among my own gentlemen freeholders and copyholders, not to speak of my falconers, huntsmen, kennelmen, and the rest. A hundred followers? Why, I could raise double that number! And then for the ten gentlemen who must lead them, there is yourself, Salisbury, Barnwell, and I suppose Harry Dunn; then there are Tilney and Abingdon, my friends among the Pensioners; I am confident they would join us, and I intend to sound them this very day. That's six; surely we could find four more – "

He broke off abruptly. Why did the number six sound ominous to him? Tichborne's next words gave him the answer.

"What is this note in someone else's hand – 'Tragical execution'?" he asked sharply.

Anthony flushed.

"Oh, I was fool enough to mention to Mr Gifford that silly suggestions of Dunn's. He was pleased to rail at me for demurring at John Savage's vow, and I – "

"Anthony, you will not mention any such matter to the Queen of Scots?"

"You see I have not," replied Anthony, a little sharp in his turn. "Even though it is held lawful by high ecclesiastical authority, as Gifford swore to me it is, I am fixed in my conscience against it, and I am very sure Queen Mary would have none of it. But what of the rest of the letter? Is it not well writ? By the Mass, Chidge, was ever so gallant an enterprise!" he cried, not waiting for an answer, his eyes ablaze with enthusiasm. "Did I not tell you all along that I would contrive her rescue? And you were pleased to doubt me!"

"You know nothing personally of this Gilbert Gifford," said Tichborne, trying to hold out against that infectious enthusiasm.

"Plague on it, Chidge!" cried Anthony crossly, "what a doubting Thomas you are! He has sworn to me that within the next few days I shall be receiving a letter from the Queen of Scots throuogh this secret post of his; will that not be proof enough that he is a most important agent of hers? And to think that Morgan and Paget, and even greater men, have selected me for this prime matter! Before this summer is out, Chidge, Mary will be on the throne, the Faith restored, the altars back in the churches, Burghley and Walsingham running for their lives, the monks returning, the shrines mended… "

So he was off in full cry, wandering about the room, striking dramatic attitudes, until at last even the realistic Tichborne could no longer resist such passionate optimism.

"But now," he concluded, coming back to mundane matters with a sigh, "to turn this long screed into cipher. I've found the secret alphabet which Morgan sent me years ago when I undertook to forward some of the Queen of Scots her letters; here it is," he went on, drawing a paper from his breast and sighing more heavily as he glanced at the rows of cryptic signs and figures. "Lord, what a task! But I dare not delay; at any hour this unknown boy may be bringing me the letter from her, and I must have the other ready to give to him."

As he had hoped, Tichborne immediately offered to help him, and throughout the afternoon they worked side by side at the table, hunting up signs in the code, laboriously turning letters into cipher characters, checking and re-checking, and finishing at last with the mysterious device which stood for his own name, -)-. To the impatient Babington the strain of such donkey-work was almost unendurable, but Tichborne kept him at it, and at last it was done.

"We will burn the original, and also Gifford's notes," said Tichborne, as Anthony sealed the enciphered letter. He took the tinder-box from the chimney shelf, struck the flint, and held the result of Anthony's early morning labours to the burning rag until there was nothing but grey ash fluttering upon the hearth. "Best sew the enciphered letter inside your doublet, Anthony, until the messenger calls." (If he ever does, he thought privately, and somehow hoped that he would not.) "And what of Tom Salisbury and the others? Shall we confide in them? You said you were going to sound these two friends of yours among the Pensioners."

"I've changed my mind," replied Anthony abruptly. "We will confide in no one for the moment."

He did not say so, but he also had a lingering doubt as to whether it was really possible that he would be receiving a letter from the Queen of Scots. And he was not going to make a fool of himself by boasting of it to friends less intimate than Chidge Tichborne, until he actually received it.

Patient though he was by nature, Mr Phelippes found it hard to abide by his chief's decision to wait three days before delivering to Babington the letter which had come from Chartley. Yet he realized that the delay was necessary; Gilbert had described Babington as a man lacking in concentration, and sufficient time must be given him for the composing and enciphering of the fatal letter which Gilbert had persuaded him to write.

So it was not until the Wednesday evening that Phelippes sent for a certain foot-boy of his, a youth who wore a dun-coloured livery with a black braid upon it, and who had a cast in his left eye and a slight impediment in his speech. Mr Phelippes gave the youth careful instructions. He was to carry this slim packet, which bore upon its outside only a curious little device, -)-, to Hern's Rents, Holborn, an old mansion standing a little westward of Southampton House, but on the north side of the street. He must go under a vaulted passage, up an outside stair, and knock on the door at the top. He must say to the servant who admitted him that his orders were to deliver this packet into Mr Babington's own hands; if Mr Babington was not at home, he must await his return; and if Mr Babington asked him any questions about whither he had come or who had sent him, his stammering must increase so as to make him incoherent.

And if, as almost certainly would happen, Mr Babington gave him a packet in return, he was to bring it back here to his master, returning to Leadenhall Street by a roundabout route and taking pains to ensure that he was not being followed. (It was unlikely that he would be; from what Gilbert had told him, Phelippes was confident that Babington was securely on the hook, and had not the slightest suspicion that he was being used as bait by the Government; but Mr Phelippes was nothing if not thorough in his precautions.)

The youth set forth very willingly. He had been employed upon such errands several times in the past, and so far had found them profitable. Nor was he disappointed on this occasion. The young gentleman with the beech-brown hair, the rich dress, and the high look in his face, who turned out to be Mr Anthony Babington, seemed to be eagerly awaiting him; he asked no awkward questions; he fairly snatched the slim packet; he kept the youth waiting outside his parlour door for no longer than three minutes, and then put into his hand another and a thicker packet, and with it a very generous tip.

As for any attempt to follow the messenger upon his homeward way, Mr Babington seemed anxious only that he should get away in haste, and have a safe journey. The foot-boy was somewhat puzzled by a whispered hope that he had a good horse, knew the road, and would contrive to avoid highwaymen and other perils; but it was none of his business, and he went whistling out into Holborn.

Valiantly resisting an impulse to spend some of his tip in the nearest ale house, he slunk along in the deep shadows, avoiding the little pools of light shed by the lanthorns of law-abiding householders, dived down an alley beside Gray's Inn, and wound a devious course through the fields, jingling Mr Babington's angels in his pouch, and wondering whether his master (who was close-fisted) might be in a sufficiently good mood as to add to them.

But Mr Phelippes was far too preoccupied to do any such thing. He was actually waiting at his door when the foot-boy returned; he snatched the thick packet exactly as Mr Babington had snatched the slim one, and without a word he scuttled into his own sanctum and locked the door.

And while Anthony Babington, sleepless with excitement, was imagining the unknown boy upon his long, dark journey into Staffordshire, Thomas Phelippes, his weak eyes glinting through his spectacles, was occupied with a task which was the reverse of that which had cost Anthony and his friend Tichborne such hours of concentrated labour on Monday. His glance darted continuously from a copy of the secret alphabet to the rows of cipher characters in the letter; and as the decipherment grew under his hand, he radiated such frenzied excitement that the very air seemed to quiver with it.

It was Mr Phelippes' habit to sleep late in the morning after working all night, and his servants had strict orders not to disturb him until he rang. On this Thursday morning, however, he was bawling for his startled chamber-boy at the hour when yawning apprentices were taking down their masters' shutters, the bells of St Paul's School were ringing the scholars to prayers, and the milkmaids were chalking their customers' scores on their doorposts. By eight o'clock, when Mr Secretary came briskly into his office in his Cheapside house, Mr Phelippes was pacing up and down it like a caged lion, the unshaven face, the untidy dress, the snatching on and off of the spectacles, all betokening news of the first importance.

"Better even than we had hoped, your Honour!" cried Phelippes, waving a sheaf of papers. "It is all here – revolt at home, invasion from abroad (and the fool believes in the existence of this 'Papal League', by the way), the rescue of the Woman from Chartley, and best of all, a demand for authority for the whole enterprise."

"And the assassination of her Majesty?"

Phelippes' face fell a little. He glanced at his chief like a dog which had expected praise and meets a rebuff.

"Nothing of that, sir, it is true. Mr Gifford hoped there would be. Babington babbled of it, said he, under the term 'tragical execution', and spoke of six gentlemen undertaking it as a ritual murder. But it is the most patent and damning treason without it; we have her for privity alone directly she receives it; and surely she will answer."

Stroking the indifferent Cleopatra, who was curled neatly in a square of sunlight upon the table, Walsingham read through the decipherment, nodding his head in approval from time to time.

"On the whole," he said at length, "it is better that Babington has not mentioned the assassination, for in her reply the Queen of Scots might well have forbidden it, and that would have been awkward. As it is, she cannot but approve. What are these packets which are to be enclosed?"

"Two letters, sir, one from Morgan and the other from Fontenay in Scotland, which it seems that Babington has had lying by him for a long while, and which contain but stale news of no importance."

Mr Secretary nodded, leaned back in his chair, and folded his arms.

"Instruct Arthur to seal up the original again, with the enclosures," he said briskly, "and then do you yourself take the packet to Chartley for delivery through the secret post. For I would have you there upon the spot when her answer comes out in the ale-cask, that you may decipher it immediately and send the decipherment to me by express."

"I'll ride post this very day, your Honour," cried Phelippes eagerly. He was no horseman, and he hated the fatigue of so long a ride, but he would have been willing to walk the hundred and fifty miles on such an errand as this. "And what of Babington himself? You will want him within reach of your arm when the moment is ripe for you to 'discover' this plot."

"Cleo*pa*tra! Arh, naughty puss!" exclaimed Mr Secretary sharply.

She was crouching, ears laid flat, mouth open in a soundless snarl, golden eyes fixed greedily upon a sparrow which had alighted on the outside sill. Mr Secretary detested the cruelty of creatures towards one another.

"I have given Poley orders to call upon Babington every day," he said. "And now he shall tell the young fool that I have approached her Majesty on the matter of a licence to travel, and am confident that she will grant it. And so she will," added Walsingham, with a flinty smile. "Before many days are out, she will have given him his licence to travel to another world."

Part Three

Chapter One

Sunday, July 10th, was one of the hottest days of that fine summer. There was not cloud as large as a man's hand as Babington walked in Lincoln's Inn Fields among the swarms of citizens who, in their Sabbath finery, were picnicking, shooting at the butts, or playing a quiet game of bowls in an ale-house garden.

Anthony did not see the crowds; his eyes looked inward upon a troubled mind. He had risen much earlier than was his habit in order to escape from his lodging before Robin Poley could call; dear Robin (they had arrived very quickly at the Christian name stage of friendship) called every day now, and Anthony simply could not bear to hear any more of that confident, enthusiastic talk about an audience with her Majesty and the certainty of obtaining the licence to travel. That was what he told himself, as he stalked along with his eyes downcast and his hands behind his back; he would not admit that he was having to fight desperately hard against the temptation to implore Robin to get the licence, somehow, immediately, and at any price.

For as soon as the unknown boy had vanished into the darkness of Holborn last Wednesday evening, Anthony had begun to suffer the inevitable reaction, and since then his irresolution had been growing upon him. More than irresolution: stark panic. He was burning his fingers in other men's fires, his fingers and those of his dearest friends. He had not, of course, abided by his own decision to confide in no one; he had not been able to resist throwing out mysterious hints (and rather more than hints) to Salisbury, Barnwell, and Dunn, and to his other friends, Tilney and Abingdon. Their reaction had ministered to his vanity and gratified his love of seeing himself as the daring young leader; whatever the nature of this mysterious enterprise at which he hinted, they would follow him gladly, they had cried.

But when he was alone, especially when he woke in the bleak dark hours of early morning, his common sense reasserted itself. It was not that he had the faintest distrust of Gilbert Gifford; Gifford had told him that he would be receiving a letter from the Queen of Scots through this secret post, and the fact that he had received one was proof enough that Gifford was an important agent. But had not he himself been childishly, wickedly over-sanguine in his letter to the Queen of Scots? In the madness of enthusiasm which had fallen upon him during and immediately after that interview with Gilbert, he had seemed to think he could muster his feudal tenants and ride to Chartley without exciting the notice of the government. And even supposing that he did succeed in rescuing the royal captive, where in the world was he going to put her for security?

He squirmed with self-shame as phrases from the flamboyant, pretentious letter of his leapt at him. How had he dared to be so impudent and boastful! She would not answer (oh pray God she did not answer!); or, if she did, it would be in the form of a well-deserved rebuke for his presumption and folly. But deep down there was another alternative he would not, could not, face. Suppose she did answer, giving her authority for the whole enterprise, including the rescue of herself from her prison? Suppose she was so desperate that she was prepared to trust him, whom she had not seen since he was a boy, and then only a mere page in her jailer's household, but who wrote now so confidently and in such detail of a scheme for the restoration of the Faith to England and the liberation of herself from weary years of captivity? What then?

He beat his gloved hands together in an agony, and the sweat that trickled down from under his hat with its fashionable bone-lace band had nothing to do with the heat of the day. For he had had a sudden sharp realization of what it might mean to this poor prisoner to have seen a hand outstretched to open the door of her cage, only to find that that hand was unable to manipulate the lock. He would have failed his heroine utterly; and all because of that old weakness of living in a world of make-believe.

He had come in his musings to the foot of a little rise in the fields, and looking up saw two men descending towards him. One was an enormous youth whose clothes all looked as though they had been bought at Rag Fair; the other was a stoutish, swaggering gentleman, with crow-black hair and beard, and an air unmistakably military. Anthony's heart leapt with relief. The elusive John Ballard had returned at last!

"Why, the very man I desired to see!" cried Anthony, hurrying towards the pair and holding out his hand to Ballard. "How do you, Captain Foscue? You are very well met."

Ballard returned the greeting with apparent pleasure, but Anthony, made perceptive by his own distress, was almost immediately convinced that under the priest's self-assurance and cheerful manner there was inward uneasiness. More than this, he soon began to suspect that Ballard was extremely reluctant to have any private talk, for suddenly he had remembered that the gallant 'Captain Foscue' was really a priest, and only to a priest could he unburden himself of the weight of personal doubts and shame under which he groaned. He was about to suggest that they adjourn to Hern's Rents, when he remembered that Robin Poley might be there.

"You must be pleased to give me your company at dinner, Captain Foscue," said he. "We'll go to the Sugar Loaf and Green Lattice in Fetter Lane." (It was a tavern where he would be unlikely to meet Tichborne or any of his other intimate friends.)

"Why, I have promised Jack here to stand him treat at a shilling ordinary," began Ballard, but Anthony was taking no excuses. The last person in the world whose company he wanted was John Savage, but no doubt the poor fellow could be got rid of when he had been fed.

"Mr Savage shall have something better than a shilling ordinary today," said he, in a tone which admitted of no denial.

Some twenty minutes later they were all three in a private room in the Sugar Loaf and Green Lattice, and Mr Savage was happily knuckle-deep in goose.

All through dinner Ballard played the part of 'Captain Foscue', larding his conversation with strange oaths, telling little anecdotes which had a military flavour; and when the meal was ended he rose with suspicious alacrity and went to put on his gold-laced cape. But Anthony stayed him with a hand on his arm.

"I must have some privy talk with you, sir. Pray, Mr Savage," he added, in the off-hand yet pleasant tone he would have used to a servant, "give us leave."

When the shabby young man had withdrawn, profuse with thanks for his entertainment, Anthony began at once, speaking, not to Ballard the agent of Catholic resistance, but to Ballard the priest:

"Father, I need your help. I wanted to ask you, as if in confession – "

He stopped. Ballard had slumped down at the table, his head in his hands.

"I know what you would ask me. I have not had the heart to own the truth to that good simple fellow, Savage, but the fact of it is, Mr Babington, I have been hugely disappointed in my recent journey. I have travelled through the North as far as Northumberland, where I parted from Bernard Mawde who is to sound the well affected in Scotland, but I very much fear he will have no better luck than I have had. Those who should be the most forward are the most slow, and the older the colder."

Anthony's face had grown pale.

"But Gilbert Gifford assured me – " he began, and stopped again, for Ballard had jerked up his head.

"You have met Mr Gilbert Gifford?"

"Yes, and he positively assured me that there would be risings. And because of his assurance, I have been guilty of a piece of unpardonable folly and presumption. I have written to the Queen of Scots."

"Have you, by cock!" muttered Ballard, his eyes beginning to burn with the old fanatical fire.

"I was mad, I suppose. But Gifford told me he had contrived a means of secret communication with her, and that shortly I would be receiving a letter from her through it – "

"And did you?"

"Yes, I did", replied Anthony shortly. (Oh why did the man keeping interrupting!) "But that's not the point. Mr Gifford persuaded me to write to her through the same channel, informing her of a great enterprise, invasion from abroad, revolt at home, her rescue from Chartley contrived by myself, and asking her authority for the whole." He beat his forehead with clenched fists. "He swore to me that her agents aboard, and greater men than they, had chosen me for this work, and like the vain fool I am, I lapped up his flattery and committed myself to it."

He wheeled round upon the priest, and threw out his hands in an agony of appeal.

Ballard had risen and was facing him, his eyes ablaze.

"A rope on it!" said he deeply. "You are the man I have looked for from the beginning. You are the leader we need."

Anthony reached for a stool and sat down. He felt curiously weak, and found that he was trembling. His mind was suddenly empty, and into it there poured the spate of the other's words.

Throughout his travels in the North, cried Ballard, he had found the young men racked with frustration, itching for action. It was only their elders who were content to resign themselves to this intolerable persecution, weakly hoping for better times. They had lost the spirit of their ancestors, the spirit of those who had left wife and child and home to wrest the holy places from the infidel, the spirit of Christ Himself, Who had taken a whip and driven out those who profaned the House of God. But even the older and more cautious would rise if they were assured of the authority of their rightful Queen; so far, no man had been found with the wit and credit to gain that authority, and until it was gained, all was but wind, and such men would do nothing. And all along there had been another essential to the success of such an enterprise, the rescue of Mary from her prison, a coup capable of being accomplished only by daring youth. And now here was Mr Anthony Babington seeking the authority of the Queen of Scots and pledged to contrive her rescue.

Anthony made one last effort to be honest and humble.

"But I am not sure that I can think of a way of contriving such a thing – "

"You will, you will!" interrupted the priest vigorously. "And you will have her co-operation. I'll swear that gallant lady, sick and middle-aged though she be, has not lost the wit and the courage which contrived her own escape from her Scottish rebels."

"But suppose she gives me her authority, how am I going to relay it to Mr Gifford? I know not how to get in touch with him; I have had no word from him since our meeting a week ago."

Ballard laughed away the objection.

"Do you suppose he would approach you on so important a matter and not contact you again? And you have heard from the Queen of Scots, Mr Babington, you say? You have actually had a letter from her who is the centre of all our hopes, the queen of all our hearts?"

It was the end for Anthony. He could not resist the temptation to rip open his doublet and fish out the much creased note from its lining.

"I carry it next my heart," he whispered. "Listen, sir, to how she addresses me, 'My very good Friend'. And hearken to this: 'I would not you should think I have in the meanwhile, nor ever will be unmindful of the effectual affection you have shown heretofore towards all that concerneth me.' She does remember, you see, ever as Mr Gifford swore she did, how I tried to serve her in the past; and by God I will again, by God I will!"

"And your letter to her," cried Ballard eagerly. "What precisely did you say?"

"I burnt it, of course," said Anthony, very solemn, "after I had sent off the encipherment, but I have it almost by heart."

So then he was pacing the room, striking attitudes, repeating fine phrases, all too conscious of an audience which hung upon every word. Chidge had been disappointingly grave and unimpressed, even, as Anthony had suspected, doubtful of the wisdom of sending such a letter; Ballard, many years Anthony's senior, an experienced campaigner in the resistance movement, and above all a priest, listened to the recital in an ecstasy, begged for sentences to be repeated, staked his salvation on Anthony's gaining the authority he sought.

So they sat talking through the long afternoon, the last remnants of Anthony's common sense swept away along with his doubts, his romantic self thrust into the role he had played so often in his private fantasies, throwing itself joyfully into the part, issuing orders, laying down conditions. Savage, he said, must be absolutely forbidden by Mr Ballard, whose authority he recognized, to fulfil his horrible vow; if he, Anthony, was to accept so huge a responsibility as the leadership, then he must decide what was lawful, and he was entirely fixed in his mind that the assassination of Elizabeth was not. As for the practical details of the scheme, nothing could be arranged until the answer came from Mary, and it was seen whether or no she would give her authority.

Very deep down in his heart there remained a secret, sneaking hope that she would never answer at all, that he would never be called upon to play out upon the national stage the part he was now rehearsing. But meanwhile how terribly delightful it was to rehearse it, with only this appreciative priest for audience, to imagine a dramatic entrance, to pretend that he knew his lines, to get drunk on the romance of the boy's adventure story in which everything is possible, mundane details can always be ignored, the hero inevitably triumphs, and the fairy princess is rescued before the final curtain falls.

On the evening of the same very hot Sunday, a much bedraggled horseman, white with dust, urged his weary steed forward to the great gate of Chartley, followed by a servant who had a couple of valises strapped to his saddle. The foremost rider, whose pock-marked face bore several scratches on it, was peevish with the guards who challenged him, and though he heartily approved of the elaborate ritual which must be gone through before anyone could be admitted to this mansion turned into a fortress, on this occasion he found it extremely trying.

"I should have been here yesterday," grumbled Mr Phelippes, when at last he was ushered into Sir Amias Paulet's chamber, "but for the difficulty of obtaining fresh horses at the Stilton post-house. And upon my soul, sir, I shall see that someone is punished for my delay. In the end they brought me a stone-horse which I swear had never been broken. It is only by the special intervention of Providence," added Mr Phelippes, remembering that hideous and humiliating last stage of his ride, "that I am here at all."

Then, stretching his aching limbs, he heard a crackle from the packet which was sewn inside his shirt, and his fatigue and peevishness vanished.

"Our labours will soon be over, my dear friend," said he. "I have brought that which will prove, please God, the Woman's death warrant." He drew forth the packet from Babington, and waved it in the air with boyish glee. "I can scarce wait for its conveyance to her. When next does the Honest Man call?"

He had to listen to a long tirade from Sir Amias upon the iniquities of the Honest Man before his question was answered, but at last it transpired that the brewer, though breaking appointments with the Substitute and 'playing the wanton' worse than ever, adhered to his original custom of calling every Sunday evening for his empties.

"As for when he will deliver his beer," declared Sir Amias, "it is impossible to say. The rogue had the gross impertinence to rebuke me for my impatience, as he termed it, when I chided him for his failure to deliver on the day I had appointed. But there is one thing can ensure the rapid delivery of this packet you have brought, and that is filthy lucre."

They went out together presently, and walked up and down the lonely road outside the gates of Chartley, Sir Amias gloomy, Phelippes exultant. The knitted purse, bulging with coins, which the knight (with great reluctance) had taken from his strong-box, would persuade the Honest Man to deliver his next supply of beer, and with it the fatal letter from Babington, the very next evening. Mr Secretary's great 'practice' was about to attain its object; the unconscious quarry, and all the stupid decoys he had used in the hunting of her, would soon be securely in the trap.

"Little does the Woman know," gloated Phelippes, glancing back at that great gloomy mansion, encircled by its foetid moat, "how soon she will be exchanging her Majesty's hospitality for hell-fire."

Then he clutched Sir Amias' arm in a fever of excitement; for at last he had heard the rumble of a heavy dray approaching. That deplorable, but, alas, indispensable character, the Honest Man, was coming as usual to collect his empties.

Chapter Two

During the following week the spell of fine hot weather gave signs of ending in a thunder storm. The air became lifeless, the woods around Chartley turned a dark, stale green; the heavens were concealed behind an unbroken pall of cloud which seemed to press further and further down upon the earth; and the stagnant water of the moat sent up a stench which penetrated into every corner of that great house.

The sullen temper of the weather was reflected in the irritability of Chartley's inhabitants. The sentries grumbled as they paced, sweating, on their beats, the men-at-arms off duty had not the energy even for a surreptitious game of cards. Frayed tempers found vent in silly little quarrels; the new supply of beer, sent in on Monday, was warm, and nothing could cool it; though ordinarily any visitor was welcome because he relieved the monotony, nobody was in the least interested in the present visitor, the little pock-marked man with the short-sighted eyes. Not even the fact that Sir Amias was in so preoccupied a mood that he overlooked certain domestic mishaps and on one occasion was absent from evening prayers could rouse his staff from their dull lethargy. Only a good thunderstorm could do that, they thought, glancing up at the brooding sky and at the trees which stood rigid as steel against it.

Sir Amias himself alternated between moods of feverish cheerfulness and depths of gloomy anxiety. When he was in the former he would clank about Chartley, his large teeth flashing, quotations from the more blood-thirsty psalms larding his orders and remarks. In his simple opinion, 'this Queen' was as good as beheaded, the end of his anxious charge was in sight, and he would not have to spend another winter in this abominable mansion with its unhealthy airs. Then down he would plunge into the depths of pessimism; 'the Queen' was as cunning as a vixen; for years Mr Secretary had tried to entrap her, but always he had failed.

Mr Phelippes, on the other hand, remained constant in a mood of suspense, the intensity of which made him silent. The fatal letter, full of stark and patent treason, from Anthony Babington, had been safely delivered through the secret post on Monday night; already, according to the terms of the Band of Association, the Government was assured of being able to catch the Queen of Scots on a charge of privity to a treasonable plot. But it would be far too dangerous to condemn her to death on such a charge; public opinion, both at home and abroad, must be satisfied; and it could be satisfied only if she replied to that letter, giving her full approval to Babington's suggestions.

And would she?

It was that question which was the cause of Phelippes' almost unbearable suspense. Daily he walked in the courtyard, glancing up again and again at the rows of windows on the prisoner's side of the house, trying to imagine the drama which must be taking place there, picturing her reading the letter, discussing it, perhaps, with her almoner, closeted with her two secretaries, composing a reply. Or burning the letter, refusing to discuss such dangerous stuff with anyone; or again, burning it in mere contempt, treating it for what it really was, the grossly over-sanguine, unfounded, boastful propositions of a silly boy.

Phelippes shuddered at the possibility. Only the right answer from Mary could force the Highest One to that from which, for eighteen years, she had shied away; to remove, openly, by judicial execution, the sister queen who menaced the new order and the new class which had risen on the loot of the Old Religion. It was true that Elizabeth was incalculable; yet surely, if the Queen of Scots set down on paper her approval of foreign invasion, revolt at home, and the rescue of herself from Chartley, the Highest One would have no excuse for refusing to sign her death warrant.

Except that in that letter of Babington's there was no suggestion of violence against Herself, no raising of that ugly spectre which alone could really terrify her, her own death.

Always when he reached this point in his meditations, Phelippes was conscious of a secret regret. He lived in the hey-day of the forger. He had been but a boy when he had heard rumours of that most outstanding piece of 'counterfeit writing', the forging of the Casket Letters which had given Elizabeth the excuse for keeping in permanent imprisonment the royal cousin who had flown to her for refuge, and had enabled Burghley's allies, the Protestant nobles of Scotland, to seize the supreme power there. He knew that Elizabeth herself had the habit of filling the spaces between the lines of her letters with tiny crosses, in order to prevent any interpolation by a forger. He had even managed to worm out the official secret that Burghley, when Secretary of State, had altered one vital word in a letter from his mistress to those same Scots rebels, substituting 'her' for 'their', and thus making it seem that Elizabeth was complaining of the Queen of Scots' misdeeds instead of their own.

But Phelippes knew also that Burghley, the real ruler of England and of the Highest One Herself, never resorted to the crude and dangerous expedient of forgery unless all other devices had been tried and had failed. He had laid this down as a rule for Walsingham when the latter had become Mr Secretary; and therefore it was, thought Phelippes, that Mr Secretary, while expressing something like regret that Babington's letter had contained nothing about assassination, had not made the obvious suggestion: that mention of it should be forged.

Patient, dutiful, really admiring of the masters he served, Phelippes humbly accepted the fact that they knew best in such matters. Yet he could not altogether rid himself of this secret regret. For he knew without vanity that if allowed to exercise his talent, not only would he show himself the greatest master of counterfeit writing his age had seen, but that on this occasion he would have removed from his Queen the last of her foolish but touching feminine reluctance to rid Herself and her ministers of a prime enemy.

To the household of the royal prisoner that week of brooding storm proved well nigh intolerable. Unlike Sir Amias' staff, they could make no excursions into the outside world, away from the foul stench of the moat and the solid stone walls which imprisoned the heat. They must not even walk upon the battlements, in case they signalled to imaginary conspirators; if they walked in the neglected gardens they were followed by Sir Amias' men-at-arms; if they sat at an open window, faces under steel caps would glare suspiciously up at them.

But it was not only the stifling weather which made old Bourgoign, the physician, depressed and uneasy during that week. Poking about with his cane among the weeds in the garden, seeking medicinal herbs, he muttered to himself; something was wrong with his mistress, something which no simples could cure. It had all started with the arrival of a packet which, he was sure, must have contained agitating news. But she would say nothing, not to him, nor, he believed, to anyone else in her household, unless it was to the Scots secretary, Curle. Yes, he believed that Curle knew something about the matter; he had been summoned to his mistress' Closet to Monday night, had remained there for a long while, and had come out looking very grave; but not a word would he say, not even to his colleague, Nau.

Nau had reported this to the physician with considerable indignation. He had always been jealous of his fellow secretary, and here was ample cause for it. Madame had confided a secret to that loutish Scotsman, and not to himself, who once had had the honour of being secretary to the King of France. Yes, yes, it must be something connected with the packet which had come in through the ale cask on Monday; it was that Monsieur Curle did the actual deciphering, but always before, Madame had shown him such letters and asked his advice before answering them.

As the week progressed the entire household became aware that some heavy matter was weighing upon their mistress. Never, throughout her trials and sorrows, had she failed to treat her servants as her friends; if she encountered a scullion or a cook-boy when she was carried out to her coach for an airing in the park, always she had had a smile and a pleasant word for them. But now she looked through them as though she did not see them; for the first time in all their experience of her, she was withdrawn. She seemed to have shut herself up with her own soul, as though there were some vital decision which she must take alone, and that until she had taken it, she was upon the rack.

Thus matters continued until the Thursday, and the sense of approaching crisis deepened every day. Waking in the night, the gentlewoman who slept in a truckle bed at the foot of her mistress' had seen the Queen rise softly, the lame feet hobble into the Closet, and then, hour after hour, the halting footsteps limping up and down. Even the little dog, Bijou, was shut out, and would sit there, whining pitifully, outside the closed door. Daily M. de Preau announced that he was saying Mass for 'a private intention'; and Jane Kennedy, kneeling beside her mistress' *prie-dieu*, noticed how often the book of devotion was open at the prayer to the Holy Ghost.

There was one odd little incident which set tongues wagging in the servants' quarters. It was on the Thursday afternoon, when Sharp, the coachman, was setting out to the stables to take his horses for an exercise. The Queen was lying on a couch in the shade, and as he passed her, she called to him, and asked if her favourite saddle-horse, Russet, was well.

"For though I cannot walk without aid, Sharp," she said (and there was a strange new animation in her look and voice, so the coachman swore afterwards), "there is never a horseman in this realm could ride ahead of me, even now when I am old and sick."

That night the two secretaries received an unexpected summons to her Majesty's Closet, and tapers burned there till the small hours of the morning. The murmur of voices was heard by the gentlewomen who fidgeted and yawned in the bedchamber, Nau's upraised in agitation, Curle's Scots brogue supplying a rumbling undercurrent, and sometimes that strangely beautiful voice, with its enchanting suggestion of an accent, breaking in upon the endless talk. Then silence, broken only by the scratching of a quill.

In the morning, red-eyed from lack of sleep, the two secretaries talked together, away from their mistress' presence.

"She must ignore this most dangerous letter," cried the excitable Nau. "You will bear me witness, Monsieur, that this is the counsel I have given her. Has it not always been her policy to refuse such proposals for her rescue? Was it not but last year that she refused the like offers from the Master of Gray and Monsieur Owen?

"Gray was a traitor and of Owen she knew nothing," retorted Curle laconically. "But it's different with this Mr Babington, who has been so strongly recommended by her agents, and who has served her in past. And och, man, dinna ye realize how sick for freedom the poor dame has grown since they mewed her up like this!" he added with sudden uncharacteristic passion.

Nau waved his hands in dismissal of such sentimentality.

"*Mon Dieu,* how many times must I remind you, Monsieur, that whatsoever she writes in reply to this letter, she will be guilty of what they call 'imagining treason' if it is intercepted."

"Why, as to that," said Curle, "if she writes not, she would be guilty of 'concealing treason'."

"So!" cried Nau triumphantly, "it is what I have said. She must reveal the whole business to the Government."

"Och away!" snorted Curle in contempt. "Ye ken fine that's a moral impossibility for such a lady as our mistress. It would bring Mr Babington and his friends to the gallows and ruin all those who are resolved to rise against their persecutors. And forbye," he added, as Nau attempted to interrupt, "you may spare your breath to cool your porridge, as we say in Scotland, for her Majesty has made up her mind what to do, taking upon herself the whole responsibility. It's for you and me just to obey orders, Mr Nau."

Friday passed, and Saturday, and still the storm clouds, undelivered of their burden of rain, pressed down upon Chartley, the parched earth cracked, the sunsets glowed livid and ominous, and men sniffed at packets of aromatic herbs when they had to pass the moat.

On the morning of Sunday, the 17th, while Sir Amias' chaplain was regaling the knight's household with one of those lengthy sermons whose text was always chosen from the Old Testament, from far away to the north there came a faint, sinister rumble, like the beat of muffled drums. It died, and all was breathlessly still again, but the worshippers shifted and listened. The storm was breaking at last.

Yet still it delayed. Several times that day a sudden little wind sprang up, whirling the dust, agitating the dull leaves, only to die again as though exhausted. Bodies streamed with sweat at the least effort; sentries defiantly discarded their corselets and steel caps; one of them caused a minor sensation by fainting at Sir Amias' feet. The Queen of Scots remained all day long in her Closet, and with her were Nau and Curle; trays of food were brought up, taken in, and later set down outside the door scarcely touched; and queerly, like a solo to the buzzing of the flies which sounded through the open casements, there came the almost ceaseless scratching of a quill.

So the day passed, and it was time for evening prayers. She was already kneeling at her *prie-dieu* when her household entered the dining room where these devotions were said; they noticed that beneath her transparent, cloak-like veil her shoulders were a little stooped as if with weariness, a weariness reflected in the hoarseness of her voice. But they noticed also that she wore a gown they did not often see, a fine gown embroidered with *fleurs-de-lis* in silver thread, and that upon the cap which concealed the grey hair there was a little diadem. It was as though she, who through every humiliation had preserved her inherent regality, this evening could be outwardly, even defiantly, a queen.

The devotions concluded as usual with the *Commendation for Death*, a prayer of which Mary was especially fond. They heard her voice, suddenly very clear, and with an odd kind of peace in it, repeating the solemn words:

> I pray that I may end my life in the true faith of Holy Church, and in perfect love and charity with all Thy creatures. Oh God, my Lord, full of truth, take my soul, for it is Thine. Do thereto as it pleaseth Thee. Oh Christ, as Thy arms were extended upon the Cross to draw all men unto Thee, even so receive me into the arms of Thy loving mercy...

So she prayed, and they prayed with her; but they were listening to something else, something familiar and prosaic enough, yet seeming this evening to have a strange significance: the wheels of a heavy dray rumbling over the drawbridge.

Chapter Three

Late that night the storm broke.

A fiery stiletto made a split in the ink-black sky, like a cipher-sign scrawled by a conspirator; a minute later a cracking roar, as of a beast loosed from its den, shattered the eerie silence. Another vein of fire, followed more swiftly this time by the tearing crash; then both together, a monstrous duel; and then at last, in a solid sheet, the rain.

The little man who, during the small hours of Monday morning, paced up and down the lonely road outside the gates of Chartley, appeared unconscious of this onslaught of natural forces, Only when the lightning evilly lit the world did he raise his head and peer with painful eagerness along the empty road ahead of him. So he paced, drenched to the skin but wholly unconscious of it, until at length, just before dawn, when the thunder was muttering sulkily far away and the rain had turned from deluge into drizzle, he heard that for which he had kept his long vigil, the sound of a horse's hooves coming from the direction of Burton, squelching through liquid mud.

He ran toward it, splashing recklessly through the deep pools in the ruts, and before the rider could dismount he had his hand outstretched, trembling with impatience. And when there was put into that hand a thick packet, smelling faintly of ale, Mr Phelippes, without a word to the

Substitute (who had been sent to Burton to await the homecoming of the Honest Man last night, with orders to return immediately to Chartley with whatever might be in the empty ale cask), went at a ridiculous clumsy run back to the house, hugging the packet to his bosom, for all the world like a lover with a keepsake.

Mr Phelippes was not seen again that day. He had given instructions that meat and drink be set ready in his chamber against his return from his solitary vigil, and that afterwards he was on no account to be disturbed. He must sleep now, with the precious packet under his pillow, that he might be fresh for the next night's work.

Sir Amias, though he knew his old friend's idiosyncrasy of sleeping by day and working by night, had hard work to restrain his impatience during that Monday; several times he clanked up to Mr Phelippes' door, once even raising his hand to knock upon it. But he forbore to do so. The worthy Phelippes needed his rest for a task of decipherment which should prove, please God, the reward for all their labours.

Paulet slept badly, presided over the changing of the guard as usual on Tuesday morning, fidgeted through prayers, snapped at the servants who brought him breakfast, almost forget to say grace afterwards, and hurried off to Mr Phelippes' chamber. Bur when he entered the room, all his ill-humour was swept away by the look with which his friend greeted him.

A weak sunlight filtered through the casements on to a paper-littered table; there was a scatter of quills, which Mr Phelippes had been too impatient to resharpen, on the floor, together with the pounce-box which had overturned, spilling sand. The air was stale, and there was a reek from the guttered candles, one of which had unfolded a long winding-sheet of wax down its stick. The little man sat in an elbow-chair before the table, wrapped in a gown, his spindly legs, the nether-stocks wrinkled, planted apart, his dark yellow hair standing up in untidy plumes, his weak eyes bloodshot, his fingers stained with ink. As his friend closed the door, Phelippes laid a hand almost reverently upon the pile of papers before him, and breathed:

"At last – her very heart!"

"In my wildest dreams," said Phelippes, when his friend was beside him at the table, "I did not look for anything as good as this. I'll not trouble with the first part of her letter, for it is mere compliment to Babington on his desire to, as she puts it, 'prevent in time the design of our enemies for the extirpation of our religion out of this realm with the ruin of us all'. But now, hearken unto this."

He took up his decipherment, shot Paulet a gleeful glance, and read:

> "Now to ground substantially this enterprise, and to bring it to good success, you must examine duly (1) What forces, as well on foot as on horse, you may raise among you all, and what captain you shall appoint for every shire. (2) Which towns, ports, and havens you may assure yourselves of, to receive succour from the Low Countries, Spain, and France. (3) What place you esteem fittest and of most advantage to assemble the principal company of your forces at the same time. (4) For how long pay and munition must be provided. (5) The manner of my getting forth of this hold."

He raised his weak eyes to the other, and the sight of Sir Amias' righteous wrath seemed only to increase his own glee.

"She is statesmanlike, you must grant her that, sir," he murmured, assuming an air of impartiality. "She will have no vague and empty plans, but demands chapter and verse.

And she stresses the need for foreign aid. She herself, she goes on to say, will write to Mendoza, and Babington also must send some trusty messenger overseas to discover the details of this invasion."

He began to read again.

> "If your messenger brings you back again sure promise and sufficient assurance of the succours which you demand, then (and not sooner, as it would be in vain) take diligent order that all those on your part make, secretly as they can, provision of armour, fit horses, and ready money, wherewith to hold themselves in readiness to march so soon as it shall be signified to you by the principal of every shire, reserving to the principals the knowledge of the ground of the enterprise."

"The cunning Jezebel!" snarled Paulet, writhing in his chair with rage. "Did I not always say that beneath her delicate airs and her show of Christian resignation she is as crafty as a vixen? But what of her proposed escape from my keeping? Eh? What of that?"

Phelippes read silently to himself for a few minutes, every now and then giving a little chuckle, or an exclamation such as 'Upon my soul, a most war like lady! Quite the she-generalissimo!' And then aloud:

> "The affairs being thus prepared and forces in readiness both within and without the realm, then shall it be time to set the ten gentlemen to work that I may be suddenly transported out of this place. This is the plot which I consider best for this enterprise; for stirring on this side before you be sure of sufficient foreign forces, that were for nothing but to put yourselves in

> danger of following the miserable fortune of such as have heretofore laboured in the like actions – "

"The Rising in the North," muttered Paulet. "She is remembering the Rising in the North, the cunning bitch!"

> " – and if you take me out of this place, be well assured to set me in the midst of a good army, or some very secure strength, where I may safely stay till the assembling of your forces and arrival of the said foreign succours. It were sufficent cause given to the Queen, in catching me again, to enclose me in some hold out of which I should never escape, if she did me no worse, and to pursue with all extremity those who assisted me, which would grieve me more than all the unhappiness that would fall upon myself."

"Unhappiness, quotha!" snorted Sir Amias. "That which shall fall upon her is a blow betwixt her head and her shoulders."

He heaved himself out of his chair, strode to the window, and flung open a casement, snuffing the fresh air like a war-horse. In his fury at his prisoner's audacity in seeking to escape from his keeping, he had forgotten his relief that she had written precisely that which it was hoped she would write.

"Do you not wish to hear, sir," asked Phelippes softly, "how the Woman suggests she may be rescued?"

Sir Amias had banged the casement shut and was back in his chair in an instant.

"Let me see," said Phelippes, peering at the sheets of paper before him, "there is a great deal of stuff with which I need not fatigue you, ere we come to that – but statesmanlike, my dear friend, we must be fair to her, very statesmanlike and showing an almost masculine practicalness. Her friends must earnestly assure themselves of the good faith of those in whom they confide (did she but know how trusting they are of Mr Gifford and Mr Mawde!); in case the foreign invasion does not take place, on no account must they proceed with the risings; but if, before they can rescue her, she is put in the Tower, then – here is a passage you will relish – 'notwithstanding what may be done to me, delay not, for God's sake, to proceed with the enterprise; for I shall at any time die most contentedly, understanding of your delivery out of the servitude wherein you are holden slaves'."

"I relish it as little as you would sugar in your muscadine," growled the knight. "A murrain on such mock heroics! Get to the point, my friend, for the love of Jesu."

Yes, it was a shame to tease him, reflected Phelippes. After all it was only natural that, as her keeper, Sir Amias should be most concerned with the Woman's schemes for getting free.

> "First," he read, "that on a certain day appointed for my going abroad on horseback, on the moors between this and Stafford, where ordinarily you know but few people pass, let fifty or sixty horsemen, well mounted and armed, come to take me away, as they may easily, my keeper having with him but eighteen or twenty horse, armed only with pistols."

Sir Amias' face was so suffused with blood that he seemed about to suffer an apoplexy.

"God's throat!" he spluttered, "I believe she has been hatching some such plot for weeks. She cannot walk, she says, but she could get her necessary exercise a-horseback; and then must that old knave, her physician, come to me and whine about her health, insisting upon the ease it would give her if she might go hawking on the moors. I have my orders, sir, said I to him, and in my simple opinion this Queen may have all the exercise she needs here in the park. As for hawking, said I, or any such-like sport, this Queen would be better employed in imploring God's pardon for her sins, and if she would hear a good minister, I would send my own chaplain to her – "

"Nay, now, Sir Amias," soothed Phelippes, "her Majesty and all the world knows how good and strict a keeper you have been, and that the Woman would never persuade you, not with all her devilish wiles, to lay aside your caution. But hear the rest."

Again he took up his decipherment.

> "Secondly, to come at midnight and set fire to the barns, which are near to the house; and whilst my guardian's servants come forth to the fire, your company, having upon them a mark whereby they may be known to one another, some of them may surprise the house, where I hope, with the few servants I have around me, I shall be able to give your people aid. Thirdly, that some shall bring carts hither early in the morning. These carts may be so prepared that, being in the midst of the great gate, they may fall down or otherwise overthrow; that thereupon you might come suddenly and make yourselves masters of the house and carry me away; so you might easily do before any number of soldiers, who lodge in sundry places, some half a mile away, could come to relieve... "

It took Mr Phelippes a considerable time to reassure his friend that there was really nothing to fear, Paulet at first refusing to listen to the reminder that such schemes were impossible, since Babington, apart from the emptiness of his promises, was under constant observation, and that in any case as soon as Mary's fatal letter was safely delivered to Mr Secretary, it would be time to act.

At last the knight calmed down, and instead of rushing out to double the guard at the gates and to bring all his men-at-arms in from the village (as at first he had insisted that he must do), he went off to his own apartments to write a little note to Mr Secretary, a note which, with the fatal letter, would go to London by express. He was full of pious congratulations; Walsingham was compared with various Old Testament worthies, was informed that 'God hath blessed your faithful and careful labours', and was committed to 'the mercy of the Almighty and the favour of her Majesty' by 'your assured, poor Friend, A Paulet'.

Phelippes wrote at greater length to his chief. Now that the major anxiety was removed, now that he knew 'the Woman' was doomed, he was anxious for the punishment of those who had been her unwitting decoys.

> I look, [he wrote], for your Honour's speedy resolution touching Babington's apprehension. I think, under correction, that you have enough of him; unless you would discover more particulars of his confederates, which may be done even in his imprisonment.

Yes, he thought happily, Mr Topcliffe could be relied upon to wrest from Babington the names of his confederates in the country, if any such existed. He suggested a search of the young man's lodging after the letter was delivered, since, despite Mary's express command to Babington to burn her letter as soon as he had memorized its contents, 'it is like, for all her commandment, her letter will not be so soon defaced. I wish it for an evidence against her, if it please God to inspire her Majesty with that heroical courage that were meet for the avenge of God's cause and the security of herself and this State.'

He paused and bit the end of his quill. He had been going to add that he was sending both the original and his decipherment of it to London by express, as he himself was a poor horseman; but suddenly he had remembered that when Mr Secretary had sent him to Chartley, and had ordered that, if the Woman answered Babington's letter, Phelippes should decipher her reply upon the spot and send him the decipherment, he had not mentioned the sending of the original. Was not he, Phelippes, justified, therefore, in retaining the original until he himself returned to London?

For suppose, just suppose, that it did not please God to inspire the Highest One with the heroical courage needed to order judicial execution, even after such stark treason was laid before her, might not a little something be inserted into the original, a little something about assassination?

He rose and walked up and down, striving to be honest with himself. He entirely subscribed to the axiom that it is lawful to do ill that good may come; he believed with all his soul that such a thing as forgery was lawful if it ensured the triumph of God's cause and the safety of the realm. On the other hand, he was aware that his own skill as a forger made him dote upon that art for its own sake. How far was he being influenced at present by his private longings to practise his pastime?

Nonsense, he thought sensibly, he was entirely concerned for the need of the speedy execution of this Woman who was so great a threat to the safety of England, both religious and political. And, of course, for the safety of the original letter. He dared not trust that precious paper into the hands of a post-boy. He would send his decipherment to Mr Secretary; undoubtedly Mr Secretary would show it to Lord Burghley; and Lord Burghley would decide whether or not to lay it before the Highest One. If, in Lord Burghley's expert opinion, the decipherment was sufficient to gain the Highest One's consent to the Woman's trial and execution, why then Mr Phelippes would hand in the original; if, on the other hand, it were deemed necessary to insert a little something before showing the letter to her Majesty... He licked his lips which suddenly had become very dry.

Taking up his quill again, he wrote Mr Secretary that for safety's sake he was sending only the decipherment, and that he himself would bring the original in the course of a day or two. He added a hope that the two secretaries, Nau and Curle, would be hanged out of hand (for they might have kept minutes and notes of the letter, and that would be awkward if there was going to be a forged insertion); he expressed disappointment at not hearing that Ballard, that really dangerous man, had been apprehended; and he hinted discreetly, not for the first time, his own poor opinion of Bernard Mawde and his fear that Ballard suspected him. He humbly hoped that all the ports would be watched, in case the priest decided to make a bolt for it, and he was 'your Honour's most humble to command, Tho. Phelippes.'

He sighed a little; it was already noon, and he had worked throughout the previous night. He was conscious for the first time of fatigue, and also of the stuffiness of this room wherein he had been shut up with his labours. So he in his turn opened the casement and snuffed the rich scents of the earth drawn out by the recent storm.

His room was on the second floor of Sir Amias' side of the house, and looking idly across at the opposite wing he realized that it was there the prisoner was lodged, and that, moreover, he could see into one of the rooms. Screwing up his pale weak eyes, he squinted intently; the casements in the chamber opposite were open, and he saw, plain in the mellow sunlight, a chair with a richly carved back and arms, and a shabby, faded cloth of estate above it.

And at the sight of that symbol of royalty, his venom took possession of him. He hastened back to his table, sealed up his decipherment of the fatal letter, and his covering note to Mr Secretary, and then, for the first time in his life, allowed exultation to override his inherent caution.

He took up a new quill, daintily dipped the point into the inkhorn, and on the outside of the packet he drew a little device. It was the outline of a gallows.

Chapter Four

The week passed in such suspense by Sir Amias and his friend at Chartley had been spent very pleasurably by Mr Gilbert Gifford in London. A note from Mr Secretary (for, for safety's sake, Walsingham communicated with GG now only by messenger) had ordered him to keep in constant touch with Babington and his friends, report everything they said and did, and urge them to go forward with their plans. It was essential, wrote Mr Secretary, that he should be able to find them when he wanted them; and since Bernard Mawde was still in Scotland, and Robert Poley was laid upon a bed of sickness, GG was the only agent for this task.

So Gilbert had called at Hern's Rents at the beginning of the week. He had slipped over to France, he told Anthony, since their previous meeting, and had reported to those whom he termed mysteriously 'the great ones' the happy news that Mr Babington had agreed to seek the authority of the Queen of Scots for their enterprise, and to contrive her rescue. So overjoyed had been these great ones, said Gilbert, that they had appointed Mr Babington the leader of the English risings, or at least of those in the northern parts where he had great credit and influence.

Throughout that stifling week, Gilbert was constantly in the company of Anthony and of his young friends, dining and supping with them in their favourite taverns, watching in pretended admiration when they amused themselves in the fencing school or on the tennis court, listening to their solemn talk when, in some private supper room which Babington's wealth and extravagance could always demand, they would babble of their empty, contradictory, treasonable plans.

One day at the barber-surgeon's above which Tom Salisbury lodged, Gilbert had a glimpse of Babington at his most typical. The youth had been imbibing pretty freely at dinner, and now nothing would content him, while he waited for Barnwell to have his hair and beard trimmed, but that an itinerant artist should paint his portrait, he cried; in so exalté a mood was he that he even invited poor Jack Savage, who was humbly tagging along with these fine gentlemen, to join the sitters. Finding a plausible excuse for declining the like honour, Gilbert thought to himself: Soon I shall be seeing these crude likenesses reproduced in the *Last Dying Speeches and Confessions* which always sell so well at Tyburn.

He could scarcely keep a straight face when, the portraits finished, Babington gravely examined the work, flung the artist a handful of money without counting it, called for a pen and ink, and scrawled beneath the picture a snippet of heroic verse: *'Hi mihi sunt comites quos ipsa pericula jungent.*

But then, of course, Chidiock Tichborne must come in, glance at the inscription, and whisper urgently:

"No, no, Anthony; it adds but another and unnecessary risk. Suppose your lodgings were searched?"

Gilbert watched the young fool waver, watched his common sense struggle with the desire for self-dramatization, watched with contempt as his quill scratched out the dangerously significant quotation and substituted the cryptic query: *'Quorsom haec alion properantibus?'*

He was a little concerned about Tichborne's influence over his bosom friend; he was almost certain it was 'Chidge' who was preventing Babington from writing to sound the influential Catholics in his own county, and this was tiresome, because naturally Mr Secretary wanted as many as possible drawn into the plot. But on the whole Gilbert was delighted with this bunch of harmless conspirators, hugging to himself the knowledge that they were being fooled, and that he himself was taking a major part in that fooling.

Again and again as he sat amongst them, the recipient of their most precious secrets, he was reminded of his boyhood in the country, of the cutting of a hayfield, and of the wild scattering of conies which had thought themselves so secure in the long grass. He had hated the rough, sunburnt boys and the lean-nosed greyhounds who had waited for the conies' dislodgement, but not because he had had any sympathy for the poor rabbits. He had hated, too, his youth abroad, the school lads with whom he had been unpopular only because he was so much cleverer than they, despised their rough sports, had a feminine elegance which they could not appreciate, could worm his way into the favour of the masters. But he had hated the masters almost as much as he had loathed his contemporaries, and in particular one master, his immediate superior in the College at Rome, who had engineered his dismissal from the College because, forsooth, he had his own ideas of recreation.

And now he was among the like callow schoolboys, grown a little older but no wiser, still satisfied with crude and sweaty sports, still talking in jargon, of jesses and imping-needles, of sly-cuts and master-hits, and of the rival merits of the French and English horns in hunting. But his own hatred of them was no longer self-torturing, for he nursed the knowledge of their coming destruction by his means.

His contempt for their innocence and harmlessness grew daily. Solemn as children, they whispered together of exploits, of impossible adventures, of derring-do. Even Ballard joined in this schoolboy plotting, and that to Gilbert was the most delightful of all, because Ballard typified for him the priestly superior by whose advice he had been dismissed from the College at Rome. And then, of course, there was Babington himself, Babington a prey to inward panic (as Gilbert's shrewd malice was quick to note); it was there in his eyes, which had begun to have shadows under them, in his increased drinking, in sudden jerky movements, in a preoccupation which made him miss an easy ball at tennis or let his opponent get under his guard in a venue at the fencing-school. And then, suddenly, he would remember that he had been appointed the leader of this absurd little secret society, and would whip up his pride, feign resolution, contradict for the sake of exerting his authority, doggedly act his part.

The two young Gentlemen Pensioners, Babington's friends at Court, had joined the group, and were full of an airy project of their own.

"It would be simple," urged Tilney, "to kidnap her Majesty and carry her to some stronghold in the country. And there we would hold her in honourable captivity until we had persuaded her to dismiss Burghley and grant toleration of our religion."

"Yes, yes," chimed in Abingdon. "It is not she, but these Ministers of hers who are at the bottom of this persecution. She is no Protestant at heart; she has a contempt for Burghley's Establishment, she was much distressed when the late Pope excommunicated her, and I know very well," he added solemnly, as though deep in Elizabeth's confidence, "that there is nothing she desires more than to be reconciled to Holy Church."

"All the same," said Barnwell, tugging at his fair beard, "it would be necessary to give her a fright, and the best way of doing that would be to set fire to her ships in the Thames. Or perhaps it would be sufficient to spike their guns – "

"I have thought of the best scheme of all," interrupted Babington. He was in one of his deceptively vigorous moods, flushed with wine, tipsily important. "It's well known that the common people, being so grievously oppressed with rack-renting by the new upstart landlords, and by the enclosing of the common lands, are ready to rise for their liberties. Thus if we put these social grievances in the forefront of our programme, we would be sure of the backing of thousands, even of those who respect little any religion at all."

"Oh, Anthony!" sighed Tichborne. "How do you suppose we are going to reach these people? Are we to ride about the country, urging them to revolt – "

"Why must you always pour cold water on everything I suggest?" shouted Babington, rounding on his friend. "If you have so little zeal for your religion, and so little trust in me, your leader – "

"He is a pupil of the Jesuits," sneered Ballard softly, "who preach that we must sit tamely down and watch the ruin of the Faith in England."

"Under your favour, sir," retorted Tichborne, quietly but with a heightened colour, "they preach the resisting not evil which has been the doctrine of the Church from the time of the Apostles."

"Damme, you'd make a good preacher yourself, my man!" cried Babington. "If you mislike our enterprise, and set yourself up to know better what is right and wrong than

Mr Ballard, why do you frequent our company, my little plaster saint?"

Tichborne did not reply in words, but his grave eyes, encountering Anthony's, gave a private answer: It is because I am your friend, and would protect you from your more reckless self.

Then up spoke the young giant, John Savage, sitting humbly a little apart from the rest, nursing a can of ale obligingly bought him by one of these fine gentlemen.

"If it had been permitted, sirs, I would have done the one thing necessary long ere this. I would have fulfilled my vow, and by ridding this land of a tyrant, I would have freed us all."

"My honest Jack!" cried Ballard, beaming on his protégé. "You shall fulfil your vow when the time is ripe – "

"He will not!" stormed Anthony. "You have accepted me as your leader, and you will please to do only what I think best."

It was towards the end of the week that Gilbert, calling on Babington at Hern's Rents one morning, found Ballard there. Babington, whose indolent habit of rising late had grown upon him, was still in bed, sitting up with his bare arms round his knees, his brown hair ruffled, pouches under his eyes telling of nervous strain and last night's session with Bacchus. Ballard, wandering restlessly about the room, had undergone a change; he still wore the gaudy clothes of 'Captain Foscue', but he seemed oddly to have shrunk inside them, and the bluff, hearty manner, the swaggering self-confidence, had disappeared. He turned on Gilbert a face which had aged in a night.

"There is the worst of news," said he, without so much as greeting the newcomer. "Certain information has reached me that Bernard Mawde, my travelling companion for so long, is a spy in the employ of Mr Secretary."

Gilbert was instantly on the alert.

"Never mind where I obtained the information," went on the priest, sitting heavily down upon a joint-stool, "but I have it for an undoubted fact that before I met him, Mawde was in the clink. He had told me that he had accused the Protestant Archbishop of York of fornication with an innkeeper's wife; what he did not tell me was that his Grace had paid him a handsome sum to keep his mouth shut. Neither did he think fit to mention that in '83 there was an enquiry into the business by the Privy Council, the affair having leaked out. The Archbishop, it seems, vindicated himself, and the council found Mawde guilty of blackmail, sentenced him to pay back all the money he had obtained, and to lie in prison for three years. Only by humbly confessing his crime did he escape mutilation. But long ere the sentence expired, Mr Secretary took him out of the Clink and into his own service, thereafter doing me the honour of appointing this rogue to attach himself to me."

Gilbert began to exclaim in righteous indignation against Mawde, but the priest cut him short.

"I blame myself," said he abruptly. "I ought to have been suspicious of the ease with which Montalto, as he called himself, obtained passports and licences. And now it may be that my folly has ruined our whole enterprise, for Mawde knew all about the proposed revolt at home, and what he knows Walsingham will know likewise."

"It can't be helped," said Babington impatiently. "He knows nothing of the developments since I took over the leadership, nothing of my letter to the Queen of Scots, or of the preparations for foreign invasion by the Papal League. But for yourself, Mr Ballard, you are in grave personal danger, for, apart from anything else, this rogue will know you are a priest and have broke prison."

"Mr Babington is right," eagerly chimed in Gilbert. "And if I might venture to suggest it, sir, you will put yourself in my hands. I know half a dozen places where you may lie very secure – "

"It's not good enough," interrupted Anthony, suddenly springing out of bed, flinging his furred gown round his shoulders, and marching to the steel-glass to comb his hair. "Mr Ballard must be gone overseas."

"You must give me leave to be the best judge of that," said Ballard, with a sudden new dignity. "Those of my sacred calling who venture into England nowadays must be ready at any moment to pay the extreme penalty."

Gilbert immediately broke in again, full of respectful admiration of Mr Ballard's heroical courage, full also of suggestions for his security. It would only be for a little while that he must lie low; very soon now there would come the answer from the Queen of Scots, and then their plans could be put into action, and the Government would have its hands too full to hunt down priests. Meanwhile, might he suggest certain lodgings where Mr Ballard could lie secure? His own work as an agent had made it necessary for him to find such places; he knew half a dozen in the City alone. He would make a list of them, and Mr Ballard should choose which suited him best.

Mr Ballard, kindly patting the enthusiastic young man on the shoulder, thanked him for his care of him, but rather disappointingly added that he himself knew of a place where he could lie low. Well, I've done my best, thought Gilbert; and dutifully wrote a note to Mr Secretary, informing him that Ballard had discovered the facts about Bernard Mawde.

Gilbert's enjoyment of his job as an *agent provocateur* had never blinded him to the risks it entailed, nor did he forget the fate of certain other gentlemen, similarly employed in the past, who, their usefulness ended, had gone to the gallows with their dupes. During this week, therefore, he was much employed upon taking measures for his own security. A crisis was approaching; as soon as Mary's answer to Babington's letter was received in London, it would be time for Mr Secretary to hunt down all the silly little conies who had fancied themselves so secure in the hay. And Mr Gilbert Gifford was quite determined that some unfortunate oversight of Mr Secretary's was not going to include himself in the bag.

When ordering GG to frequent the company of the conspirators, Mr Secretary had deemed it safer for him to remove from Mr Phelippes' house in Leadenhall Street and take another lodging. Forth from this lodging he sallied daily upon business of his own. It was never the habit of Mr Secretary to inform individual agents of all the details of a 'practice', and he had not thought fit to tell Gilbert that Mr Phelippes had gone in person to Chartley to supervise the smuggling in of Babington's letter to Mary and to await her reply. But Gilbert had his own ways of finding out these things; his artlessness, his boyish charm, his appealing innocence, all made him popular with servants, and he had his confidants among these lowly folk, in Mr Secretary's own household, in that of Mr Phelippes, and elsewhere.

The one in Mr Phelippes' house was a certain homely-faced serving-man whose name was Simon, and who wore a blue coat. Gilbert had selected him partly because, during the time when he himself had lodged in Leadenhall Street, he had observed that the man was often employed by his master in carrying important letters, partly because Simon had a mysterious internal ailment, described by him as 'an 'umour in me stomick', and if encouraged to enlarge upon the symptoms, very easily could be led on to indiscretions concerning his master's business. Thus had it come about that Gilbert knew that Mr Phelippes had gone in person to Chartley at the end of the previous week; and why he had gone there, Gilbert needed no telling.

There remained the vital questions: Would the Queen of Scots answer Babington's letter, and, if so, when would her answer reach London? It was because he sought a reply to these questions, so important to his own safety, that Gilbert called every day at Mr Phelippes' house and listened very patiently to a rehearsal of the misbehaviour of the homely-faced one's stomach. But it was in vain. Mr Phelippes' household had received no word as to when their master might be expected home.

The following weekend passed, and Gilbert became anxious. Remembering that it had always been the habit of that really delightful character, the Honest Man, to call for his empties on a Sunday evening, he made his calculations. If the Queen of Scots replied to Babington's letter, her answer almost certainly would have come out in the empty ale cask on Sunday night; Phelippes would work at the decipherment all Monday, and in all probability, instead of bringing it to London himself, would dispatch it through her Majesty's post. An express post, who had a fresh horse waiting for him at every ten-mile stage, could cover as much as seventy miles in a day; therefore it was possible that this particular post-boy, supposing that he rode through the previous night, might be expected in London late on Tuesday.

After a dutiful call on Babington on Tuesday morning, Gilbert changed his lodging, taking a room at a little tavern in Highgate, convenient to the post-house there, where the posts from the North got their last remount. He had made it his business to gain the confidence of the post-boys employed between London and Chartley, and thus was certain of being able to discover when this fateful letter arrived.

No post-boy called at Highgate on that Tuesday. On Wednesday Gilbert sent his servant with his usual daily note to Mr Secretary, as though from his former lodging, informing his employer, with a regrettable disregard for truth, that he was dining with the conspirators as usual, and was going to bull-bait with them afterwards. Actually he sat all day long at the window of the Highgate tavern, with the casement open so that he could hear the horn which announced the coming of a post-boy. But it was not until the following morning that his patience was rewarded. He was actually awakened by the distant sound of the horn, and was out of bed, had thrown on his clothes, and was stepping, dainty as a cat, through pouring rain when the post-boy, plastered with mud and riding a weary horse, toiled up the hill.

Gilbert greeted him as an old friend, was all solicitude for his sad condition, and insisted that ere calling at the post-house for a fresh horse, he come into the tavern and drink a pot of mulled ale.

"Mighty anxious were they at Chartley," grumbled the post-boy, his clothes steaming before the fire, "that I make no delay on this journey, caring nothing, forsooth, that I might catch my death by riding all night in such weather. Mighty important must be this packet I am to deliver into the hands of Mr Secretary, and between ourselves, sir," he added, lowering his voice, "I'd give much to know what it contains. For it bears a strange kind of mark upon the outside, a kind of secret mark, I doubt not. Look you here."

Gilbert looked. He looked at the thick packet addressed in Mr Phelippes' delicate handwriting to 'The Right Honourable, Sir Francis Walsingham, knight'; he looked at the inscription in one corner, 'Haste, haste, post haste!'; and he looked at the little device drawn in the opposite corner, the shape of Tyburn's fatal tree.

It was scarce an hour later when Gilbert came bursting into Babington's lodging at Hern's Rents, to find Anthony still a-bed as usual, and Mr Ballard eating some breakfast in the same room.

Playing heavily the part of secret agent, Gilbert explained that he had been summoned to cross to France immediately by no less a person than the Spanish Ambassador, his Excellency, Mendoza himself. It must be, he whispered, in connection with the coming invasion. He was full of regrets that he would not be here when the all-important letter from the Queen of Scots arrived; certainly it must be on its way by this time. But he would not fail to communicate with his dear friends, Mr Ballard and Mr Babington, once he was overseas, and while there he hoped to hear that their plans had been translated into action, and that their great crusade was launched.

Then, without giving them time for questions, he knelt, with a great air of piety, for the priest's blessing. The voices of Ballard and Babington, begging him to have a care of himself, wishing him a safe journey and a quick return, followed him down the stair.

He went straight to the French Embassy in Bishopsgate. He had vital news, he told the Ambassador's secretary (with whom by this time he was in high credit) to carry to the Queen of Scots' agents in Paris. Had they a man going over whom he could accompany in the guise of servant, so that he would escape being searched at the port? It so happened that they had. One Dujardin was just back from Scotland with letters, and was crossing to France with the diplomatic bag that very night.

For the first time since a certain moment in Highgate that morning, Gilbert breathed freely. When he was safely in France he would write to Mr Secretary, and, drawing freely upon his excellent imagination, explain the reason for his sudden departure without leave. But the great thing now was to slip out of England before the catching and slaughter of all those silly little conies who were hiding in the hay.

That night, while Gilbert, carrying the valises of the French messenger, was toiling down the quay at the little port of Rye, in the upstairs supper-room at the Plough tavern outside Temple Bar, Anthony Babington was talking apart with John Ballard, earnestly expressing a hope that all was well with their good friend, Mr Gilbert Gifford, and that soon they would see him again.

They never did. But neither, for that matter, did Mr Secretary Walsingham.

Chapter Five

"And so," concluded Lord Burghley, "the Red Bull of Norraway turned into a handsome prince, and he married Princess Beauty, and they lived happily ever after."

He beamed upon the little prattlers who had hung upon his words, then rose from the dining-table, took his walking-cane from the hands of his page, and limped painfully towards the room where he transacted his business. These meal times, when he was wont to entertain his grandchildren with fairy tales or with stories from Pliny's *Secrets and Wonders of the World,* were his only hours of relaxation. Never in his long life had he hunted, danced, hawked, or played at tennis. He detested the frivolous Court where he must spend long hours flattering, bowing, standing about on his gouty feet. Even more did he detest the ritual Progresses upon which the Highest One embarked during the summer, jolted over appalling roads, applauding elaborate masques, all too often playing the expensive part of host at his own palace of Theobalds.

He was happiest when he was at work, here at Cecil House in the Strand, with his coat of arms (or rather the Sitsilts') painted in the window-glass, displayed in shields on the newel-posts, carved in the panelling, embroidered on cushions, coverlets, and hangings. Slowly pacing the two hundred foot gallery, with its rich cabinets and pictures, he could weave his elaborate web of statecraft in peace, taking the air when it was fine upon a little mule in his carefully laid-out gardens. Sitting at his table in the Great Chamber, he presided over the whole administration of the realm, the conduct of foreign affairs, the cases in the Star Chamber and the lucrative Court of Wards, poring over memorials of policy, petitions, drafts of instructions, correspondence with his agents and ambassadors abroad, as much in love with work as when, during his student days at Cambridge, he had hired the bell-ringer to call him every morning at four o'clock.

He sat down at his table on this particular Thursday as the bells chimed the half hour after noon, and immediately became immersed in business. He signed a warrant for the burning of an atheist, read through the minutes of a recent Council meeting, and was beginning a letter of flowery compliment to King James of Scotland when one of his gentlemen entered to announce that Mr Secretary had called and begged the favour of an interview.

A quarter of an hour later, Burghley raised his venerable head from Mr Phelippes' decipherment of the Queen of Scots' reply to Anthony Babington, and for several moments pondered in silence. Walsingham regarded him with surprise and some disappointment, for he had expected congratulation.

"My dear Mr Secretary," said Burghley at last. He stopped, as though he had begun to dictate a letter and did not know how to continue. Then, abruptly: "We will go to Richmond, and seek a privy audience with the Highest One." He rang a hand-bell to order his coach.

"But will not your lordship take this decipherment with us?" asked Walsingham, noting with astonishment that Burghley was putting the papers into a strong-box.

"God has blessed me with a retentive memory," replied the Great Man, not without complacence. "I have ever been able to recall to mind anything I have seen, done, or read. No, Mr Secretary, we will not take this letter with us. We will (or rather, I shall, for I think it best that you are not present at the audience) first acquaint her Majesty with the progress of this 'practice' of yours."

Walsingham was hurt and bewildered, and particularly by that last phrase. For he knew that it was the Great Man's habit to speak of 'my device' if he foresaw that some tortuous piece of statecraft was on the eve of success, and of 'your practice' if he thought otherwise.

On the uncomfortable journey to Richmond, whither the Court had just moved, they jolted up and down in silence, now absurdly thrown towards each other when the wheels encountered a pot hole in the road, now rising and immediately falling side by side upon the cushions when a hillock of mud was surmounted. Mr Secretary did not dare to break the silence, and was angry with himself that he did not. He had a great deal to say; he had done admirably in the Babington business; he had worked hard and long and patiently, and with the Queen of Scots' reply the last obstacle had been overcome.

Only when the trees of Richmond Park came into view did Burghley break the silence. He sighed a little, and murmured:

"I wish this letter had arrived when the Highest One was anywhere but here at Richmond."

It was an odd remark, but Mr Secretary knew exactly what it meant; and his heart sank.

Richmond Palace was commonly known as the Queen's Wardrobe, for here was stored that famous collection of dresses which popular opinion estimated at no less than three thousand. And at Richmond, from her Ministers' point of view, the Highest One was at her most trying. For she regarded herself as being on holiday; she would attend to no public business; she passed her time in elaborate picnics, in hunting and hawking, and in the company of a succession of young fops, her 'little dogs', her 'apes', and her 'pussy cats', as she termed them. She indulged in the baby-talk she had made fashionable, flirting and girlishly giggling, and playing at being a nymph, wearying her ladies with the number of times a day she must change her dress, listening to verses composed by courtiers who harped upon the theme that she was immortal.

And if thwarted in these recreations, if a word of public business was uttered in her presence, she would fly into one of her devastating rages, and lay aside her baby-talk for that robustly obscene hectoring which she had learnt from her father. On the whole, reflected Mr Secretary, he was relieved to think that he would not have to be present at the coming audience; my Lord Burghley was used to having to manage the Highest One in her more difficult moods.

Mr Secretary paced softly up and down the ante-room to her Majesty's Cabinet, sometimes pausing and cocking his head as the murmur of Burghley's voice sounded through the closed door. Yes, he comforted himself, Burghley had always been able to manage the Highest One, appealing now to her vanity, now to her greed, now to her very considerable intelligence; and if all else failed, insinuating into her mind a fear of her life, even writing out with his own hand instructions she must follow to prevent mythical assassins from accomplishing their wicked designs.

Mr Secretary had reached this comfortable conclusion when, with sick sensations in his stomach, he realized that on this occasion my Lord Burghley was not being able to manage the Highest One.

From beyond the closed door he heard a voice interrupt the grave tones of the Lord Treasurer. Majesty was speaking, or rather it was beginning in an ominous rumble which rapidly rose to a shout. Walsingham listened in fascinated horror; in that spate of abuse he caught phrases – 'raised you from the dust', 'grandson of a low innkeeper', 'woundy upstarts that dare dictate to Us', accompanied by the repeated crashing of a heavily ringed hand upon a table. He shuddered and turned pale as a dull thud, as of some object being hurled, sounded as the storm rose higher; he took a step towards the door as though to venture into the holy of holies, but instead applied his eye to the key-hole.

His thoughts whirled round. Steeped in the queen worship of his day, he was honestly bewildered by these glimpses of Elizabeth the woman. As for feeling any pity for this ageing, barren spinster, who dared not look in a mirror, whose physical bi-sexuality was reflected in a natural duplicity of temperament, whose abiding fear was of the common lot of death, that to Walsingham would have been lese-majesty, even if he had possessed the virtue of compassion. But what particularly bewildered him on this occasion was the cause of the storm. It could not be only that she was being plagued with public business when she was on holiday; she had known from the beginning of the secret post and its object; she had been thrilled by it; and yet now, when it had accomplished its purpose, she –

Mr Secretary stepped hastily backwards, as footsteps sounded from beyond the closed door, arranging his body into that low reverence with which Majesty must be greeted; but it was Burghley, and not the Highest One, who emerged, backing out on gouty feet and softly closing the door behind him. Glancing at him, Mr Secretary had the fantastic suspicion that that soft white beard had been pulled.

It was never the habit of Burghley to comment upon such distressful scenes, even to his intimates. His soul was as ruffled as his beard; he was getting too old for this sort of thing; but outwardly he was as calm and upright as ever when, in the apartments always reserved for him in the palace, he said abruptly to the bewildered Walsingham:

"You have enough, and more than enough, to apprehend Babington and the rest, and to stage a good spectacular plot. You can lay your hands on them at any moment, of course?"

"Yes, indeed, my lord," replied Walsingham. "The good GG is constantly with them. But surely," he added, unable to contain himself any longer, "we have enough likewise to condemn the Queen of Scots."

Burghley raised his pale and furtive eyes and looked at the other.

"The Highest One is not pleased to think so." He lifted a hand for silence, as Walsingham would have exclaimed in dismay. "I quoted freely from the Queen of Scots her letter, stressing its patent treason. But the Highest One, while naturally indignant, would not admit it as sufficient to take her cousin's life. And for these reasons: First, the Queen of Scots refrains throughout from giving her authority to the subjects of another queen. Instead, she bids Babington use his own. Next, there is nothing in her letter to indicate that she hopes to use this enterprise for the gaining of the Crown of England while her Majesty lives; her anxiety is clearly for liberation from her imprisonment and for the restoration of the Old Religion."

"But my lord," fairly bleated Walsingham, "she approves in every line the rebellion of her Majesty's subjects. Is that not treason?"

"Treason in a subject, but not in an independent sovereign such as the Queen of Scots has always insisted that she is."

"And foreign invasion?"

"The same applies to that. You will remember that we have stated time and again as our excuse for keeping the Queen of Scots a prisoner, that she is our enemy. She may contend, therefore, that being restrained by force, in peril of her very life (for she is not unaware, I think, that suggestions have been made for her secret assassination), and regarded by us as our enemy, she is not bound to forbid a rising of men, or even a foreign invasion, the objects of which are the restoration of her religion and the liberation of her person. The Highest One, she would say in effect, has made war on her by detaining, against her will, an independent sovereign; therefore is she justified in fighting defensively by what means soever come to her hand."

Walsingham gaped at him.

"Your lordship has said from the beginning that it was necessary to incriminate the Queen of Scots in a treasonable conspiracy – "

"My dear Mr Secretary, I am being *Advocatus Diaboli,*" murmured the Great Man, adding kindly, "which means 'the Devil's Advocate'."

"With respect, my lord," went on Walsingham, a little flushed, "I cannot imagine anything more treasonable than her answer to Babington. What can you ask more than her approval of armed revolt at home, invasion from abroad, and her forcible rescue from her Majesty's keeping?"

"Approval of taking her Majesty's life," replied the Lord Treasurer quietly.

"But there was nothing in Babington's letter to her about that," cried Walsingham. "GG endeavoured to provoke him to it, but failed. And on the whole I thought it as well; the Queen of Scots would have been too cunning to have expressed approval of it, and might even have forbidden it."

Burghley did not answer for a moment. He was looking out of the window, apparently absorbed in the view. Then he said, with seeming irrelevance:

"The letter from Babington to the Queen of Scots and her reply to it are very long letters indeed. Perchance sufficient time was not given to your worthy Mr Phelippes to make a careful decipherment; it may be that here and there he missed a few words."

Walsingham tensed like a hound, and blood began to flood his face.

"It may be so," he murmured, his glance fixed keenly on the other.

"A *few* words," repeated Burghley. "Possibly a postcript which could be used and then cut off when it has served its turn. Or even a trifle of suppression here and there, or the alteration of a word or two. It is marvellous what may be done only by the rearrangement of a sentence."

"I understand your lordship," said Walsingham eagerly. "Her Majesty will not be induced to take the life of the Queen of Scots unless proof is given her that that Queen has plotted against her own Person. You feared it might be so, and that is why you would not show her Majesty the decipherment of this letter."

"I wondered," said Burghley, with gentle condescension, "when you would arrive at that very simple conclusion, my dear Mr Secretary. Now, as soon as your Mr Phelippes returns from Chartley, you will bring him to me, together with the original letter from the Queen of Scots and also the copy of Babington's letter to her. For you will understand," he added, making it sound as though Walsingham could not arrive at so obvious a conclusion unaided, and thus taking it out on his inferior for his own humiliation at the hands of the Highest One, "that the two letters must be adjusted one to the other before they are shown to her Majesty."

Mr Secretary returned to Cheapside full of renewed confidence. A crucial stage of the entrapping had arrived, and now he was sure of getting his quarry. A little exercise of that art of 'counterfeit writing' in which Mr Phelippes was such an expert, and the Highest One would be frightened into signing the death warrant of the Queen of Scots. In case Phelippes had not already set out from Chartley, Mr Secretary sent an express recalling him to London without loss of time, bringing the original letter with him.

Meanwhile, Babington and the rest of the dupes must be kept under constant observation. Mr Secretary had not been unduly troubled by the information sent him by GG that Ballard had discovered Bernard Mawde's true character, for there was GG himself, who had proved so expert an *agent provocateur*, daily in the company of the priest and the youths, completely trusted by them, and daily sending Mr Secretary little notes reporting their treasonable talk.

When Mr Secretary returned from Richmond this Thursday, however, there was no little note from GG Walsingham thought nothing of it, being completely absorbed in a study of the decipherment of Mary's letter (which Burghley had returned to him), examining and re-examining it for passages suitable for interpolation. But when the next day, Friday, passed without a word from GG, Mr Secretary was not pleased; and when on Monday morning he had still heard nothing, his displeasure turned to downright annoyance. He sent his private secretary, Francis Mills, to Gilbert's lodging, with orders to bring GG to him immediately, and not return without him.

Another twenty-four hours passed before an extremely agitated and haggard Mills returned; and GG was not with him. He had hung about outside Mr Gifford's lodging, said Mills, all yesterday and throughout last night, but of Mr Gifford there was no sign, nor did his landlord know what had become of him.

Mr Secretary's annoyance gave place to panic. For five whole days he had lost contact with the conspirators, and heaven knew what might have happened during that period. The discovery by Ballard that Mawde was a spy might have caused the whole bunch of them to scatter. And now whom could he 'use' towards them? GG had disappeared; it was unthinkable to introduce a strange agent at this stage. There remained only Robert Poley.

He was by no means an ideal choice. He knew nothing of the plot, either from Babington or from Mr Secretary; and moreover Walsingham remained unsatisfied of his full allegiance to the Government. But there it was, there was no one else to 'use'; and Mr Secretary sent Mr Poley a curt message, ordering him to present himself at the former's office without delay. Actually it was some two hours before Mr Poley presented himself, and by that time Mr Secretary was very wroth indeed.

"I was constrained to find a litter to carry me hither, your Honour," explained Poley, holding on to a chair-back and gasping for breath. "I have kept my bed for a fortnight, greatly troubled with my chest – "

Mr Secretary cut him short. He had a commission for Poley, and it must be embarked upon without loss of time. Trifling ailments must not be weighed in the balance against her Majesty's service. Poley must go at once to Anthony Babington's lodging; if the young man was not there, he must be found, or at least some news of him. When found, he must be kept under the strictest observation, careful note being taken of all he said. It should be easy enough; the youth trusted and liked Mr Poley; and Mr Poley could detain him in London by renewing his hopes of obtaining a licence for that old project of his going overseas.

Chapter Six

Anthony sat at the window of his parlour, an opened letter lying on the seat beside him, his eyes dreamy as he looked down upon the little courtyard. A water-carrier was going his rounds, one of his servants was grooming a horse, a girl with a basket on her head intoned monotonously 'Live peri*wink*les! Live peri*wink*les!' He neither saw nor heard. In imagination he was at home of Dethick, whence this letter had come from his wife.

How good she was, how patient! It was more than two months since he had paid a visit home, and yet there was not a word of reproach in her letter, which had a postscript written by little Meg: 'Sir mi Father, see how I can rite thee criss-crosse rowe at the top of mi horne-booke: Christ's crosse bee mi speede, in all virtu to proceede.' He could imagine the two of them sitting in the Summer Parlour at Dethick, the child's head, with the brown hair which was so like his own, bent over the paper, a pink tongue protruding with the effort as the small hand carefully and laboriously formed the words between the guiding lines, wife and daughter dutifully not asking him, both of them secretly longing to ask him, when he would come home.

And outside the window where they sat together the rolling parkland, the formal gardens, the fresh, sweet country air, the deep woods with their shade; the mews where his falcons sulked for lack of sport, the dogs growing fat in the kennels, the busy life of husbandry lacking the master's keen eye, the tenants beginning to whisper that, after all, Master Babington had become an absentee landlord, seduced from the life of his fathers by the delights of the town.

The delights of the town! What pleasure had he in this foul-smelling, raucous London? What kept him here? The Queen of Scots would never answer his letter now. It must be nearly a month since he had given it into the hands of the unknown boy in the dun-coloured livery; either she had not received it, or she had decided to ignore it. It might have been intercepted; that was a very unpleasant thought; but after all he had written in a cipher impossible to translate save by herself and her secretaries who had the key. If by any unlikely chance it had been not only intercepted but deciphered, he would have been under arrest by this time. No, she had decided to ignore it; of course she had; had he not always suspected that she would?

He would go home to Dethick this very week, he thought, rousing himself. He would meet the others this evening and tell them so. Nothing could be done unless the Queen of Scots gave her authority; that had been agreed on from the beginning. And since she was not pleased to give her authority, well then – nothing could be done.

"What is it? What is it?" snapped Anthony irritably, becoming aware that one of his servants had entered the room.

"If you please, sir," said the man, "there is a gentleman desires to wait upon you. His name is Mr Poley."

"My sweet Robin," cried Anthony, enfolding Mr Poley in a warm embrace, "where have you been this age? Why have you not called on me? Nay, you have been sick," he went on, looking with compassion at the grey face, the thin hands clasped on the chest as though they would press down the pain within, "you have been mortal sick, and you never let me know it."

Poley sank down upon a stool, and remained for a few moments fighting for breath.

"This late humid weather," he gasped, the sweat shining on his forehead. "Ah, how often have I not longed to see you, dear lad, but I would not presume upon our short acquaintance to send to ask you to visit an invalid."

With characteristic impulsiveness Anthony snatched a diamond ring from his finger, and catching the other's hand drew it gently on.

"There!" he cried, "it is a token. Whensoever you want me, you have but to send me that ring and I will come, even though I am in Derbyshire."

Clumsily he fussed about his sick friend, arranging cushions, calling to his servants to prepare a posset. Never ill himself, he had strong youth's awkwardness in the presence of the sick, but he was kind, he really liked this elderly man, and he was flattered by Poley's obvious affection for himself.

"You are going to Derbyshire?" asked Poley, sipping his posset a few minutes later. "How I envy you, dear lad. And tomorrow I must go to Richmond, whither the Court has moved. Apart from my weak condition, I detest the necessity. To have to bow the knee to those who are our persecutors, to have to flatter and dissemble, it hurts me, it cuts me to the heart," murmured Mr Poley, again laying a hand upon that organ. "At one time, when you desired to obtain a licence to travel, I entertained a foolish hope that you would – nay, forgive me, it was presumption even to think of such a thing."

"What did you hope, Robin?" insisted Anthony, a little breathless.

"That you would take me with you," replied Mr Poley, shamefaced.

"Why, so I would."

"But you were pleased to put the project out of your mind. I make no doubt at all that you know best – "

"I have not put it out of my mind."

Only into the back of it, thought Anthony, and God forgive me that I did not keep it in the forefront. Had he followed up the matter all those weeks ago when he had actually been in touch with Mr Secretary, he and Margaret and little Meg would have been safely overseas by now, the first pangs of exile passed, the first homesickness for Dethick dispelled by the novelty of travel and the consciousness of having secured the safety of his loved ones. And why had he not followed it up? Because he had been persuaded to the contrary by a younger stranger, Gilbert Gifford, and the indiscreet priest, John Ballard.

"Robin," he said earnestly, sitting down and looking into the sad, hound-like face of his friend, "if you love me you will remind Mr Secretary of my desire of a licence to travel, and bring me word what he says."

Mr Secretary was wise in not altogether trusting Mr Robert Poley. For though Mr Poley had acted as a spy in government service for several years, both at home and abroad, and was so plausible and pathetic that he easily gained the confidence of the unwary, he was never a whole-hearted traitor.

The house he lived in, called The Garden, in Bishopsgate Without, had been specially rented to him by one Hall, a Queen's Messenger, for the purpose of entertaining Catholics, harbouring priests, and reporting their names to Walsingham. He reported some, but not all. He possessed a conscience, a poor thing though it was. He was a genuinely sick man, needing comfort and security, and he could obtain these only by entering the odious service of the Government. But he would ease his conscience by occasionally harbouring a priest or succouring some distressed fellow Catholic for whom he had conceived a liking, without informing Mr Secretary.

Such a fellow Catholic was Anthony Babington. From the first moment of their meeting, Poley had felt a warm regard for the young man, and being old, childless, and sentimental, had seen in this headstrong and handsome lad the son he would have liked to have begot. He had been truly glad when the boy had seemed so keen on obtaining a licence to travel, unselfishly glad for the boy's sake. And now here was Anthony as keen as ever; and there was Mr Secretary tempting him with hopes of it, yet most undoubtedly determined to block such a means of escape.

Well, there was nothing he could do about it, thought Poley with a sigh, but obey Mr Secretary's orders and hope for the best. On Wednesday morning, therefore, he presented himself at Richmond (where Walsingham was attending Council meetings), waited humbly until Mr Secretary was at leisure to receive him, and reported progress.

Mr Secretary pondered in silence for a while. Babington was still very keen to go overseas, was he? That might well be because of the discovery of Bernard Mawde's true character; or, on the other hand (a distinctly unpleasant possibility) because he had somehow got wind that the Government was aware of his plotting. Mr Secretary was extremely loth to suspect GG of having tipped the plotters the wink, but the fact remained that GG had suddenly and most unaccountably disappeared. Also that since GG's disappearance, Mr Secretary had lost track of John Ballard.

He roused himself and gave Poley instructions. Poley was to return to Babington at once, and tell him that he had spoken to Mr Secretary on the matter of the licence to travel. That if Mr Babington would remain in London, Mr Secretary would communicate with him in the course of the next few days. But that if the licence was granted, it must be on the same conditions as those laid down when he had requested such a thing before; he must put into writing the nature of the services he had offered to do her Majesty if permitted to travel.

Anthony was very surprised to see his dear friend Robin again that same day, and not as pleased as he might have been with the message. It made him faintly uneasy, though he could not for the life of him think why. However, he sent a reply by Robin to the effect that, with all due respect, he would prefer to discuss the situation with Mr Secretary rather than to set down in writing anything which might seem to reflect upon his honour.

Having dispatched Robin with this evasive message, Anthony ordered his servants to saddle his horse, and, with a sparrow-hawk on his fist as though bent on sport, he rode out that same evening to the little village of Marylebone where, at an inn kept by one Robert Gage, a secret Catholic, Ballard was lying low.

As they walked beside the Tyburn stream, which ran through the fields at the back of the village, Anthony was frank with the priest. He had decided, he said briskly, that, hearing nothing from the Queen of Scots, he must think of his wife and child, and therefore had revived his old project of going overseas. He owed it to Mr Ballard, he added, to tell him this, and also that, through his old acquaintance, Mr Poley, he had applied to Mr Secretary for a licence.

"You cannot think of abandoning the enterprise!" cried Ballard. "Your honour is involved, and you have accepted the leadership. But," he went on, before Anthony could protest, "your application to Mr Secretary may come in very handy. For I tell you, Anthony, I cannot get this rogue

Mawde out of my mind. I curse myself for ever trusting him, for it is like I have brought my friends into peril."

"But how?" asked Anthony, with an inward qualm.

"Suppose, for the sake of argument, that Mawde has reported that he has seen you and your young friends in my company, I who am a marked man. Then almost certainly you are being watched. Therefore it is of the utmost importance, not only for your personal safety but for the success of this noble enterprise, that you remove Mr Secretary's suspicions of you."

"And how is that to be done?"

"By revealing to Mr Secretary all that you know about me," replied Ballard calmly.

Anthony stopped dead, and stared open-mouthed at the other.

"You cannot know what you say, sir! Reveal the enterprise on which you were engaged when first I met you, reveal Savage's vow – "

"Not that last," interrupted Ballard sharply. "Savage's name is not to be mentioned; I will not have that good simple fellow implicated in any way. But as for me, I am well able to look after myself, and in any case would think my life well lost if it might bring your own enterprise to fruition. Do you not see, Anthony? By revealing to Walsingham my discarded scheme, you may push on underhand with the real one without exciting suspicion. If he thinks you are willing to inform against me, not only as a priest but as an instigator of revolt, he will not concern himself with your doings, but will regard you as a man he can use."

Anthony's colour had risen. He said curtly:

"I cannot do it."

"A rope on it, do it you must!" cried the priest, gripping the young man's arm. "Not for your own safety, not even for that of your friends, but for the success of this enterprise of which you have been appointed leader. But put nothing in writing; a request for that is a favourite bait of theirs. Give them a line or two in a man's hand and they can hang him. They have clever forgers among them."

"I tell you I can do nothing," argued Anthony (oh God, they were back again on the old treadmill!), "unless I have an answer to my letter to the Queen of Scots, and how long must I wait for that?"

During a restless night he came to a resolution, which, while it cost him some uneasiness of conscience, seemed the only possible one. He would act on Ballard's suggestion to the extent of hinting to Mr Secretary that he had valuable information to impart as the price of a licence to travel; but as soon as he got that licence he would use it without delay.

The next day, Thursday, passed uneventfully until evening when, according to an appointment made by messenger earlier in the day, Anthony met Robin Poley for supper at the Castle tavern near the Exchange. Poley had another message from Mr Secretary; the latter was very much occupied with Council matters, but hoped shortly to be able to give Mr Babington the interview he had requested. But indeed, said Poley, he would most willingly go to Richmond again next day, and inform Mr Secretary that Mr Babington had information to impart which was of the utmost importance to the safety of her Majesty and the realm. For the rest of the evening he tried to pump his dear friend as to the nature of this information, but his dear friend had suddenly become very close.

An extraordinary fatigue fell on Anthony when, having parted from Robin outside the Castle, he walked westwards towards his lodging in Hern's Rents. He had drunk but little, he had lounged about all day, yet his head spun, his limbs felt leaden, and his mind was like a whirlpool, throwing up disconnected flotsam of thought.

Could he bring himself to betray Ballard, even though Ballard had commanded it? Was he being a coward and a renegade, or a sensible man and a loving husband and father? Into what a maze had he got himself during the past few months! What had happened to Gilbert Gifford, from whom there had been no word since his sudden departure to France? Why had he himself not acted on his mother's consistent warnings against living in a world of make-believe? A man who daydreams, she had told him so often, loses touch with reality, and was not that precisely what he had done?

Depression fell upon him with every step as he left the City by the empty space where the old Lud Gate had been pulled down and a new one was in course of being erected. It was an evening of thick cloud, and, though the sun was but newly set, in the narrow street with the upper stories of the houses almost touching one another across it, it was night. The lanterns on the Fleet bridge cast queer shadows, and he was conscious of his servant fingering his cudgel, keeping a sharp look-out for foot-pads. But it was not foot-pads Anthony feared. He had a feeling of being watched and spied upon, had had it all day. Suppose that rogue Mawde was shadowing him? Ballard himself did not know Mawde's whereabouts; he had not seen him since they had parted in the North.

"Pox take you, hold that link steady!" cried Anthony to his foot-boy.

The outline of Temple Bar loomed up, lit by the fire-pot of a watchman who paced up and down before the wooden gate. The stink of burning pitch and resin fought with the odours of the Fleet ditch and a nearby lay-stall, and made Anthony retch. He would not seek to go out of the liberties by way of Temple Bar; the watch could always be bribed to open the postern after sunset, but tonight he was taking no risks. He turned into Chancery Lane; here was a blind alley which had a gate into Lincoln's Inn Fields, a gate which the residents in the alley carelessly left open, so that it was always possible to get in and out of the liberties when Temple Bar was closed. Chidge found it very useful in his work as Conductor Companion; dear old Chidge, thought Anthony; he's coming to collect me for a duck-hunting expedition to Islington first thing tomorrow morning; we shall be two ordinary young gentlemen indulging in ordinary recreation. That is the real world!

The night was cool, almost chilly, yet his forehead was burning and his body in a sweat. Perhaps I am going to be ill, he thought, and found a strange pleasure in the prospect. To lay everything aside, even the hope of obtaining this licence, to go home to Dethick, to lie in his own bed there, to be tended by Margaret's gentle hands, to sleep – yes, he thought, with a wave of self-pity, to sleep and never again to wake up in this confusing, unsatisfactory, dangerous, tedious world. Well, at least he would sleep tonight, and tomorrow he would give himself a holiday from all his problems.

He was dog-tired when at last he came to Hern's Rents and entered the vaulted passage which led into the courtyard. And suddenly, as on a previous occasion, he halted dead, and his hand leapt to his sword-hilt; for a figure had stepped from the gloom of a doorway and was addressing him in a low, conspiratorial tone.

"Mr Babington? I am commanded to give you this packet, and to ask you when I may call for an answer."

Mechanically Anthony stretched out his left hand, his right remaining on his sword-hilt. His heart was beating so fast as to sicken him; he stared at the stranger, almost believing that he was reliving that night when he had come back here after a long, happy Sunday spent with

Chidge in Lincoln's Inn Fields, and, at this very spot, had encountered for the first time that mysterious person, Mr Gilbert Gifford.

"Bring the light closer," he snapped at his foot-boy.

But it was not Mr Gilbert Gifford who was disclosed by the ruddy light of the flambeau: it was a stranger, a homely-faced serving-man in a blue coat. Anthony's eyes strayed to the packet which had been put into his hand; it was very thick; and it bore upon its outside only a cryptic device, '-)-'.

PART FOUR

Chapter One

An excited barking of spaniels sounded from the courtyard of Hern's Rents, followed by the cheerful voice of Chidiock Tichborne on the staircase.

"Hallo there, Anthony! I hope you are up betimes for once. It's a fine day for our sport, not too hot – "

He broke off abruptly, slammed shut the door of the parlour, leaned against it, and stared at his friend in dismay.

Babington looked ten years older than when last they had met. He sat slumped in his elbow-chair before the table, his eyes red-rimmed, a fever-spot burning upon either cheek. Beads of sweat glistened on his unshaven chin; his doublet was thrown aside, and he sat in shirt and hose. As Tichborne stood regarding him, he let out a groan which had no trace of play-acting in it.

"By the Mass, I have done!" he muttered. "I was on the point of surrender a dozen times during the night, but I have driven myself to complete it."

"To complete what?" began Tichborne, and then his glance fell upon sheets full of cryptic signs, and others scrawled over with Anthony's untidy script, spilling over on to the floor. His face grew grave, and instinctively he turned and bolted the door against which he had been leaning.

"It has come at last, then, the letter from the Queen of Scots? But how was it delivered?"

"By some serving-man or other," replied Anthony. "Oh for God's sake don't plague me with questions!" he snapped suddenly. "See for yourself what she writes."

He rose, staggered to the casement, threw it wide, and, with another groan, sank down upon the window-seat.

There was a long silence, broken only by the crackle of paper. Methodical and patient, Tichborne gathered and sorted the various sheets, and fell to examining them. There was a brief covering note, anonymous, but promising that the writer would 'discover himself in the next dispatch'. It warned Anthony to avoid inquisitiveness, to read carefully the enclosed, and to have his answer for which the same bearer, a serving-man in a blue coat, would call at his convenience.

And the enclosed, deciphered by Babington during the long hours of the night, was from the Queen of Scots herself.

Phrases from that lengthy letter kept leaping like savage dogs at Anthony's mind, defenceless with fatigue after a sleepless night. 'Now to ground substantially this enterprise and bring it to good success... What forces, as well as on foot as on horse, you may raise... Which towns, ports, and havens you may assure yourselves of... To yourself in particular I refer to assure the gentlemen whom you choose for commanders of all that shall be requisite on my part... Take heed of spies and false brethren... Whatever issue the matter taketh, I do and will think myself obliged, as long as I live, for the offers you make to hazard yourself, as you do, for my delivery... Fail not to burn this quickly... '

Fail not to burn this quickly. It was the only command in the whole letter which he could carry out!

He heard footsteps on the stair presently, a tap on the door, Tichborne rising to open it, a whispered exchange, and then the excited voice of Ballard:

"So your patience is rewarded, Anthony; she has answered after all – "

"What are you doing here?" cried Anthony shrilly. "Why do you come here, Mr Ballard? Have you no care for my safety, as it seems you have none for your own? Like as not you have been followed – "

"Anthony," broke in Tichborne, "pray take a hold on yourself and remember to whom you speak."

"I came because I was anxious for news," said Ballard mildly. "I am too old a hand not to know when I am being shadowed."

"Well, now you are here," said Anthony ungraciously, "you may as well read what was brought to me last night. The encipherment is in the hand of Curle, the Scots secretary; I know it well, for he always enciphers her letters."

He went and sat down on the window-seat again. Even in the enormous dismay which filled him he could not help being a little proud. She *had* answered his letter, and with such warmth and approval, and at such length! And he, who had a reputation for indolence, had spent the whole of last night at the decipherment. The murmur of the two men's voices came to him like the hum of bees, of bees in summer outside his windows at Dethick. They lulled him; his head dropped forward on his breast; until suddenly a sentence spoken by Ballard aroused him:

"We had best take notes of the salient points."

Anthony leapt to his feet, wild-eyed.

"No!" he cried violently. "You see what she says – 'Fail not to burn this quickly'. What use to burn it if we take notes of such hanging matter?"

"But they are most vital and detailed instructions, Anthony," protested the priest, "which you cannot possibly commit to memory – "

Anthony interrupted him by snatching the papers out of his hand.

"It is my letter," he cried childishly, "written to me; and I say it shall be burned, both the original and the decipherment, now at once."

His hands shook so that he could scarcely hold the tinder-box; the burning papers dropped from his fingers, scorching his fine silk nether-stocks; he ground his heel upon them, stamping again and again, leaping from one to the other as they scattered among the rushes on the floor, seeming as though he engaged in some fantastic dance. Then, suddenly drained of all energy, he lurched into his bedchamber, waving his friends away, crying only to be left alone, and flung himself face downwards on the bed.

He slept heavily all that day. It was dark when at last he awoke, and groping his way out into the parlour found it empty and set in order by his servants. Well, they would have found nothing suspicious; thank God he had insisted on burning both the letter and his own decipherment of it. He called for his chamber-boy, washed, undressed, ate some supper, and returned to bed. But now he had become hatefully wakeful; and now he must face it, the coming of the letter he had thought would never come, and of the contents which had engraved themselves for ever upon his memory.

He had been caught in the trap of his own day-dreaming. Someone, and that someone his heroine and his rightful Queen, had taken his empty boasts seriously, and expected him to translate his solemn promises into action. He was like a child who, feeding his imagination on a picture of himself as St George, was suddenly confronted with a very real dragon, and with a maiden of flesh and blood tied to a tree. And he had but a toy sword for the slaying of the dragon, and no means whatsoever for the rescue of the dragon's victim.

What particularly dismayed him was the difference between the image he had created of the Queen of Scots, and the real Mary who had written that letter. He had invested her with a personality utterly unlike the one she possessed. The whole tone of his letter to her had been grandiloquent and exaggerated; her reply was masculine, mature, businesslike and far-seeing. He had pictured her as frail and languishing; and every line of her letter revealed a spirit as strong as tempered steel.

She had taken it for granted that he really intended to do something, that actual plans had been made. Airily he had written of risings in various parts of England; she ordered him to appoint commanders. In the same manner he had written of the necessity to seize ports for the reception of the invaders; she ordered him to select and seize them. She instructed him to see to the providing of pay and munition for the army he had given her to understand he could raise; where in the world was he to obtain such things? Even his most cherished daydream, the rescue of her from her prison, now that she had made practical suggestions for it, appeared impossible to accomplish. Oh, he could ride with a hundred or so friends and followers to Chartley, but if he did succeed in rescuing her, where in England could he place her for security?

For the risings at home he had made no plans at all, excusing himself on the grounds that he could do nothing unless or until he obtained the authority of the Queen of Scots. As for the foreign invasion, that was not his business, except that she bade him send some trusty messenger to Mendoza to discover the details. He had no such trusty messenger; now that Gilbert Gifford had disappeared, he had no contact with those 'great ones' overseas who had appointed him the English leader.

A thin ray of comfort lit the darkness in his mind. The Queen of Scots had not given him her authority; she bade him, in the role of leader, use his own. And in her letter she insisted that without foreign succour it was useless to think of revolt at home. Very well, then; he had not succeeded in obtaining that authority which both Ballard and Gifford had asserted was necessary to the enterprise; and unless he heard from Gifford it was impossible for him to be sure whether the invasion was going to take place or not. In a word, he was justified in doing nothing.

Then his mood changed. He had pledged his word to her, to his boyhood heroine, the lady in whom lay the only hope of the restoration of the religion to which he was devoted. He could not fail her now. He was committed in honour to attempt something, for she trusted him, and so did his friends. He had strutted and boasted before them; how could he, at this stage of all others, when the Queen of Scots really had answered his letter and had accepted him in the role of leader, tell her and his friends that he was incapable of acting the part?...

So he tossed feverishly through the dark hours and woke from nightmare with his mind beaten flat.

Poley called in the morning, looking very pleased with himself, but instantly distressed to find his dear lad so wan and strained. A walk in the fields, he suggested; the day was fine, and exercise would do Anthony good.

It was a Saturday morning, and Lincoln's Inn Fields, which later would be thronged by the citizens, were deserted at this hour, save for the washerwomen spreading clothes to bleach. It had rained again in the night, and there was a smell of country; here and there, like new-minted coins, yellow leaves hung in the elms.

"A letter from Mr Secretary," said Poley, drawing a thin packet from his breast. "And from his manner when he gave it me, I believe it contains good news."

Anthony opened the note, read its contents, and frowned.

"He gives me permission to deal with those whom he terms 'the principal practisers against the State'. What does he mean by that?"

"Why, that you may consort with them for the purpose of discovering their intentions. A dangerous work, dear lad, unless you are covered by his warrant. And you remember that you asked me to inform him that you could impart valuable information which was of the utmost importance to the safety of her Majesty and realm."

Anthony walked on in silence until they came to a spot where a bank made a natural seat in the sunshine.

"Let us sit for a while," he said. And then, abruptly: "Robin, if I were to impart to you something very secret, could I rely on you not to reveal it to any man?"

The sad hound's face was turned to him, the eyes guileless, the thin hand reaching out for his.

"It is within my power," said Anthony, retaining his friend's hand and idly playing with the diamond ring, the token he had given Robin, upon it, "either to maintain this state and religion as they now stand, or to change both, and to bring in a new government and an old religion. There is a third course: to gain this licence, forswear matters of State, dedicate myself to a life of study overseas, and leave the future of my country in the hands of God."

Poley glanced covertly at the boy, and his heart smote him; the young face was so solemn, so naïve, and so troubled. It was with an effort that he roused himself to say:

"I will tell you this, sweet Anthony, that so great is the love I bear you that I myself am ready to follow you in any of these courses, even before you impart to me the details of the first two. Upon my salvation I swear it," he added, as solemn as the other.

Anthony flushed with pleasure. Really, he thought, it was extraordinary what influence he wielded over his fellow men. Nature seemed to have designed him for the role of leader.

"And which," went on Poley, "of these three courses do you yourself prefer, dear lad?"

The answer came so unhesitatingly that Poley was taken aback.

"To go overseas, and so secure my family and be free to practise my religion, and afterwards, if it please God to send a better England, to return and take the fruit of other men's labours, exempting my family from the danger which accompanies change."

A starkly honest answer. In other words, thought Poley, left to yourself you have a preference for inaction. And if only I could get this licence for you, you'd take me with you, entertain me without charge in some sunny clime, where my health would improve, where I could become a good Catholic again, and repent my sins in peace. He had to wrestle very hard indeed with himself to remember that he was in Mr Secretary's employment before he managed to say:

"My dear boy, though this were best for your personal convenience, I have ever deemed you one to reckon little your own advantage when there is a question of the public good. Therefore my advice to you needs must be that you continue in your heroical endeavours (whatsoever these may be) to reform this State and to liberate it from the heretic persecutor."

The young fool nodded, so solemn, so weighed down by a burden too heavy for his years, that Poley had to take out his handkerchief and wipe his own eyes which suddenly were wet.

Always subject to rapid changes of mood, Anthony refrained, on this occasion, from taking Poley further into his confidence. He turned the conversation on to ordinary matters and firmly kept it there; but he made an appointment to sup with Poley next evening at the Black Boy and Rose in Fleet Street, and from his manner when he made it Poley felt sure that secrets were to be revealed.

The old man was first at the rendezvous on Sunday evening, and presently watched the tall young figure come striding through the postern at Temple Bar, with his stuff-crowned hat set on the side of his head, his sword in its velvet scabbard swinging at his side, his long legs striding confidently, a couple of servants behind him. But for all the self-confidence in his walk, Poley noticed how the youth glanced over his shoulder one or twice, and when Anthony greeted his friend it was with a preoccupied air. Taking Poley's arm, he dived suddenly into a narrow alley-way, through a courtyard (still glancing over his shoulder), and finally through the back door of the Black Boy and Rose.

"A private room," said he to the landlord in his high-handed way. "A flagon of your best Canarian, and supper anon when I call for it."

When the two were alone in an upstairs room, Anthony drew off his embroidered gloves and flung them on the table. Poley noticed then that his nails were bitten to the quick.

"I have had a notion lately that I am being followed," said the boy. He walked to the window, threw it open, and looked this way and that. "I am a fool, I suppose, and yet – "

He wandered back to the table and poured the wine. His hand shook a little, and a twitch made one eyelid seem to wink. He took a gulp of wine, grimaced, and set down the cup.

"Sour as vinegar," he grunted. "That rogue of a landlord – "

He walked briskly to the door, halted there, seemed to forget his purpose, and came and sat down at the table, leaning his chin on his fist.

"There is some heavy matter weighing upon you, sweet Anthony," murmured his friend. "Will you not let me share it? I have given you my word that your secrets shall be locked within my breast; I am old enough to be your father, and indeed I have presumed to look upon you as the son I never had."

It seemed as though Anthony had been waiting for this, for immediately he began to unburden himself with a vengeance. He acquainted Robin with the whole enterprise, his own as well as Ballard's, keeping back one thing only, the names of all except Ballard himself.

Poley did not need to feign his dismay at the story. All he had known hitherto was that Babington was under some sort of suspicion, and that Mr Secretary wanted him kept within reach of his arm until such time as he chose to apprehend him. And now here was this disclosure of an 'enterprise'; and though, from what he knew of his young friend, Poley suspected that it was not and never could be in the realm of reality, it would none the less be sufficient to bring this lad to Tyburn and the hideous death of a traitor.

"You must pardon me for asking this, for I ask but out of my love for you," said Poley, laying his thin hand on the other's. "This noble enterprise of yours – has it substance?"

He saw the young face redden.

"I know the ways of youth, though I am old," went on Poley, tender and without patronage. "You are but a lad, and as such you dream dreams, good dreams but, alas, seldom capable of being made reality. Was not this enterprise just a gallant vision of a youth racked in spirit to see his religion trampled upon and his rightful Queen held prisoner?"

Anthony turned away to hide his tears, Here indeed was the spiritual father he had sought in John Ballard, and had sought in vain.

"I would admit it to no one but you, Robin," he said shakily. "Yes, I've been a romantic fool, and am caught in the web of my own daydreaming."

Or in the web of some 'practice' of Mr Secretary, thought Poley with an inward shudder.

"Nay now," he soothed, "you must not despair. No harm is done, thank God; you have this man Ballard's permission, nay, his positive command, that you reveal his abortive plot to Mr Secretary."

He broke off, and sighed. He had been about to say that by revealing Ballard's plot, Anthony would put Walsingham so deeply in his debt that the licence to travel would be granted immediately. But Poley was old in the ways of espionage, only too well acquainted with Mr Secretary's subtlety and ruthlessness, and he had a strong suspicion now that it was not only Ballard Mr Secretary was after.

It was eight o'clock and some of the shops were shutting, when they came out of the Black Boy and Rose. Candlelight gleamed in the windows, running footmen went before a coach, bawling 'Way! Way!', watchmen in their rug gowns, with their bells and cressets, emerged from the watch-house at Temple Bar to go upon their nightly rounds, and from the slums of Whitefriars slunk furtive figures, the bullies and the foot-pads who preyed on London after dark.

And now it was Poley who seemed uneasy, as indeed he was, torn between his genuine affection for this boy, and the consciousness of on which side his bread was buttered.

"Anthony," he whispered, putting his arm round the youth's shoulders, "I cannot forget what you told me about your fancy that you are being shadowed. For does not Ballard come to your lodging? If a watch is being kept on him, he may well have been tracked thither. Suppose he were arrested there? They might take you too, and that would be a disaster," went on Poley with an effort, "before you were able to speak with Mr Secretary and clear yourself by divulging Ballard's plot. Hern's Rents is unsafe, sweet Anthony; come and stay with me at my house outside the City wall; come now, tonight."

Anthony made a show of demurring, but with suspicious quickness allowed himself to be persuaded. He had come to hate his lodging; it seemed to smell of wild talk, empty promises, mysterious callers, nights spent poring over secret alphabets, mythical plots.

They went down to Temple stairs and called 'Eastward ho!' to the watermen lounging on a bench. They would land at St Katherine's stairs beyond the Tower, whispered Poley, and walk thence through open country to his house. As they were rowed down-river each was silent, staring out upon the wharfs piled high with bales and casks, the flocks of swans, the tilt-boats and barges, the richly painted craft moored at the landing-stages of the houses of nobles and City merchants, the light of lanthorns making bright waving ribbons in the water.

Oh, thank God I have purged myself of it all, thought Anthony, and have found such a friend as Robin, someone before whom I need not play the silly hero, someone who understands and yet loves me, loves the real Anthony, infirm of purpose and vainglorious though I am. Let me see, today is Sunday; by the end of the week at furthest I should have got my licence to travel, and can go home to Dethick to make arrangements. How excited little Meg will be at the prospect of seeing foreign parts! And Margaret and I will be together again; we have been married seven years, and for at least half that time I have been absent from her. I'll make it up to her now; no longer will she be forced into the role of Penelope. I shall have to get in touch with Chidge and the others, he thought with secret shrinking. He was going to have to drink very deeply of the cup of humiliation when he told them that, despite the letter from the Queen of Scots, he was not going to act upon his promises to her.

I wonder if we could both make a bolt for it, thought Poley. His reasons for inviting Anthony to stay with him had been very mixed and he was unable at present to sort them out. Mr Secretary had commissioned him to keep the youth under constant observation; in Anthony's distracted mood he might slip home without telling his sweet Robin; therefore sweet Robin was doing his duty as Mr Secretary's man in making sure that Anthony remained under his eye. On the other hand, he was not at all sure that he was going to inform Mr Secretary that Anthony was staying with him... Well anyway he would think about it, once the pair were safely home at The Garden, and decide at leisure what was to be done.

He shuddered and huddled himself further into his cloak. They were passing Tower wharf, and in the ruddy light spilling from a torch in the wall he could see the portcullis of Traitors' Gate grinning like the fangs of some beast in its lair.

Chapter Two

When Mr Phelippes had arrived back from Chartley on the previous Monday, he had received from his employer a sharp rebuke. What had he been thinking of, cried Mr Secretary, to have drawn that gallows mark upon the packet? More than likely it had bred suspicion; post-boys were apt to talk, and GG, he feared, had been 'inward' with the post. At all events GG had completely disappeared, and thereby had caused Mr Secretary a great deal of trouble and uneasiness; not only had he lost a most valuable *agent provocateur* who might yet have succeeded in persuading Babington to implicate influential Catholics in the country, but he had very nearly lost contact with Babington himself.

This lecture completed, Mr Secretary bundled his crestfallen henchman into his coach and drove him off to Richmond. And here there was disclosed to Mr Phelippes a secret which threw him into an ecstasy of delight. It had been considered necessary, Lord Burghley told him, to insert a little something into the two fatal letters, Babington's to Mary and her reply.

It would prove, Burghley warned him, a very considerable task, even though the insertions would be trifling. For first of all an exact forged copy of the original encipherment of Mary's answer must be made, and this, in due course, would be delivered to Babington. The real encipherment they would hold, because, said the far-sighted Burghley, they might need it when Mary's two secretaries came to be examined. Yes, yes, he realized that Mr Phelippes was so expert a forger that Curle, the Scots secretary, might have no suspicion if shown something which only purported to be his own encipherment; but one could not be too careful; he might have put some secret mark upon the original whereby he could be sure of knowing it again.

Next Mr Phelippes must make a copy, counterfeiting Babington's hand, and inserting such interpolation as Burghley had decided was sufficient, of that youth's long letter to Mary; this copy, they would tell the Highest One, had been found in his lodging, kept by him after he had sent off the encipherment at the beginning of July. And lastly, not only a decipherment, again with interpolations, of the Queen of Scots' answer must be made, but an encipherment which purported to be the original as written by Curle, but with the same interpolations.

The Great Man did not see fit to explain why he needed this last. The fact of the matter was that, the Highest One being in a particularly difficult mood, it was quite on the cards that she might profess herself unsatisfied with a decipherment made by an agent of the Government, and containing approval of her own assassination, and might go to the trouble of deciphering for herself, with the aid of the key, the letter which would be laid before her as the original.

By Thursday Mr Phelippes had reached a stage in his colossal task when, in the evening, he was able to put a thick packet into the hands of a certain homely-faced serving-man of his, Simon by name, and bid him deliver the packet to Mr Anthony Babington at Hern's Rents. Next day he dispatched a messenger to Mr Secretary at Richmond; a forged copy of the Woman's encipherment, containing no interpolations, had been safely delivered to Babington, he wrote, and Babington had told the serving-man to call again in a few days' time when he might have a letter for him.

So much remained to be done that, contrary to his habit, Mr Phelippes worked at his desk all that Friday; he did not pause for dinner, but had something sent up to his room, eating with one hand and writing with the other, happily absorbed. During that evening, however, a faint cloud passed across the sun of his happiness.

It came in the form of a note from Mr Secretary in answer to his, but it was not concerned with Babington and the letters. Mr Secretary was becoming more and more anxious about the complete disappearance of Ballard. He had not been seen at any of his usual haunts, and discreet enquiries for 'Captain Foscue' had elicited nothing. 'Sorry I am,' reiterated Mr Secretary irritably, 'that GG is not here. I marvel greatly how this manner of absenting himself is come upon him.' While it was essential that the plot was not 'discovered' until Mr Secretary thought fit (in other words, until the Highest One had been persuaded to try and to condemn the Queen of Scots), Ballard being a really dangerous man must be arrested immediately if found. The charge against him could be that of his priesthood only, which would prevent Babington and the others from taking fright.

Saturday and Sunday passed without news. On Monday Mr Phelippes decided to do something on his own account. Acting on the principle that conspirators sometimes hide in the most obvious places, he sent a menial (not the homely-faced one) to Hern's Rents, armed with some plausible excuse and a good fat bribe for Babington's servants, to discover whether Ballard was there. The menial returned with the devastating news that not only Ballard but Babington himself was absent from Hern's Rents. He had last been seen, so the landlord of the lodging had told the menial, on Sunday afternoon, and since then there had been no sign of him. The menial had handsomely tipped such servants as remained; and was convinced they were telling the truth when they professed themselves equally ignorant of their master's whereabouts.

Mr Phelippes was thoroughly alarmed. First Ballard and now Babington! Either someone must have warned them, or else Babington, goaded into action by Mary's letter, had gone down into the country to raise his friends and tenants. If the former alternative was the correct one, then the most likely person to have warned them was Robert Poley, a man of whom Mr Phelippes had always retained the lowest possible opinion. And in that case, Poley himself would have fled.

Mr Phelippes dispatched a man to The Garden, with orders to scout around and discover whether Mr Poley was there or not. The man returned shortly with information which was in the nature of an anti-climax: Mr Babington was staying with Mr Poley at The Garden, and in fact had removed thither on the previous evening.

On that same Monday afternoon, some hours after Mr Phelippes' menial had called at Hern's Rents, Babington sent his foot-boy thither to fetch the rest of his servants to The Garden, and to tell any of his friends whom the boy might find there that he was the guest of Mr Poley. To Anthony's dismay, the foot-boy returned with Ballard.

The friend Anthony had hoped to see was Chidge, from whom he had heard nothing since Tichborne had called at Hern's Rents early on Friday morning and found Anthony distracted with the receipt of the Queen of Scots' letter. He had been, Anthony remembered, rather rude to Chidge, but it was unlike the other to take offence, still less to sulk. And now, instead of Chidge, here was Ballard, the last man in the world he wanted to see, and here was Ballard still urging him to disclose the discarded plot to Mr Secretary, and under cover of the disclosure to go forward with his own. Anthony was very short indeed with the priest, reproaching him for coming hither when, for all he might think to the contrary, almost certainly he was being watched.

That night Anthony and his dear friend Robin had a long talk, the latter suggesting that they might both contrive to slip overseas without waiting for the licence; but though the idea was tempting, Anthony resisted it. He would not, he said, risk reprisals against his family if he managed, against the law, to secure his own safety that way. No, Robin must go to Richmond again tomorrow, and persuade Mr Secretary to give Anthony the promised interview at the earliest possible date, and at this interview he would disclose Ballard's plot as arranged.

No sooner had Robin departed on his errand next morning than Anthony, left alone, began to waver. The thought of Chidge remained in his mind. Chidge had been against the enterprise from the beginning and without actually saying so had had an, unmistakable air of doubting whether Anthony was capable of fulfilling his part as leader. And now Chidge was pleased to shun his best friend's company only because of a few hasty words spoken when that friend was quite distracted.

Very well; he, Anthony, would prove to himself at least that he was not a dreamer and a boaster. He had appointed the homely faced serving-man in the blue coat to call again at Hern's Rents in the course of a few days in case there might be a letter for him to take to Chartley; that the homely-faced one would succeed in tracing him to The Garden seemed unlikely, for Anthony had not informed his landlord where he was. However, he would while away the time till Robin's return by composing a reply to the

Queen of Scots' gracious letter, and hope that somehow he would find means to dispatch it.

It was no easy composition, for what could he say? He remembered only too well what she had written to him, and he knew the kind of businesslike, practical answers she would require to her suggestions and instructions. He sat fraying out the feathers of his quill for minutes together, made several false starts, irritably tore them up, combed his brown hair with his fingers, applied himself to Robin's wine to see if that would help, and at last hit upon an idea. Of course! The discovered treachery of Bernard Mawde was the reason why at present he could do nothing. His pen began to race across the paper.

Most Gracious Sovereign,

Your letter I received not until the XXVIIIth of July. How dangerous an accident hath fallen out by my next letter shall be enlarged upon. In the meantime your Majesty may understand that one Mawde (that had attached himself to Ballard) is discovered to be for this State. By whose treachery, unto what extreme danger myself hath been and the whole plot is like to be brought, and by what means we have in part prevented and purpose by God's assistance to redress the rest, your Majesty shall be by my next informed.

He read it over, and frowned. It sounded very feeble, and it was not entirely honest, but what else could he say? Shying away from the answer to that question, he took refuge in appearing at least on paper the active, resolute young leader the Queen of Scots believed him to be.

Till then, my Sovereign, for His sake that preserveth your Majesty for our common good, dismay not,

> neither doubt of happy issue. It is God's cause, the Church's, and your Majesty's, an enterprise honourable before God and man, undertaken upon zeal and devotion, free from all ambition and temporal regard, and therefore no doubt will succeed happily. We have vowed, and we will perform or die.

His eyes were full of tears. He meant every word of it; all his old zeal for his religion and his devotion to his boyhood heroine had come flooding back.

> In the meantime, [he concluded, observing, not without pleasure, that a tear blotted the ink], I rest infinitely obliged to your Majesty for the great confidence it hath pleased you to repose in me, which to deserve by all faithful service I vow before the face of our Lord Jesu, Whom I beseech to grant your Majesty a long and prosperous reign; and us happy success in these our virtuous enterprises.

He read it over several times, not entirely pleased with it, tempted to insert some of those classical allusions and Latin tags with which he loved to embellish his letters. But no, stark simplicity was best in this case. With only the faintest of sighs he turned to the task of encipherment.

Mr Poley returned from Richmond looking glum. He did not say so, of course, but he had been rated most soundly by Mr Secretary for his delay in passing on the news that Babington was staying with him, and the only result of his plausible explanations had been to draw forth a detailed description of what would happen to him if he proved false.

"Mr Secretary bade me tell you, dear lad, that he is too busy to see you tomorrow, but offers to give you an interview on Thursday morning at eight of the clock."

Anthony, who had been dozing on a couch, leapt up instantly, exclaiming:

"I detest and suspect these delays. Did you give him my message in full? Did you make him understand how important is this information I am prepared to reveal to him?"

"I did, I did, sweet Anthony." Poley sank upon the couch and coughed weakly and pathetically for some moments. "But it seems," he panted, sniffing at the medicinal herbs enclosed within the silver knob of his cane, "there is ill news from Ireland, and that Mr Secretary is kept at the Council board day and night. But the delay is trifling, and from what he hinted to me I believe you will have audience with the Queen herself. Then you may be sure of getting what you desire, for she dotes upon handsome young gentlemen and can refuse them nothing. All you have to do in the meanwhile is to stay quietly here, where you are safe, and not to return to your lodging."

That, indeed, was a precaution Anthony was prepared to observe. But despite all Robin's assurances, his mind was a prey once more to a thousand doubts, including, for the first time, a horrid little stab of uneasiness concerning the good faith of Robin himself. But he drove it from him; it was basely ungrateful after all sweet Robin had done.

Wednesday passed in increasing suspense. The obliging Robin had agreed to his dear lad's request that he should go again to Richmond and make sure that Mr Secretary would keep the appointment at eight next morning, and Anthony, never fond of his own company, grew more and more distraught. Several times during the long hours by himself, he was on the point of going into London to seek out his old friends; but the confusing events and the indecisions of the past few days prevented him. What could he say to them? How answer their inevitable questions?

It was not until evening that Poley returned, and then his manner was agitated and his eyes refused to meet those of his friend. Mr Secretary, it seemed, was full of regrets, but the Queen was unwell and was giving no audiences. Moreover there was so much business that Mr Secretary himself must be at the Council table all Thursday and Friday, but he would see Mr Babington without fail on Saturday morning, if that young gentleman would present himself at Richmond at eleven o'clock.

Anthony's face had paled long before this message was finished. He refused to discuss the situation; he snapped at Robin that he was sick and tired of being cooped up here like a prisoner, and that they would take a late supper in the City. They could go by boat from St Katherine's stairs and return the same way, so that they would not have to pass through the gates which were closed at sunset. The very first person they encountered when they had landed at Thames Street stairs was Robert Gage, and the sight of him belatedly reminded Anthony of Ballard and his peril.

"Give Mr Ballard a message from me," said Anthony, taking Gage aside. "Say that Mr Secretary is acting in a manner which I consider very peculiar and suspicious, and that my urgent advice to Mr Ballard is that he lose no time in slipping overseas if he can contrive it, or at least that he keep very close in your house."

Returning to The Garden an hour later with Robin, Anthony's anxiety for Ballard turned to resentment. It had been he, a much older man and a priest, who had embroiled youths like Anthony in these perilous courses; and now, a marked man, he had been so careless of his friend's safety that he had called upon him in his new retreat. As he walked with Robin up the narrow lane which was bounded by houses on one side and by the Tower moat upon the other, again, and much more strongly, he had the feeling that he was being shadowed. But they reached The Garden without mishap, and Anthony, saying shortly that he was tired, was going upstairs to bed, when there came a soft knock upon the outer door.

He stood petrified, one hand tightening on the banister rail, his very thoughts frozen. Standing there in the shadows, he watched Poley take up a candle, watched him cross the hall and open the door. A moment later, after a whispered conversation with someone unseen, Poley came hastening to where his friend was standing.

"There is one here come enquiring about a letter to be collected from Mr Babington," whispered Poley.

"What manner of man is this messenger?"

"A serving man wearing a blue coat."

Anthony stared at him for a moment. Then, acting like an automaton, he took the stairs three at a time, drew his recently written letter to the Queen of Scots from its hiding-place, hastily added the date in cipher, sealed it, and, waving aside Robin who was standing at the stair-foot, himself carried it to the outer door. In the light of the branched candlestick he held, he saw that the man waiting there was indeed the same homely-faced one who had brought him the long letter from the Queen of Scots last Thursday night.

He put his reply into the outstretched hand, and was about to question the man as to how he had managed to trace him hither from Hern's Rents when, without a word, the messenger disappeared into the darkness.

Several times that night Anthony awoke and lay listening intently; several times he sprang out of bed, and without lighting the candle stood straining his eyes through the closed casements. But always there was nothing unusual to see or to hear, only the rustle of the trees, the hoot of an owl, and the snoring of his chamber-boy in the truckle-bed at the foot of his own. Yet the impression was strong upon him all through the dark hours that there were figures prowling and lurking out there.

It was only just growing light when he was awakened by the sound of his door being opened. He took one look at his visitor, then he was out of bed, aiming a wild kick at his sleeping chamber-boy, bundling the dazed youth out of the room.

"You are mad to come here!" he cried wildly to John Ballard, slamming and locking the door. "Did you not receive my message by Gage?"

"I received it," said the priest quietly.

Anthony was about to break into a hot denunciation of such folly when he realized that it was a new Ballard he was seeing. Gone was not only the old fanaticism, but also the uneasiness which had fallen on him since his discovery of the treachery of Bernard Mawde. No trace remained either of the swaggering, raffish 'Captain Foscue' or of the agent of Catholic resistance. Here was just a human being, broken in spirit, remembering too late that he had dedicated his life to the service of God.

"Anthony," said Ballard, very quiet, seating himself on the bed and drawing the young man down beside him, "I have had leisure to think during the time I have been skulking in Marylebone (I who never skulked in my life before), and it has been revealed to me that I have done you and your friends a great wrong. That maybe after all the Jesuits are right in their constant preaching that we must bear persecution with Christian resignation and leave the issue to Almighty God. I cannot tell. Theologians are divided on the question, and not only the laity but priests are much perplexed."

He paused. His head was downbent, the dyed hair dull in the thin dawn light.

"But what torments me is the thought that it was I who persuaded you young men into what is termed 'imagining treason'. You are innocent in the sight of God; what plans you formed were made out of a true devotion to your religion and to your lawful Queen; but that innocence would not save you from the death of a traitor."

Anthony drew a sharp breath. The death of a traitor! How often had he seen those dismal processions pass down Holborn, figures strapped prone upon hurdles, pelted by the mob, bound for the rope, the quartering-block, the disembowelling-hook. In all his dreams of 'exploits' his imagination had presented him with a very different picture of his own death. His hands clutched the bed-linen to steady himself. He was no coward, but months of strain, weeks of drinking too much and sleeping too little, temporarily unmanned him now.

"I cam hither this morning," went on the priest, "for three purposes. First to ask your forgiveness for the wrong I may have done you – *mea maxima culpa*. Next to tell you that, if God gives me grace, no word shall ever pass my lips, even if they put me to the Bloody Question, which can incriminate you and your young friends. And lastly to beg you after all to lay aside this most perilous enterprise, and to go overseas, you, your family, and your friends, by any means you can contrive, and without delay. I pray God with all my heart that if any must suffer for this business it shall be myself alone. And I would it might be for my priesthood only, though I have little deserved the honour of martyrdom."

There was such a quiet despair in his voice, such simple humility in his look, that Babington forgot both his fears for himself and his resentment against this man. He knelt and asked a blessing, and when the priest had gone he remained there on his knees, his arms outstretched across the tumbled bed-linen, his face buried in it, praying in broken words for God's mercy on them all.

He was still kneeling there when he heard a confusion of sounds from below. There was a knocking upon the outer door, a strange voice speaking, the rattle of steel, hurried footsteps within, a slight scuffle, and then the banging of the door again, and silence. But oddly it meant nothing to him; he had sunk downwards into his own soul, drawing strength and peace from the familiar words which he repeated over and over again:

"Miserere nobis."

Then, breaking through his absorption, shattering the newfound peace, the hammer of footsteps on the stair, the bursting open of his chamber door, the sight of Robin Poley, ashen-faced, gasping, his voice shrill with panic:

"Ballard is taken!"

Chapter Three

"That such a thing should happen in my house!" wailed Poley for the dozenth time. "This house which has proved so sure a retreat for our poor persecuted brethren!"

Anthony made no answer. For an hour he had been pacing up and down his bedchamber, his bedgown slung over his shoulders, his face grey with strain, the twitch in one eyelid working continuously. Every now and then he dashed his hand against his mouth and bit it as though to prevent himself from screaming; sometimes he made for the couch where his clothes were lying, snatched up his shirt, and flung it down again.

"But my dear lad," went on Poley soothingly, "we must not despair. Mr Ballard was arrested by ordinary pursuivants (I marked the badge upon their doublets) under the Statute of 1584, for being ordained abroad and returning to England. I do not think for one moment that the warrant came from Mr Secretary; it is far more likely to have been issued by that rogue, Justice Young, a most officious priest-hunter, and who only last week arrested the Jesuit who calls himself Mr Edmondes."

"What does it matter *why* Ballard was arrested?" snapped Anthony. "They'll kill him just the same."

Poley went up to him and took him gently by the shoulders.

"It signifies very much, sweet Anthony. If Mr Ballard has been arrested for his priesthood only, then you may still obtain your licence by revealing to Mr Secretary Ballard's plot. But if he has been arrested for that plot, then – "

He broke off, and gnawed his thumb-nail for a while, seeming to ponder deeply.

"Now I will tell you what I will do, dear lad," he went on briskly. "I will go again to Richmond, now at once. I have friends there from whom I can discover the truth of the matter. Meanwhile do you stay here; if you yourself are in any danger (which I do not for a moment think you are), this is the safest place, since if they had suspected you were here and were desirous to catch you, you would have been arrested with Ballard."

Among his many prevarications, Poley had told Babington one truth: that Mr Secretary was very busy.

Phelippes had finished his monumental task of forgery, and the results were now being laid before the Highest One; but so far without any startling success. Oh, she was thoroughly frightened; she had accepted without question that which purported to be a copy of Babington's long letter to the Queen of Scots, and she was determined to have his blood. In her terror and fury she rounded upon her Ministers, accusing Burghley and Walsingham of having so little care for her life that this wretch Babington had been allowed to remain at large in London for weeks, nay months.

They had known for at least a month, she cried, of the contents of this letter; did they not control the secret post? And according to this letter six unnamed gentlemen had been appointed to assassinate her. There it was in black and white, she stormed, jabbing a ringed forefinger at Phelippes' main interpolation: 'For the dispatch of the Usurper, there be six gentlemen; all my noble friends, will undertake, the tragical execution.' Why were these villains not arrested? What was the use of Mr Secretary's precious spy-system if it could not protect her Person? God's blood! it was expensive enough; look at these accounts... '

Again and again, patiently and gently, Burghley endeavoured to bring her back to the point. Mr Secretary could lay his hands upon these conspirators at any time he chose; they were all under observation. But what of the answer from the Queen of Scots? Would her Majesty be pleased to look at this: '(6) By what means do the six gentlemen deliberate to proceed?' And this: 'The affairs being thus prepared and forces in readiness both within and without the realm, then shall it be time to set the six gentlemen to work, taking order, upon the accomplishment of their design, that I may be suddenly transported out of this place.' The 'design' was none other than the assassination of her Majesty, and the Queen of Scots here expressed her approval of it.

The Highest One muttered, snatched Phelippes' doctored decipherment of Mary's answer to Babington, and read it through again. Burghley sat on tenterhooks. Would it have been wiser after all to include the postscript which at first he had suggested might be added? But no; the asking for the names of the six gentlemen would have been too crude. There was a ring of regality about the whole of the original letter, and the interpolations, amounting only to a few words, in the body of it, had been difficult enough to frame.

He glanced covertly at the Highest One. His pitiless eyes noted how sweat was making the paint shine on that raddled face, how the heavily ringed hand shook a little as it held the papers. He realized the agony of indecision of which these things were the outward signs; he knew that the considerable intelligence was at war with an old desire to find some excuse for putting a rival out of the way.

Next moment he was congratulating himself upon his foresight, for the Highest One, squaring her lean shoulders, demanded what she supposed was the original letter from Mary, together with the cipher key, and announced her intention of re-deciphering the whole thing herself, if it took her a week. And, she added, grimly, my Lord Treasurer and Mr Secretary should keep her company at her task; if she was to be deprived of her well-earned holiday, she would keep her Ministers' noses to the grindstone as well as her own.

The two men did not confer with one another during those days of suspense, but in both their minds dwelt the same frightful possibility: Would the intelligent Highest One perceive the fraud? Would she notice, for instance, that *after* being made to speak of the assassination, Mary went on to express her fears that if Elizabeth caught her again she would place her 'in some hold forth of which I should never escape', and would 'pursue with all extremity those that had assisted me'?

But the Highest One did not notice this discrepancy. Her intelligence was overlaid by the mortal struggle which raged within her. She wanted to accept the letter as genuine; she wanted just such an excuse for taking the life of the woman she had wronged. But judicial execution! How would it be regarded abroad? Might it not precipitate a Catholic rising? How frightful a precedent it would set! A sovereign to die by the axe! Such a thing had never been known. It would strike a mortal blow at absolute monarchy. His own conscience, began Burghley piously, but the Highest One interrupted him with an oath. He had no conscience, she told him tartly, only his precious Establishment.

Thus she wavered back and forth, as weathercock as the poor dupe, Babington; and until she made up her mind, Mr Secretary's great 'practice' was at a standstill.

"Poley is here, sir," said Mr Phelippes, entering Mr Secretary's apartments in Richmond Palace on Thursday morning, "though he had precise orders to stick close to Babington. Upon my soul, sir, I would take leave to advise your Honour to put the man in ward. I have always deemed him a notable knave, and – "

"And a useful one," interrupted Walsingham curtly. He was in a very bad temper, bewildered by the Highest One's inability to make up her mind, longing to 'discover' a good spectacular plot, acutely missing the peace of Barn Elms and the company of his pets, and tormented by the beginnings of another of his boils. "You have your men keeping a close watch on The Garden? Very well, then. And what of this letter Babington gave to your serving-man last night?"

"I have deciphered it, sir, and find it most disappointing. There is no mention of any who are in league with him in the country; indeed it was not worth waiting for," added Mr Phelippes in disgust.

Mr Secretary did not enlighten his underling as to what they were really waiting for before they arrested Babington and his friends and made public this plot. After dismissing the little man, he sat thinking for a while. On the whole he thought it would be safer to ward Poley; the man had been behaving in a very suspicious manner of late. If he mended his ways he might be used for other 'practices', for he was in high credit with the Catholics, and such men were becoming increasingly rare. But someone else must be 'used' towards Babington until it was time to pull him in, and that would be, please God, in the course of the next few days at longest.

Mr Secretary rang his hand-bell and sent his servant to find Mr Scudamore, a gentleman of his chamber. To Mr Scudamore he gave a warrant for the arrest of Anthony Babington, and also some careful instructions. On no account was Scudamore to execute this warrant until he received an order to that effect, and he must keep in constant touch with Mr Phelippes at his house in Leadenhall Street. Mr Scudamore was to go at once to The Garden, taking another of Mr Secretary's gentlemen with him; he was to present Mr Secretary's compliments to Mr Babington, tell him that Mr Poley had suffered a physical collapse and was being tended at Richmond, and beg Babington to accept the advice offered in a note written by Mr Secretary's own hand.

Babington, meanwhile, had succumbed to stark panic. He was incapable now of reasoning; the situation had grown so complex and confused that it was impossible for him to think out. Dark doubts beset him concerning Robin's good faith; a sudden and belated fear joined them in regard to the homely-faced serving-man in the blue coat. Who was he? Whence had he come? Why, in God's name why, had he, Anthony, been so childishly trusting of this stranger? Why, in so perilous a business had he trusted anybody?

He could not remain alone in the house. Company he must have, and. there was only one whose company he desired, his best and oldest friend, the friend who, though he might have taken offence at some hasty words, had never failed him yet.

Careless now as to whether it was safe or not, not once glancing back to see whether he was being followed, Anthony hastened to the nearest stairs and hired a wherry. Landing at the Temple, he pushed his way across crowded Fleet Street to Chancery Lane. He could have wept when Tichborne's servant informed him that his master was not at home. He had been laid up with a hurt leg since Friday, said the man; today was the first occasion of his being able to go abroad. But whither he had gone, the servant could not say.

The nightmare deepened upon Anthony, even though he now knew the reason why he had not seen Chidge this past week. He felt himself utterly forsaken by all his friends, Ballard arrested, Gilbert Gifford disappeared and no word from him, Chidge he knew not where, Robin a possible traitor. Cursing the crowded streets, fiercely elbowing his way along, he hurried from one to another of the taverns he knew that Chidge patronized, but there was not a sign of his friend. Almost in despair, he decided to call at Salisbury's lodging, though in his present distracted state he dreaded Salisbury's inevitable questions.

He was about to ascend the stair which led to the lodging, when he paused abruptly, and stood peering through the window of the barber-surgeon's shop below. For beyond the neat rows of corn-cutting instruments, the basins stuffed with red rags to represent blood, and the rotten teeth tastefully laid out upon a white cloth, he had caught a glimpse of a familiar figure – Chidge himself!

Tichborne, who was having his leg dressed by the proprietor, glanced up in surprise as the door was thrown violently open; then, seeing who it was who had entered, exclaimed with pleasure.

"Why, Anthony, I feared you were gone out of town without letting me know. I had no answer to the notes I sent to your lodging "

He broke off, for he had noticed the wildness of his friend's look. There was silence while the barber-surgeon completed the dressing, and Tichborne paid him. Then, leaning heavily on a stick, Tichborne slipped his other hand through Anthony's arm and hobbled out of the shop, drawing his friend into an alley which ran at the side of it.

"What is to do, Anthony? "he asked in a low tone. "You look – "

"Ballard is taken. They arrested him early this morning in the very house where I have been staying this past week."

"God pity him," said Tichborne quietly.

Anthony wrested his arm from that of his friend.

"God pity him, quotha!" he cried violently. "You had better be praying that God has pity upon us whom he seduced into these treasonable practices, as he himself admitted to me. And unless we get out of London immediately, we shall share his fate."

"Anthony, you are beside yourself. Come back to my lodging and let us talk – "

"Talk! Talk! There has been too much woundy talk! You must warn the others; I dare not, for I am sure I am being followed. And get away from London, all of you, now, at once!"

Then he was plunging out into the street again; scarce knowing what he did, whither he went.

He found himself back at The Garden presently, and called eagerly for his friend Robin, but Poley had not returned. What use to wait for him? And yet supposing after all his fears were groundless, and Poley returned with good news? He owed it to Robin to wait here at least until darkness fell. Then, if there was still no sign of Robin, he would ride through the open country north of the City and try to make for home. He took a flagon of wine, and paper, ink-horn and quills to a little rustic arbour; while he was waiting he would try to calm himself by writing a letter to his friend.

Gulping down the wine to give himself inspiration, he experienced again the sensation that he was being watched, that figures were lurking behind the clipped yew hedges. Instinctively, to save his reason, he fell back upon his old self-dramatizing. He was the dashing young hero of his boyhood dreams, who had saved his friends by warning them in time, who sat calmly here remaining at his post till the last. Yes, that was it; he would perform or die, as he had written to the Queen of Scots. And if they closed in round him, those unseen watchers, he would sell his life dearly, he thought, drawing his sword and laying the naked blade upon the table. In a mist of wine he saw himself with his back to the wall, heard his voice shouting for Queen Mary, and her voice, choked with tears, commending his gallantry, praying for his soul...

> Robin [he wrote],
>
> '*Sollicitae non possunt curae mutare aranei stamina fusi*! I am ready to endure whatsoever shall be inflicted – *Et facere et pati Romanorum est.* What my course hath been towards Mr Secretary you can witness; what my love to yourself, yourself can best tell. I am the same I always pretended. I pray God you be, and ever so remain towards me. Take heed to your own part, lest of these my misfortunes you bear the blame. *Est exilium inter malos vivere*! Farewell, sweet Robin, if, as I take thee, true to me. If not, Adieu – *omnium bipedum nequissimus*!'

Of all two-footed things the wickedest! A just epithet if Robin had betrayed their friendship.

> Return me thine answer for my satisfaction, and my diamond, and what else thou wilt. The furnace is prepared wherein our faith must be tried. Farewell till we meet, which God knows when,
>
> Thine, how far thou knowest,
>
> Anthony Babington

So remarkable a literary effort had eased him; the fine phrases rang in his head as he reached for the flagon again. 'Nor care nor cautel ever mends of spiders' threads the broken ends' – 'Both to do and to bear is worthy of Romans' – 'To live among the wicked, what an end!' He leaned back against the rustic-work of the arbour and his eyelids drooped; suddenly he jerked upright, wide awake again. For he had heard the click of the garden gate.

Constables? Robin returning? One of his friends? His hand closed on the hilt of his naked sword; he rose and stood *en garde*; and so watched two strangers walking towards him through the twilight.

"Mr Babington," began one of the strangers, a pale-faced person with two dark eyes set close to a hook nose, and a little, rather silly, dark moustache, "I fear you will not remember me, but I had the honour of being introduced to you by Mr Poley when you were at Greenwich early in the summer. Allow me to present myself, sir; my name is Scudamore, and this is Mr Hunsdon; we are both of Mr Secretary's chamber, and we bring you his Honour's compliments and this note."

Very red in the face; Anthony slipped his sword into its sheath, and returned the greeting, trying to force his exhausted and wine-dulled mind to take in what Mr Scudamore was saying.

Mr Scudamore was courtesy itself. Poor Mr Poley had suffered one of his attacks when he came to Richmond this morning; alas, poor good gentleman, a martyr to his lungs! And therefore Mr Secretary had sent two of his own gentlemen to call on Mr Babington, went on Scudamore, gently and tactfully manoeuvring Anthony into the house, calling for candles, and presenting a sealed billet.

It was a surprisingly friendly little note, almost deferential. Mr Secretary begged Mr Babington not to be disturbed by the arrest of one Ballard at The Garden. It had been made by the orders of Mr Justice Young who, of course, was perfectly within his rights in acting so. It pained Mr Secretary to have to tell Mr Babington that the safety of the realm necessitated an intensification of the hunt for priests ordained abroad, but the Government had no wish to disturb peaceable Catholics who paid their fines. However, since certain of the justices were somewhat over-zealous in these matters, Mr Secretary strongly advised Mr Babington (and here the words were underlined) to keep close in the company of the two gentlemen he was sending with this note, until arrangements could be made for his coming to Richmond for the interview to which Mr Secretary was greatly looking forward, and at which Mr Babington had promised to disclose some important information.

Anthony excused himself to the two gentlemen on the score of extreme fatigue, and leaving Poley's servants to attend to their needs, staggered up to bed. He slept deeply for the first time for many nights, and awoke at a late hour feeling more himself than he had felt for weeks. He remembered Mr Scudamore now; he was the gentleman who was to have had the four hundred pounds which Anthony had offered for his licence to travel, when he had gone to see Mr Secretary at Greenwich. No wonder Scudamore had been so polite and almost servile last evening; he was still hoping to get his hands on that bribe!

Oh God, the relief of it all! What a melodramatic fool he had been yesterday. Why did he always believe the worst? Why had he suspected sweet Robin of treachery, and never entertained the possibility of some other explanation of Robin's failure to return home? And all the while poor Robin had been lying on a sickbed. He blushed with shame as he remembered the note he had written, his wild careering about London earlier, his panic-stricken urgings of Chidge to flee.

Messrs Scudamore and Hunsdon were waiting upon his pleasure when he came downstairs, greeting him very properly as one of superior social rank to themselves, anxious to know whether he had slept well, suggesting that he dined with them, as it was now near noon.

"You will be my guests, if you please, sirs," said Anthony, in his high-handed way. "I'll conduct you through the fields to the Plough outside Temple Bar, where I am well known and can command the best food in London."

Behind his back, Mr Scudamore nudged Mr Hunsdon. Excellent, said the nudge. We can put it down to expenses and keep the money. And the Plough of all places! Probably the whole gang will be there.

But as they rode out from Mr Poley's stables, Anthony suddenly changed his mind. Not the Plough, of course, not any of his former haunts. He would not like to be seen by his friends in such company until he had been able to explain the situation to them.

"You must excuse me, sirs," said he, reining his horse under the arch of the Bishop's Gate, "if we take our ride afterwards, for my appetite is too sharp to brook delay. The Mitre here in Bishopsgate is a good hostelry, they say; let us see if it lives up to its reputation."

They were dismounting from their horses in the yard of this tavern, when Mr Hunsdon suddenly clapped a hand to his forehead and exclaimed:

"Pox take me, what a fool am I! I had near forgot I had an errand to do for Mr Secretary in the City. Pray, Mr Babington, don't stay dinner; I deserve none for being such an ass."

"A head like a riddle, has my friend George," chuckled Mr Scudamore, as his companion rode out of the yard again.

They heard him break into a canter as he turned into the street; evidently Mr Secretary's errand was an important one. And indeed it was. Mr Hunsdon rode as hard as he could to Leadenhall Street, to tell Mr Phelippes that, if wanted within the next couple of hours, Anthony Babington was to be found at the sign of the Mitre in Bishopsgate Within.

Anthony enjoyed a pleasant meal. Mr Scudamore was attentive and even flattering, showing no trace of either that hostility or contempt which Anthony was accustomed to from Protestants. Politics were not mentioned; nor was religion; and gradually the reserve with which Anthony had treated his companion faded away. By the time they had arrived at the stage of eating a tart of almonds, he found himself patronizingly instructing Mr Scudamore on the art of 'manning' a falcon, his companion having confided to him his ambition of buying a little country estate when he retired.

"It is the too hasty discarding of the rufter-hood on a young bird," declared Anthony, "that ruins many a good hawk. It must be kept on until she no longer starts at the sound of a voice, otherwise you will never cure her of bating. Now – "

He broke off, for Mr Hunsdon had rejoined them, panting somewhat, and looking strangely excited. Without so much as greeting his host, he sat down close to his friend, and passed him a note.

Immediately, though for no reason he could imagine, Anthony's suspicions reawoke. On the excuse of standing up to reach for the wine-flagon, he contrived to get a fleeting glimpse of the note which Scudamore was reading. He saw only his own name and part of a sentence; but it was enough. For the few words he read were:

'...execute your warrant immediately...'

"If you will excuse me, sirs, I will pay the shot," said Anthony, his voice calm, his manner perfectly natural.

Never in his life had he acted with real decision, but he did so now. He left his rich cloak and his sword in its velvet scabbard hanging on the back of his chair; he strolled out of the room, bawling for the landlord, careful to leave the door open; he forced his legs to descend the stair without haste.

But as soon as he was at the foot he made a bound for the outer door, debouched into the yard, waved aside his servants, seized the nearest horse, leapt into the saddle, and spurred towards the Bishop's Gate and the open country beyond, galloping breakneck for his life.

Chapter Four

In his apartments at Richmond, Mr Secretary was writing a letter to Sir Amias Paulet. He was in the highest of spirits, even his incipient boil forgotten; for at long last the Highest One had consented to appoint a Commission to try the Queen of Scots on a charge of conspiring against her life. The great 'practice' had achieved its end; and as for the silly dupes who had been used in it, Ballard was safely under lock and key, and by this time Scudamore would have received from Mr Phelippes the order to execute his warrant for the arrest of Babington.

> With all convenient speed [Mr Secretary wrote to Paulet], you are to remove the Queen of Scots from Chartley, under colour of taking the air, to some secure house in the neighbourhood. As soon as she is removed, you will arrest her two secretaries, taking care that they speak not one with the other, and send them, close guarded, to my house in Cheapside. Then must you break open all the coffers and trunks within her apartments, making sure search for secret places; and all papers of whatsoever nature found therein you must send in sealed bags and under a strong guard to London.

Having completed these instructions, which would ensure that all the victim's papers, which otherwise might prove embarrassing to the Government, would be safely in his own hands in readiness for doctoring or burning as circumstances might require, Mr Secretary began a note to Mr Phelippes on the subject of John Ballard.

> If he do not disclose, it were fit to commit him to the Tower with two trusty men to attend him, that he may be examined out of hand and forced by torture to utter.

He paused for a moment, and frowned. He really did detest giving a warrant for torture; it was a foolish little weakness in him, but there it was. With a small sigh, he was about to continue, when an express messenger was admitted, bringing him the news that Babington had given Scudamore and his friend the slip, and had got clean away.

Mr Secretary was pardonably wroth, and it was as well for Mr Scudamore that he had not brought the news in person. But further consideration convinced Walsingham that perhaps it was all for the best. Babington could not get far; and the very fact that he had fled would give the appearance of guilt, and help enormously in the staging of a sensational manhunt and a national alarm. For it was not only the Highest One who must be terrified; it was of vital importance that the public should believe that this plot, which actually had been instigated and nursed from the beginning by the Government, was a conspiracy by desperate Papists.

Mr Secretary set briskly to work. He issued warrants for the apprehension of all those whose names he had obtained from Gilbert Gifford, and, for form's sake, for Gilbert himself. He sent couriers galloping with a command for a watch on the ports, others into Derbyshire in case Babington was making for home. He warned the Lord Mayor that a hellish conspiracy, which included a burning of the City and the cutting of all Protestant throats, had been discovered, advising a closing of the gates and the barricading of the principal streets. He set clerks to work writing out Hues and Cries to all justices in the Home Counties:

> These are to charge you in the Queen's Majesty's name upon pain of death, to make diligent search and hue and cry for Anthony Babington, Chidiock Tichborne, Henry Dunn, Thomas Salisbury, Robert Barnwell, John Savage, Charles Tilney, Edward Abingdon, and Gilbert Gifford, who are fled and proclaimed traitors, to lay all highways, and to keep a standing watch day and night until you receive orders to the contrary...

Poor GG But then he had known from the beginning that he would have to be proclaimed and eventually indicted with his dupes; and he ought to have known also, thought Mr Secretary severely, that to go and sneak overseas like that (as undoubtedly he had done) before the quarry was in the bag, was no way to retain Mr Secretary's good opinion of him.

The irresolute, when faced with real danger, are apt to display a surprising coolness; and so it was with Babington as he galloped through the sparsely inhabited district north of the City wall. He had plenty of physical courage, and the need for simple urgent action was a relief after the indecisions and suspense of the past month. What luck that he had decided to ride instead of taking a boat when he had set out from The Garden with Mr Secretary's bloodhounds! And now his first necessity was a change of clothes, for already Scudamore would have raised the alarm and issued a description of him. His best hope of obtaining this necessity was to ride to Ballard's old hide-out in Marylebone. Ballard was taken, and therefore there would be no longer a watch on the house.

(At the back of these practical thoughts there raged bewildered questions: What was it all about? Why had Scudamore pretended that Mr Secretary was friendly when all the time he had a warrant for his arrest? How had Mr Secretary come to know about that silly, up-in-the-air enterprise of his? But he crushed down his bewilderment; there was no time to indulge it now.)

Avoiding the hamlets, keeping as far as possible to the woods, he came safely to the little inn on the outskirts of Marylebone where Ballard had stayed. His luck had not deserted him. The only occupant of the yard at the back was Ballard's friend and former host, Robert Gage, who was busy feeding his hens.

"Why, Mr Babington," said Gage, coming up to the other's stirrup, "I'm right glad to see you. For Mr Savage came hither in a great pother this morning, full of a rumour that Mr Ballard was taken, and there the poor fellow sits in the chimney-corner, weeping like a wench."

The young giant, his face blotched with crying, sprang up as Anthony strode into the room, and implored the newcomer to tell him that the rumour was false. Mr Ballard was the best friend he had ever had, his spiritual father –

"It's true enough," interrupted Anthony harshly, "and unless you would share his fate, you had best run for your life. For I'll tell you this, my man, we have all been damnably tricked, and Mr Secretary's hounds are hot upon our trail."

The youth stared at him, but without betraying any fear.

"If you had permitted me to keep my vow, Mr Babington," said he, mildly reproachful, "Mr Ballard need not have been taken, and by this time all our troubles would have ended."

Anthony stared in his turn; and there stabbed at him the humiliating truth that among them all this low-born fellow was the only one who possessed the resolution to act instead of talk. Then he thrust the thought from him. Savage must be got away at all costs; he, Anthony, owed that to Ballard. Refusing to listen to the boy's protests, he forced him on to a horse and bade him put as many miles as he could between himself and London before nightfall.

Then, and not till then, did he turn to the problem of his own preservation. Frantically stripping himself of his fine clothes, he threw on an old suit of Gage's, bidding the latter stuff his own silk doublet and hose, his hat with its jewelled band, and his be-ribboned shoes down the well in the yard. Then, with Gage for guide, he fled through fields and along bridle-paths until they reached the shelter of St John's Wood, that considerable forest which stretched northwards from Marylebone to Hampstead, where it merged into the Heath.

His luck still held. The night was fine and warm, and there was no moon; London and its terrors seemed a world away; and the only alarm turned out to be yet another piece of good fortune. They were standing under the trees, getting their breath, when they heard voices, and had scarce time to duck into the undergrowth before Anthony recognized the soft Irish voice of his friend, Robin Barnwell. A cautious hail, an astonished answer, and Anthony was embracing Barnwell, whose companion was none other than little Henry Dunn.

"We have been skulking here since yesterday," explained Barnwell. "Salisbury came bursting in upon us at the

Plough where we were supping, warning us to flee, though neither he nor we know what it is all about. We decided it would be better to separate, so Tom Salisbury has made a bolt for his home in the North, Tichborne and Tilney are trying to reach some secure island in the West (so Tom said), and I believe Abingdon is making for his native Worcestershire."

"We are near famished," wailed Dunn, who presented a most ridiculous appearance, for he had lost his wig and had concealed his baldness under a kerchief, "for we have not dared to approach a house to buy food."

It was found that Gage had thought to snatch up some provisions ere leaving his inn, and sitting down under a tree the party ate and drank. And then, of course, they must begin bombarding Anthony with the questions he had dreaded. Why were they fleeing? What had they done? As bewildered as themselves, he snapped at them. He did not know; someone must have betrayed their plans, someone whom they had trusted, perhaps even Ballard himself. They looked at him in reproach, for he had been their leader all along. Trying to rouse himself, he cried that he would save them yet. How many priests and seminarists had he not smuggled in and out of the country, harboured, supplied with skilful disguises, and got safely to and fro under the very noses of pursuivants and priest-hunters.

He had forgotten that he lacked now the one thing he had always taken for granted: money.

During the night he was full of his usual vague plans. Lying there under the trees he talked vivaciously. They must start walking before dawn, still making northwards; the forest was extensive, and so long as they avoided the one highway, Watling Street, which skirted it on the way from London to the North, and the track which connected the villages of Hampstead and Highgate, they would be safe enough. When they reached the northern outskirts of the wood, they must lie hid until night fell, and then scout around to find some horses. If only they could get into Derbyshire, why, there were a score of houses where they could lie secure until they found a chance of slipping overseas, a multitude of kinsfolk and friends he could call upon for aid. (Privately he cherished the possibility that the whole thing was a false alarm, though he would look pretty silly if it were.)

They were ravenously hungry again by noon, Gage's provisions having been eaten the previous evening. Gage being the one least likely to be in danger, since he had taken no part in their talk of plots, he volunteered to go and buy some food at an inn on the outskirts of Hampstead. He was back almost directly, empty-handed and agitated.

"There must be a hue and cry after you gentlemen," he panted. "There are mounted constables patrolling the road, and the village folk yonder are cackling like geese about some plot being discovered."

They stared at him in silent dismay.

"Mr Gage," said Anthony shortly at last, "you had best think of your safety. They have nothing against you – "

"I harboured Mr Ballard," interrupted the innkeeper gruffly, "and as you know, sir, to harbour a priest is death. Nay, I'll take my chance along of you gentlemen, if you please."

"But what are we to eat?" moaned Barnwell, a young man devoted to the pleasures of the table.

"I'm ashamed of you Robin," snapped Anthony. "If you have forgot your country arts by living so long in a town, I assure you that I have not. There are fish-ponds here, conies in plenty, and if all else fails I'll make shift to rob a henhouse."

But once again he found that his brave words were words only. His mind in a turmoil, his heart sick with dread, he had not the energy for contriving snares, for fashioning a fishing-rod. The days and the nights began to merge into one another, so that the fugitives forgot which day of the week it was, how long they had been skulking. Time was endless and aimless, as aimless as their talk.

Barnwell and Dunn talked incessantly. At first the latter had been the soul, if not the life, of the dismal little party, prattling of hardships cheerfully borne for conscience' sake, comparing himself and his companions to the early Christians, who had crouched in dens and caverns from pagan persecutors. All this was trying enough; but it was worse when he and Barnwell began a futile speculation as to where the hidden treachery had lain. It could not be Mawde; he knew nothing of Anthony's enterprise. What about Poley? They did not know the man, but what did Anthony think? Who was it who had introduced Poley to him? It was Tom Salisbury – or was it Tichborne? If only Salisbury and Tichborne were here now, they could ask them how they had become acquainted with Poley. And what about this secret agent, Gilbert Gifford?

"I never liked him," said Dunn, shaking his absurdly kerchiefed head. "I never believed he was truly devout. He let fall an oath in my presence such as no good Catholic would use, and he spoke disrespectfully of – "

"Oh, pox take you!" shouted Anthony, his temper snapping. "What does it signify now?"

They stared at him; then began all over again.

Surely it could not be Ballard who had betrayed them, ruminated Barnwell. Dunn rounded upon him; to suggest such a thing of one of God's priests! Almost certainly they would have put him to the Bloody Question, retorted Barnwell, and many a good man had succumbed to that, especially at the hands of this villain Topcliffe, who was so valuable to the Government that he was actually allowed a private rack in his house.

"Ay, and it's not only the rack they use," chimed in Gage darkly. "I knew a man who worked as porter in the Tower, and he told me of some instrument they term the Scavenger's Daughter, which trusses a man into a ball until the blood sprouts from divers places in his body. And the worst of all, says he, is the hanging up by the hands – "

Anthony scrambled to his feet with an oath, and stalked away from them. What was the use of these futile discussions? he asked himself, not daring to admit that a certain fantastic suspicion was the cause of his torment: that they had been deliberately exploited by the Government itself.

On the fifth day of their wanderings the weather broke, and it began to rain. It was the last straw. They were almost starving, they were filthy, their clothes in rags, their unshaven faces haggard with fatigue. Hunger making them light-headed, often they would find themselves wandering in circles; the craving for food had tempted them to gnaw roots and grasses, and this had brought on a kind of dysentery. Once or twice they had strayed within sight of the highway and had had a glimpse of constables patrolling; several times in the distance they had heard men beating the very forest which was their refuge.

As the rain poured down upon them, Barnwell cried hoarsely that they must give themselves up. The spirit of this lively Irishman had shown signs of breaking from the start, and now it had snapped entirely. As they began to argue with him, Robert Gage, the simple innkeeper, spoke suddenly and firmly.

"There is one thing we could do, gentlemen, though I would not mention it until we were come to this extremity. On the outskirts of Harrow there's a moated house called

Uxendon, and the owners of it, Bellamy by name, are staunch Catholics. I believe they would give us succour, for they are known to be charitable folk."

The others looked at Anthony, touchingly seeking guidance from him who had been their leader. His conscience forced him to refuse the suggestion; it was unthinkable to imperil strangers. But they were innocent, cried Dunn, and it was a work of mercy to succour the innocent. So the interminable argument raged; it was their only outlet now, to argue and to bicker. Still quarrelling fiercely they found themselves, that same evening, on the edge of the forest, looking down through the rain upon a tall chimneyed house, with a moat about it, and candlelight gleaming in the many-paned windows.

"Uxendon," said Gage quietly.

They had agreed to wait till nightfall before sending Gage to the house to beg for some food; but an hour before dark they spied from the shelter of the undergrowth a tall boy of about sixteen approaching across the fields towards them. He was dressed in rough country clothes, yet had an air of breeding; there was a bow slung on his shoulder and a sheaf of arrows at his belt; and as he walked he sang loudly and cheerily a favourite ballad extolling country life.

The fugitives were arguing in whispers whether or no to accost this young stranger, when his dog, which had been nosing in a hedgerow, began racing towards them, barking furiously. The boy, after vainly calling his dog to heel quickened his pace in the direction of the wood, unslinging his bow as he came, and evidently believing that the dog had got the scent of some marauder. It was useless now for the fugitives to think of flight; and Anthony, crouched in the bushes, watched the lad's progress.

He had come to that state of physical weakness when the mind is free to receive small indelible impressions. Never as long as he lived, he thought, would he forget this trivial little picture which typified the normal life to which, perhaps, he had said goodbye for ever: the long-legged, active country boy, in a belted doublet which reached to his knees, his boots of plaited straw with a fringe about the ankles, his cap with a broken pheasant's feather in it set at a jaunty angle over his curly hair. His step had freedom, his unset face expressed both the gravity and the vitality of youth, face and hands were tanned by the long hot summer, and as he marched he still sang as though he could not help it:

'The morning lark which shepherds love
Here sings at break of day:
And nightingale in yonder grove
Where flowers perfume our way – '

He stopped abruptly, for he had caught sight of the little bunch of gaunt and ragged men half concealed by the undergrowth. His young face grew grave, but without fear; it was plain that he was on his own land and that if these were poachers he would know how to deal with them. In a tone of command which would brook no disobedience he summoned his dog, and standing there facing the fugitives he asked courteously but firmly who they were.

"We are unfortunates who beg for charity in God's name," replied Anthony hoarsely, parting the wishes and staggering towards the boy. "I know not of what religion you are, young sir, but perhaps you have been taught that to feed the hungry is one of the corporal works of mercy."

The boy smiled gravely, and lifted his chin.

"I make no secret of my religion, sir, though it be proscribed. That likewise I was taught. My name is

Bartholomew Bellamy; I am the younger son of Mistress Bellamy whose house stands over yonder. If you will come with me – "

"It is only right," interrupted Anthony, "that first you know who it is you would succour. I am Anthony Babington, and these others are my friends. Does that mean aught to you?"

The boy looked at him keenly, though still there was no shadow of fear in the clear eyes.

"You are in very grave peril, Mr Babington. The whole countryside is in a ferment for your capture. It is put about that you have plotted to murder the Queen, fire the City, kidnap my Lord Treasurer, and proclaim the Queen of Scots." He gave a short laugh of contempt. "Oh, and I forgot the supernatural warnings of your villainy. A woman of eighty has given birth to a monster armed cap-a-pie, and the great bell of Westminster has tolled of its own accord, as it did before the coming of the Jesuits when I was in the 'coats."

Then his expression changed to one of pure compassion.

"I keep you talking here in the open when you should be lying hid." He thought a moment, the smooth brow furrowed. "Until it grows dark you must stay here in the wood, but when dusk comes I will guide you to one of our barns. I don't think the house would be safe; the pursuivants have discovered all our priest's-holes except one, and that is not great enough to contain you all."

"Your mother may well refuse to imperil her family for the sake of strangers."

"You must allow me, sir," replied the boy, with touching youthful dignity, "to know my mother better than you can do."

There were tears in Anthony's eyes as he watched the active young figure go striding back towards the house;

and they were not tears of mere exhaustion. How many times had he not imagined himself in just such a romantic role as the one Bartholomew Bellamy was playing now? How would he have acted that part if the dream had come true?

Dusk had just fallen when Bartholomew returned, accompanied this time by his elder brother Jerome, a stolid youth of eighteen, who was obviously the follower of his quick-witted junior in all important matters. Bartholomew had thought of everything; he had brought smocks and fustian *mockados* for the gentlemen to put on, clogs for their feet and old-fashioned flat caps for their heads. Their hair must be close-cut in the fashion of countryfolk, and their faces stained with walnut-juice. He had some wood-bills for them to carry, and he had even remembered to bring a spade, that he might dig a hole in the ground and bury their own clothes for safety. Yet he was boy enough to fall a-laughing at the difficulty of carrying out these tasks in the fading light.

That night, for the first time for a week, the four exhausted fugitives lay under cover, secreted behind piles of sweet-smelling hay in one of the Bellamys' barns.

Anthony awoke next morning from a dream that he was at home at Dethick, and stared bemusedly at the grave young face of Bartholomew peering down at him through the hay. The unsentimental compassion in it reminded him poignantly of Chidge.

"I have brought you food, sir," said the boy. And then abruptly: "We have had a fright, but I think all is well. A constable knocked at our door an hour ago, demanding to know whether we had seen you; it was a good thing Jerome was fetched to him, because I have a tiresome habit of blushing when I have to lie. But Jerome is excellent at that sort of thing, not at lying, of course, but well, yes he is, in a good cause. He looks so absolutely dependable that even pursuivants have believed him when he has told them flatly that there is no priest in the house, when all the while we have had one secreted up the chimney."

"Your mother – " began Anthony doubtfully.

"She bade me bring you her greetings," said the boy, before the other could continue. "And to say that she asks your pardon that she cannot give you more fitting hospitality. Oh, and to say further that she has begun a novena to Our Lady of Perpetual Succour for the safety of you all."

When he returned at evening with food and drink, he brought other news.

"There is a priest arrived at Uxendon," he whispered excitedly, "one, Mr Davis, who has just broke prison. We have said nothing to him of you, for we would not do it without your consent, but if you will that I disclose your secret, you may make your confession and hear Mass tomorrow morning. It will be said in the Upper Parlour before it is light. Of course the servants will be present, but there is not one of them you need fear."

A mood of extraordinary emptiness, almost resembling peace, lay on Anthony, as he knelt with his friends, a little apart from the Bellamy household, in the parlour transformed into a chapel. He had made his confession to this priest who, like himself, was a hunted fugitive; and not only had he purged his soul of its burden of sin but his mind of a suspicion so fantastic, so intolerable, that he could not have imparted it save under the seal of sacramental confession.

"I believe we have been drawn into these courses, father, by those who abused our zeal for religion. That we have been used, for what purpose I cannot tell, and that in this our enterprise Mr Secretary has been the contriver and chief actor all along."

Putting that foul suspicion into words, he had been appalled by the void which it opened beneath him. For if there could be such evil in men who held the reins of government, who were respected, even revered, by the country at large, whom could he trust? God alone, the priest had replied very simply.

God alone. The words went echoing into his empty mind as he knelt there on the rushes assisting at Mass; and he held to them as though clutching a life-line in a stormy sea.

The world, both within and without, was very quiet. The rain had ceased; there was no wind. A melon-slice of the old moon looked in upon the worshippers, and the trees in the garden stood like silent sentinels. They were all together in an upper room, and the door was shut for fear of the Jews, he thought; and never had he experienced so sharp a realization of the romance of his religion. It was not with him now as it had been on so many similar occasions at Dethick. The centre of the romance had shifted from himself to someone else. He was no longer an actor, but a spectator.

The fact he had always accepted because it was the very heart of the Church's teaching, suddenly became real to him: that it was the Passion of Christ that was being re-enacted there at the old chest turned into an altar. That again, and eternally, the human nature prayed that the cup of agony might pass, the Divine prayed only for the fulfilment of God's will; that the man craved the comfort of intimate friends, shrank from unjust death and the revilings of the fickle mob; but that the Word Incarnate stretched willing arms upon the Cross, forgave His enemies, had compassion and not resentment for the friends who deserted, the friend who betrayed, the friend who denied.

"Miserere," he prayed, holding fast to that life-line.

He went with the rest to receive Holy Communion, thinking suddenly of poor John Savage, and of how he had once said that he hoped he would be shriven and receive his viaticum before he fulfilled the vow which must cost him his life. The Food for the journey, that journey which all must take alone.

"Ite missa est," said the priest, 'Go, the Victim has been offered.'

And in that same moment there came from below the crashing of halberds against the outer door.

Chapter Five

Anthony stood flaccid, pushed and jostled by figures which, anonymous in the gloom (for the candles had been instantly extinguished), frantically stripped the altar, flinging crucifix, sacred vessels, and altar-stone into a recess behind the panelling.

"You'll understand," said the breathless voice of Bartholomew, "that for you and your friends, Mr Babington, we can do nothing; the priest must be our first consideration."

Deafened by that crashing from below, he watched in dull stupor as the priest, still in his vestments, was assisted into the wide chimney. Then the outer door gave, there was a wild scrabble of feet upon the stair, and the light of lanthorns invaded the parlour.

"It is they, the whoreson traitors!" cried a voice in triumph. "We arrest you in the Queen's name, every man and woman present, and we charge you to obey us. Jeffson, and you, Gray, take the women to the watch-house and guard them close. The rest of you truss up these men."

"You can't take my grand-dame!" shouted Bartholomew, suddenly a little boy again. "She is eighty-two years old, and she – "

"Old enough to know better than to harbour traitors," roughly interrupted the serjeant-at-arms. "And as for you, my stripling, you'll certainly hang for it."

Hoisted on to a horse, his ankles strapped beneath its belly, his elbows pinioned behind him, Anthony stared in stupid bewilderment at the crowds which thickened in the streets as the dismal procession approached London. So many times had he seen himself as the central figure in some drama; but never such a sorry figure in never so senseless a drama as this. The Trained Bands were parading; shopkeepers stood besides their booths, armed with axes; the church bells clamoured in triumph; there were chains across the streets, cannon planted in front of public buildings. On every face was fierce exultation, from every mouth issued cries of hate; and still from the belfries iron tongues proclaimed London's thanksgiving that he, poor harmless Anthony Babington, had been caught.

He had lost all notion of where he was when at length, lurched forward over his horse's neck, blood trickling into his mouth from a well-aimed stone, he realized that the nightmare journey was over. So dazed he was that he did not recognize Ely House into which they carried him, not even this familiar Holborn where he had lived for so long, where he and his young friends had walked with their servants behind them, lesser folk giving them way, beggars besieging them for alms, shopkeepers respectfully saluting them, where they had dined and supped in private rooms in taverns, strolled to the fencing-school or the tennis-court, and now and again, when it pleased them, attended lectures at Lincoln's Inn.

He lay where they had thrown him, on the floor of a small chamber, thankful only to be alone, away from those hundreds of hostile eyes, those hands flinging filth, this London which suddenly and unaccountably had become his enemy.

It might have been hours or days later when he found himself being marshalled along corridors, ringed about with armed men as though he were some violent maniac, and into a handsome apartment filled with sunlight that made him blink. He had a vague memory of being given some refreshment ere they brought him hither; at all events his mind, mercifully numb before, was able to register certain impressions. The frightful stench from his clothes, still plastered with the mud the crowds had flung at him, distressed him; acute humiliation brought tears to his red-rimmed eyes as he saw the trim, well-dressed gentlemen, sitting behind the long table set beneath the windows, staring at him in contempt.

Then the questioning began.

It was surprisingly mild at first. Had he been at the Plough tavern outside Temple Bar on such and such a day in March? Did he know one Ballard, and one Savage? Did he know that Ballard was a priest? Had Ballard ever spoken to him of a 'practice' which involved invasion from abroad and revolt at home? He answered truthfully, his courage reviving. For their questions seemed to indicate that they knew only of Ballard's discarded enterprise, and he had the priest's full permission to speak of that. But all the same he must be careful in his answers, for he observed that they were being taken down by a clerk, who sat at a little table by himself, an insignificant man with a pockmarked face and short-sighted eyes glinting behind spectacles.

"Did you know of Savage's intended practice against the person of her Majesty?"

He hesitated. Ballard had insisted that Savage's name was to be kept out of it. But evidently they knew about Savage and his vow, and it was useless to try to shield the poor fellow.

"It was told me, but I rejected it upon the first knowledge thereof."

"Because you would have it done another way."

"That's not true!" he shouted violently.

"You would have it done by six gentlemen who were to undertake it as a ritual murder, terming it a 'tragical execution'."

Christ! how did they know of that? It had been Henry Dunn's idea; Dunn, that little rat, must have blabbed.

"I would not have it done by any means," he cried. "I absolutely forbade it – "

"Then you must have had authority, so to have ordered the rest. Come, Mr Babington, was it not suggested that six gentlemen should undertake this 'tragical execution'?"

"It was suggested, but I – it was put by."

"What communication has there been betwixt you and the Queen of Scots?"

The sudden change of subject set him off balance for a moment, and he felt a sharp stab of fear. Had they caught Gilbert Gifford? Had he also blabbed? –

"We are waiting for your answer, Mr Babington."

"It is true," he said, deciding to bluff, "As I told Mr Secretary, that several years since I contrived to convey to the Queen of Scots some letters directed to her by her friends. But I laid aside the practice when Sir Amias Paulet became her keeper."

He tensed himself for the next question, but it did not come. One of the gentlemen, whom he recognized now as Mr Vice-Chamberlain Hatton, made a sign to the guard, and Anthony was taken back to his cell.

A foot roughly prodded him from sleep. He was marched back to the handsome apartment, and saw that the shutters were closed and candles burning on the table. The wax was perfumed, and this, together with the scent of sweet herbs mixed with the rushes on the floor, made him think for the moment, that he was at Dethick...

"You are acquainted with one, Charles Tilney, now a prisoner?"

So they had caught Tilney. And how many others, he wondered with a shudder.

"Say what you know of his practice against the Queen's Majesty."

What in the world were they talking about? Then his face cleared. Of course; Tilney would have confessed to that high-flown scheme of his of kidnapping the Queen. Well, that was nothing to be ashamed of.

"Mr Tilney suggested on one occasion (it was but idle talk) that it might be possible to enclose her Majesty in some secure place, treating her with all due reverence but persuading her to grant toleration to her Catholic subjects. Mr Tilney being of the Court assured me that her Majesty had no wish to persecute any man for his religion, so he be a loyal subject – "

"Who were the gentlemen who were to undertake this practice?"

"I do not know."

"You were present when Mr Tilney suggested it?"

"Yes, but – "

"State the names of the six gentlemen chosen."

"But there were not six gentlemen chosen."

"This morning you said there were."

"No, no, that was for the tragical execution – "

He broke off short as he saw them look at one another and smile.

It was Mr Secretary himself who conducted the third examination of Anthony Babington.

Everything was going very well. All Anthony's friends, with the exception of Edward Abingdon, had now been captured, and two of them, Tichborne, whom GG had described as Anthony's most intimate friend, and Ballard, were in the hands of Topcliffe. It was true that both were proving extremely obstinate, but Topcliffe was confident that if he persevered they would break within the next few days. The Queen of Scots' papers had been seized before she could hear of the arrests; her two secretaries were safely under lock and key in Walsingham's own house. No examination of them would be made until after Babington had been trapped into confessing to the forged interpolations in the two fatal letters, but meanwhile they were being thoroughly frightened.

As for Babington, Mr Secretary was satisfied that he was becoming so confused by the usual tricks of cross-examination (including the assertion that his friends had confessed), that it would soon be time to come to the point to which all these preliminary questions were leading.

"When and where was it you talked with Ballard concerning the excommunication of the Queen's Majesty?"

"I don't remember."

"What was the very speech when Ballard told you that the excommunication was sufficient warrant to take the life of her Majesty?"

"Mr Ballard held expressly that it was, but I rejected it."

"Mr Ballard says otherwise. In what month, and upon what day of the month, was it that you promised him you would sound your friends upon this assassination?"

His pale face flushed with fury. So Ballard had told them that! Ballard, for all his fine words at parting, his desire that only he himself should suffer, his swearing that no torture should make him incriminate those whom he had drawn into these treasonable courses, Ballard had blabbed. Not thinking what he said, no longer striving to pick his words, Anthony launched into a tirade against Ballard, relieving his overwrought nerves in a spate of denunciation.

"Where and when," came the inexorable voice, "did Ballard prevail upon you to accept the leadership?"

His head whirled. How much had Ballard confessed? And what of Gilbert Gifford? His name had not been mentioned in this barrage of questions. Or had it? If only he could remember; if only they would give him time to think.

And all the while the little pock-marked man, with his weak eyes held close to the paper, his quill scratching industriously, took down notes.

Next day there were no questions. Instead, the pock-marked man read aloud, rapidly and indistinctly, the confessions Anthony was said to have made during the past few days. He kept trying to interrupt; it was impossible for him to follow, he cried, if the clerk read so quickly. He demanded the right to read over these confessions at his leisure; they could not deny him that when his life was at stake.

As a special privilege, they told him, he should read them, but it must be here and now. A hand thrust a sheaf of papers towards him; but joy that he had won his point was quickly stifled when he tried to read through this mass of stuff. He could not concentrate; the words in the delicate handwriting swam and danced before his eyes; even when they stood still for a moment they might have been written in some foreign tongue. Only one phrase, repeated over and over again, was clear, and horridly ominous, 'the practice against her Majesty'. He seemed to have admitted to it every time they asked him about it, and he was so confused that he did not know whether when they used the phrase they were referring to Savage's vow, to Ballard's plot, or to Tinley's highflown suggestion of kidnapping.

"I did not confess all this," he cried desperately.

Including the clerk, said Mr Secretary in a stern voice, there were four witnesses to what he had confessed. They had it word for word. (In point of fact, of course, Mr

Phelippes had written up these 'confessions' at his leisure from his notes made during the examinations, taking several answers out of their proper context.) Naturally Mr Babington could not be expected to remember all he had said, especially when he had denounced Mr Ballard at such length; and did he presume to suggest that they, her Majesty's representatives, were asking him to sign a document which was inaccurate?

Naturally slapdash, hideously confused, he lacked the moral courage to say Yes. He scrawled his untidy signature at the foot of the confessions, and threw down the quill. At least they knew nothing of his fatal letter to the Queen of Scots, or of her reply. There had not been a single word of either throughout the examinations; he was sure of that. And now it was all over, and they would allow him to get some rest.

That same day he was taken by water to the Tower, entering the fortress by way of Traitors' Gate.

Chapter Six

It was to the Bell Tower, the first in the Inner Ward, that they took him, and to the upper of its two chambers.

"You must consider yourself honoured, Mr Babington," said a very spruce gentleman who was one of those who had received him on his landing just now, a gentleman whose bright red lips smiled perpetually between well-brushed moustaches and dagger-pointed beard. All the while he was looking Anthony up and down in a curious, somehow unpleasant fashion. "Ordinarily no man under the rank of viscount is confined in the Bell Tower, but we are rather pressed for space just now. And you will be able to console yourself with the knowledge that two of your favourite Catholic martyrs, Bishop Fisher and Sir Thomas More, spent their last days on earth in this very tower."

Anthony glanced at the eight-foot-thick walls, the slit of window, the bare stone floor.

"Come, come, sir," said the spruce gentleman reproachfully, "you must not look askance at the lodging her Majesty has assigned you. It is the custom for gentlemen in your unfortunate situation to provide their own food and firing, but then you are a rich young gentleman, and it will be no hardship. Order what you will, and as long as you can pay for it, it will be brought you."

"There is but one thing I desire, sir," said Anthony stiffly, "and that is a bed. I am much wearied and in need of sleep."

The other stroked his beard, seeming to ponder.

"Why now that, alas," said he, "is an article of furniture of which we are extremely short. But do not, sir, distress yourself unduly. You will soon forget your desire to sleep, in the entertainment with which we shall take care to provide you."

A knife-blade of terror made Anthony flinch before he could control himself, but the gentleman went on with a bright little laugh:

"Now, now, Mr Babington, I believe you have mistaken me. You are not to be put to the Question, and indeed why should you be? seeing how free and frank you have been in your confessions. No, no, sir; you are to be made as comfortable as we can contrive it, and any sad thoughts you may have will soon be dispelled by good company. Unlike most of our guests, you will not be, solitary. Oh no, you will not be solitary, sir," repeated Mr Topcliffe, with his sunny smile.

'You will not be solitary.' He did not understand the significance of that remark at first. When he found that two warders were locked in with him, he imagined it was because they feared he might try to kill himself (when he was at Ely House they had refused to allow him a razor for shaving). He shrugged his shoulders in contempt; he was not that kind of a coward.

It was horrible when he had to relieve himself in front of his warders, he so fastidious and accustomed to refinement, but he was not going to give them the satisfaction of seeing how such a thing tormented him. He had been a fool, and worse than a fool, in his daydreaming and his involving his friends in his wild schemes, but at least he would preserve his dignity to the end. He must concentrate upon the arranging of his private affairs, write his last letters, send Margaret all he had left to send her, his love, and prepare his soul for death.

But first he must sleep, for such sleep as he had had at Ely House had been broken and hideous with nightmare. It was curious that they would not provide him with a bed, for which he would have paid highly, and which afterwards, in the custom of the day, would have become the perquisite of the Lieutenant; but he was so weary that he would make shift with the floor. He was curling up in a corner when a rough hand shook him, and a coarse voice said:

"Come and take a 'and at the cards, Mr Babington, with me and me mate 'ere. Or we'll throw the dice, if you please."

"Let me be!" cried Anthony, shaking off the hand. "I'm in no mood to play. There is nothing I desire but to sleep, and that is one thing you cannot deny me, even in my situation."

They dragged him to his feet; he struggled, but he was still very weak and they were big, powerful men; in a moment or two they had sat him violently down at the table. He stared from one to the other in furious amazement; until something in their expression told him that in the grisly catalogue of tortures Gage had described when they were in hiding, there was one he had omitted to mention.

They kept him without sleep for two days and two nights before his next examination. Each time his head nodded, he was shaken by the shoulders and marched up and down the room. Day and night there were two warders with him; all night long, candles burnt in his cell.

He wandered in a strange inferno. Sometimes he would stand for an hour at a time staring at the pitiful inscriptions which former prisoners had cut into the walls, skeletons and armorial bearings, favourite verses, a crucifix with the words *Adoramus Te* scrawled in a hand like a child's in its first attempt to write. Sometimes he would fling himself upon his knees before his warders, offering them everything he had if they would grant him but one hour's sleep. And then again he would find himself staring out of the slit of window, seeing phantoms there, King Henry III in the midst of his gorgeous Court receiving from the Patriarch of Jerusalem a phial containing a drop of the Precious Blood, Sir Thomas More walking up the steps above Traitors' Gate with the axe's edge turned towards him, and his daughter breaking through the guard to fling herself into his arms.

Hearing became unnaturally acute, so that the shuffle of the greasy cards with which his warders eternally beguiled the time was like a great wind battering at him, the click of the dice made him wince, the bell in its wooden turret above, ringing the curfew at sunset, made him cower against the wall, his hands clapped over his ears, and when the wild beasts in the Lion Tower roared, he cried out in terror because he thought they were in the room. The heaviness of his limbs was worse than any pain; his eyes were mere blood-rimmed slits; his mind was invaded by an army of fleeting images, horrible, grotesque, or meaningless.

And sometimes, in moments of semi-clarity, he would glance at the immensely thick door, and each time he seemed to see a pair of eyes, very bright and lively, peeping at him through the judas.

"What month was it when you conveyed a letter to the Queen of Scots?"

He stared stupidly about him. He was not in his prison room, but in one which was vaguely familiar to him. (It was an apartment in the Lieutenant's Lodging, where all prisoners were registered and searched when first brought to the Tower.) There were hard-faced gentlemen sitting at a table; there were papers on the table, ink-horn, pounce-box, and quills. At the foot sat the little pock-marked man whom he had seen at Ely House.

"W-what did you say?"

A hand emerging from a clean ruff put a cup to his lips and forced him to drink. Fire burnt his mouth, and he gasped and choked, but his head cleared a little. They were examining him again; he must be careful (careful, careful, the word went echoing on in his empty mind).

"It was years since," he said, when the question had been repeated. "I do not remember the month."

"Was it June, or perhaps July?"

"It may have been."

"Who were those who should have taken away the Queen?"

"Taken away the Queen?"

"Was not that an essential part of your enterprise?"

Of course it was; how silly of him. For years he had been resolved to take away the Queen of Scots from her prison. And he would have done it, too, if he had had more support.

"Who were the six who should have joined with you in this practice?"

"Not six, there were to be ten – "

"Are you sure it was ten? In previous examinations you told us six."

"I think it was ten, but it may have been six. But those for taking away the Queen were not decided upon."

"But you would have taken away the Queen?"

"Yes, damn you!" he cried with sudden weak violence. "Why should I not take away the Queen from her imprisonment?"

He was brought before them twice a day thereafter, still denied sleep. The questions were like gun-fire now, barking from left to right, jumping backwards and forwards. When and where? What was the very speech? Who and by whose authority was this to be done? How many were present? What was your opinion touching this practice? What did you move to be done? Where was the discourse spoken?

"Let me sleep," he whispered. "For Jesu's sake let me sleep."

"When you have made a full confession, as others have done."

"I have told you all I know."

"No, Mr Babington, we would hear more of this letter to the Queen of Scots."

"But it was so long ago, several years I think and I cannot remember – "

"Can you remember this phrase: 'I vow and protest before the face of God that I will keep my word or die happily'?"

"No, no!" he cried. (They were murdering his fine phraseology.) " 'I vow and protest before the face of Almighty God, Who miraculously hath long preserved your sacred person, that what I have said shall be performed, or all our lives lost in the execution thereof'."

His cracked lips smiled, his mind, partially unhinged, was full of an old fire; his own voice, not as it was now, weak and hoarse, but the voice of a young hero of romance, rang in his ears, swearing that he would rescue his princess. He saw them smile as though in admiration. Could he remember any more of such elegant writing? they asked him encouragingly. Yes, he thought he could. What was that passage of which he had been particularly proud... ?

That afternoon, instead of firing questions at him, they read aloud long portions of his fatal letter to the Queen of

Scots. He sweated in horror as he listened; surely he could not have quoted all this. He had quoted a great deal of it they told him, adding significantly that all his friends had been captured now.

He forced his brain to take in what they meant by that. Who had been with him when he had written that letter? No one, surely; he had sat up alone all one night composing it. But wait! Had not Chidge come in next morning and helped with the enciphering?

"Oh Christ!" he cried, shaking his clenched hands together in an agony. "If Chidge Tichborne has betrayed me there is no faith left in this world."

They exchanged glances. He had given them what they wanted. It was plain that Tichborne (who, despite all Mr Topcliffe's ministrations, was still refusing to 'utter') had seen that letter.

"Mr Tichborne has confessed everything. But we must have it from you also. Did you write this – and this – to the Queen of Scots?"

"Sleep," he muttered, exhausted by his late outburst. "For the love of Him who had compassion on all men, let me sleep."

He should sleep anon, they promised. They even described to him the kind of bed he should have, of feathers, the linen sweet smelling from wash-balls scented with musk, curtains shutting off the light, down pillows. It should be given him as soon as he had answered these remaining questions. Now let him attend carefully; had he written as follows... ?

Mockingly his fine phrases were fired back at him. When they paused, he answered, 'I don't remember', for indeed he had come into a state when he could not remember his own name. But they hung on to him like bulldogs; they would have Yes or No; and the thought of that bed they had described made him say Yes. Only once did he try to make a fight of it. In the mumbling of the clerk he caught a phrase, 'there were six gentlemen, all my noble friends, for taking away the Queen'.

"Not six, but ten," he insisted.

"You have told us many times it was six, and so has Mr Tichborne. Now which was it, Mr Babington, six or ten that were to take away the Queen?"

Six-ten, *six*-ten, said the brass-faced clock on its bracket. Then, after a preliminary clearing of its throat, it struck. He winced, and then began counting it aloud, like a child or an idiot:

"One, two, three, four, five, six."

'There were six gentlemen for taking away the Queen's Majesty,' wrote the clerk, smiling to himself.

The day after that they kept him standing before them, supported by two warders, for hour after hour, while the clerk's voice droned and mumbled on, reading out his confessions, including what he had written to the Queen of Scots. It was just a babble of sound to him, without sense or meaning. Even if he could have heard distinctly, even if they had offered him his life, he could not have answered honestly whether or no this was a true version.

They had to guide his hand when he put his pitiful, straggling signature at the foot of the pile of papers; and when they told him he could sleep now, he was too broken to understand what they said.

Chapter Seven

His mind was blank, and he was conscious only of something resembling boredom when, on September 13th, a month after his capture, he was brought before a Commission of Oyer and Terminer to be tried under a Statute of Edward III for 'imagining treason'. The judges in their robes, the jury filing into their box, the Attorney and Solicitor Generals in their gowns, the craning, rowdy spectators filling every available inch of space, all were dummy figures without significance or interest.

He was the first to be set in the great dock, and it was only when he heard footsteps coming up the steps to join him that a needle of emotion jabbed him into awareness. His fellow prisoners whom he had not seen since that morning when, in the improvised chapel at Uxendon, he had received the Food for that journey he was soon to take. And others besides those who had been captured with him. All his friends had been caught, the hard-faced man had told him. And there were two among those friends, the two on whose constancy he had had most reason to rely, who had betrayed him.

He drew himself up; he would not look into their false faces. Yet whether he would or not, his eyes were drawn to a man who at first he took to be a stranger, and who was set on his left in the dock. Who could he be, this wreck of humanity whose legs dangled helpless as he was carried in by two turnkeys, whose arms were bent at an unnatural angle, whose limp black hair showed an inch of grey at the parting, and from whose ashen lips there came a little whimper of pain as his dislocated limbs were jarred by the rough carrying. Then from those lips there came a whisper:

"I kept the pledge I made you when last we met," said John Ballard. "I told them nothing, Anthony."

So it had been Chidge, and Chidge only, his best friend, who had betrayed him. He jerked his head round, and saw Tichborne standing next to him on his right. His own face hardened as a first glance told him that Chidge had not been racked. And yet there was something odd about him; he was wearing a curious sort of mantle with very wide sleeves. Then Chidge laid a hand on his friend's, the sleeve fell back, and Anthony saw that both hand and arm were swollen into two mountains of flesh, bridged by a wrist on which was an iron bracelet. 'And the worst of all, says he, is the hanging up by the hands.' Who had said that and where? But it did not matter. For he was looking into his friend's eyes, and in them he saw a fidelity, a constancy, a love impossible to doubt.

Then the hard shell of his numbness cracked, and a flood-tide of pure contrition washed over his heart. These two had been tortured beyond belief, yet they had told nothing, whereas he – what had he told? Oh God, what had he told, to what lies had he signed his name? He and his friends were innocent of the crimes of which they were now being accused in a long indictment; but he was guilty as a human soul. His vanity had made it possible for a corrupt government to condemn a group of young men whose only desire had been to maintain the cause of the true religion; in the eyes of God, before Whom he must soon give his account, whose was the greater sin... ?

"Savage," said Sir Christopher Hatton, slowly and impressively from the Bench, "I must ask you one question. Was all this willingly and voluntarily confessed by yourself – without menacing – without torture – without offer of any torture?"

"Yes, your Honour" replied John Savage, who alone among the group of prisoners was the same as he had ever been, eager to please, upright and healthy-looking, nodding once or twice with simple pride as they had read out to him his confession of his vow to kill the Queen.

This good impression of governmental leniency having been made on the spectators, the other prisoners were asked the formal question, 'Guilty or Not Guilty?' One by one they replied in the negative; but when the question was put to Anthony Babington he answered, not to the court but to a higher Justice:

"I am guilty," and he beat his breast.

An execution for high treason had always been one of London's most popular spectacles compared with which plain hangings were tame. But the execution of the conspirators in the Babington Plot was going to be a spectacle of spectacles, and in tavern and shop, in market-place and street, nothing else was talked of during this latter half of September, 1586.

For first of all there were to be so many victims, no less than seven on the first day, Tuesday, the 20th, and five the next. There ought to have been even more, but it seemed that the boy, Bartholomew Bellamy, had committed suicide in prison, and that a Mr Gifford and a Mr Mawde had managed to escape overseas. Next it was rumoured that there was to be something out of the ordinary in the manner of their death. Those citizens who had managed to squeeze into the court-house during the trials had heard the judge say in pronouncing sentence that 'considering that this manner of horrible treason against her Majesty's own Person hath not been heard of in this kingdom, it is reason that the manner of their death for more terror be referred to her Majesty and her Council.' But most folk were sceptical about this; no death ever devised could be more frightful than that of being half choked by the rope and cut down alive for mutilation and quartering.

Then there were the personalities and circumstances of the victims, and these were full of interest. With the exception of the Popish priest, Ballard, the innkeeper, Gage, and a minor victim, Edward Jones, who was condemned for lending Mr Salisbury a horse to aid his escape, they were all so young. Mr Tilney and Mr Abingdon (and the latter had very nearly got clean away, disguised as a woman, it was said) had actually been of the Gentlemen Pensioners, the Queen's immediate bodyguard; why, it was an absolute miracle that they had not accomplished their hellish design of murdering her. And the rest of them, except the youth, Jerome Bellamy, had been such familar figures in London for so long; everyone had seen the swaggering, devil-may-care 'Captain Foscue', and had heard his lying talk of his military experiences in the Low Countries (though of course there was no one now who would admit to having been taken in by it).

As for the young gentlemen, Mr Babington and his friends, there were dozens of tailors and mercers and tavern-keepers, not to speak of the masters of fencing-schools, and owners of cockpits, all eager to relate little anecdotes of these fine gallants, of how free they had been with their money, of how they must always have a private room when they would dine or sup at a tavern, of how the relaters had suspected all along that they were up to no good.

The plot itself, too, was so sensational, even though there was a similarity between it and former Popish plots. London was to have been fired, the Lord Mayor hung from his own doorpost, every Protestant throat cut with consecrated daggers, the Parliament House blown up by gunpowder, and a long list of great ones, headed by my Lord Treasurer, were to have been slaughtered by some dreadful Popish instrument the details of which never transpired. As for her Majesty's death, opinions were divided on the manner of it; some maintained that Savage had received from the hands of the Pope himself a specially blessed stiletto, others that the pommel of her saddle was to have been poisoned, others again that the whole bunch of conspirators had planned to do the deed, giving her stabs to the number of Popish priests whom she had executed during her reign.

But the supreme interest lay in this young spark, Anthony Babington. For it seemed that he was infatuated with the Queen of Scots, and some said had actually been her lover when he was a page in my Lord Shrewsbury's household. (The fact that he was a child of ten or eleven at the time was not, of course, allowed to spoil a good story.) Whether or not she had connived with him in his plot to slaughter the Highest One was not clear; there had been no mention of it at the trial of the conspirators. But it would not be the first time, some folk said darkly, if she had; everyone knew she had blown up her second husband, poor Lord Darnley, at Kirk o' Field, in order to marry Lord Bothwell, and it was said that she had poisoned her first husband, the poor young King of France.

The entire population of London, therefore, stood squeezed along the route from the Tower to Lincoln's Inn Fields on the morning of September 20th. (The victims were to die on a specially erected scaffold in the fields, where they had hatched their horrid treasons.) Most of the crowd had taken up their chosen positions during the night, some favouring the Tower precincts to see the condemned strapped on to the hurdles, and especially to get a sight of the priest, Ballard, who had been racked until he could neither stand nor walk. But the majority wanted to see the actual execution, and Lincoln's Inn Fields was one vast seething mass, a pick-pocket's paradise, a gold-mine for the sellers of gingerbread, hot cockles, ballads, and *Last Dying*

Speeches and Confessions already printed by enterprising booksellers.

There was so much to see before the bloody play began. Yonder was the actual house where Mr Babington had lodged, not more than a bowshot distant; on the scaffold was Bull, the hangman, dressed up in a great apron, very brisk and businesslike, adjusting the seven nooses, sharpening his knives, flinging more pitch into the reeking cauldron which presently would receive the victims' legs and arms before these were stuck on the spikes of London Bridge. Children were lifted up to get a view; voices chattered and exclaimed in relishful horror. Here and there groups stood silent, only their lips moving in prayer, hands, concealed beneath cloak or shawl, surreptitiously telling their beads. Then there were the fine gentlemen to stare at, Privy Councillors, some said, guarded by halberdiers, talking gravely to one another from their bejewelled saddles, the Sheriff in his coach, the City Marshal on his richly caparisoned horse, the peace-officers, the javelin-men, the constables.

"Ooh!" breathed the crowd, as the broken figure of Ballard was lifted from the foremost hurdle and propped against an upright of the gallows.

"That's Babington!" bawled an excited voice, as the second horse was brought to a standstill and a fellow stooped to cut the bonds of a figure, plastered with mud and refuse, which lay prone on the hurdle at the horse's heels. "By cock! 'e don't look very 'andsome now!"

But other voices cried for silence. It was customary, besides being fair play, to let the condemned speak for the last time from the scaffold. Usually what they said was pretty dull, especially when the victims were Papists; they couldn't lay by their wicked superstitions even on the brink of Eternity, it seemed. Highwaymen gave far better sport, boasting of their exploits, kicking off their shoes in a last gesture of defiance as the cart was drawn from beneath them. Nevertheless, it was established by long tradition to hear all victims in silence, and London was proud of her reputation for fair play and abiding by custom, let it be at a bull-bait or at an execution for high treason.

Five minutes later the crowds began to shuffle and to murmur; for immemorial custom was being outraged with a vengeance. The time Bull allowed to elapse before he cut the victim down to commence the butchery upon him, varied considerably; if the condemned was popular, or had friends who could afford a handsome bribe, he would be left to hang until he was quite unconscious, even, in some cases, dead; but even the most unpopular or friendless victim must be allowed sufficient time partially to lose his senses. But on this occasion, after one swing of the rope Ballard was cut down, just as his dislocated arm had tried to raise itself to bless his companions who were to follow him into Eternity.

A shout or two of execration was directed at Bull; but then it was observed that when John Savage, the next to be turned off, broke the rope with his great weight, the Sheriff himself gave the signal for his disembowelling even as he was struggling to his feet again. The crowd's demeanour immediately became dangerous, and the deputation from the Privy Council, observing this, conferred agitatedly among themselves. But there was no help for it; the order for this protracting of the pains of death had been issued by the Highest One Herself, and the remaining five victims must be similarly treated. All the gentlemen could do was to send a messenger galloping into London to fetch more constables and halberdiers.

"Silence! Silence!" roared the crowd, as Anthony Babington was set upon the scaffold.

He was trying to speak; at least his lips were moving silently. A rumour went through the close-packed ranks that he was repeating the name 'Mary' over and over again, and this seemed suddenly so romantic and pathetic that when he too, after one swing of the rope, was cut down for the butchery, the multitude gave one united roar of execration and began to pelt not only Bull but the group of fine gentlemen.

But those who were really near enough to hear the word which Anthony Babington repeated so long as he could breathe, knew that it was not 'Mary' but *'Miserere'*.

An angry and disgusted London awoke next morning to hear a proclamation being read at Temple Bar and other public places. Her Majesty, it seemed, being informed of the severity used in the executions of the previous day, and 'detesting such cruelty' had given express orders that the remaining conspirators were to be permitted to hang today until they were quite dead before they were cut down, disembowelled and quartered.

London cheered to the echo this new evidence that Elizabeth was not only Gloriana, but Good Queen Bess.

Epilogue

England early in the month of February in the year fifteen hundred and eighty-seven.

In a room in Whitehall Palace, Elizabeth of England strode up and down, up and down, her drum-shaped verdingale, weighted with jewels, rustling and clinking to her restless movements, her ringed hands clenched on her fan, her painted mouth drawn into a line of pain.

"Where is my Lord Burghley?" she demanded of Secretary Davison, who remained upon his knees because she had forgotten to give him the signal to rise. "I commanded him to present himself this morning that I might speak further with him concerning the death warrant of the Queen of Scots. What did you do with it?" she snapped suspiciously, "when I was prevailed upon to sign it yesterday?"

"P-please your Majesty," stammered the agitated Davison, "I took it to Cecil House."

"Well, it must be held back a while. Some other way must be thought upon."

Leicester had always told her there was some other way; dear Robin knew it was intolerable that so great a weight of responsibility should be thrown upon Herself. Surely there was someone among her devoted subjects who would do the deed privately and decently, making it seem like an accident. Sir Amias Paulet was the obvious choice, the man on the spot; he had always professed so deep a hatred of the Queen of Scots, so passionate a devotion to Herself. And only last week she had written to him almost in the style of a love-letter, beginning 'My Amias'.

But beneath these thoughts there raged the real agony of indecision which had racked her throughout the winter. Oh, she had been absolutely convinced of the guilt of Babington and his friends, and so genuinely terrified by their plot that she had betrayed herself into giving that vindictive order that their death-pangs be protracted to the uttermost. But her very shrewd intelligence continued to suspect that the incriminating of Mary was but a Cecilian 'device' employed by her Lord Treasurer for the consolidating of his New Order and the preservation of himself and his kind after her own death.

"I fear your Majesty did not sleep very well," murmured Davison, surreptitiously easing his knees upon the boarded floor.

"If you were in the habit of seeing such things in your bed as I do in mine," snapped the Highest One, "you would not sleep either. I dreamed last night," she muttered, staring into the fire, "that I saw the Queen of Scots lying headless and bloody in a great room. It is fortunate for some that it was only a dream."

The wretched Davison felt the sweat break out upon his forehead.

In his Great Chamber at Cecil House, Lord Treasurer Burghley made notes upon his tablets. The winter sunlight, stained with colour from the heraldic devices in the casements, cast a benison upon his venerable head. He had been up since six o'clock, at which hour he had summoned a meeting of the Privy Council, and in their presence had affixed the Great Seal to the death warrant of the Queen of Scots. Immediately this was done he had dispatched Robert

Beale, Clerk of the Council, to Mary's new prison of Fotheringay, to see the warrant executed.

'Details of Burial,' he wrote neatly. Something splendid, he thought, a magnanimous gesture which should placate the Catholics, at home and abroad, and tickle the Highest One with the thought of her own generosity. Naturally the Queen of Scots' last request, that her body should be carried over to France for burial with her royal kinsfolk there, could not be allowed; relations with France were going to be delicate enough as it was.

He made another note: 'The State of the Cause as it ought to be conceived and reported concerning the Execution done upon the Queen of Scots.' Now the composing of that would require a great deal of skill. The Highest One must be protected at all costs, and it must be inferred, if not expressly stated, that the execution of an independent sovereign had been carried out against her wishes. She had ordered the delay of the warrant even after she had signed it; and therefore a scapegoat must be found to bear the blame of disobeying her order.

Davison, he thought. Yes, Secretary Davison was just the right person to cast for the role of that unfortunate animal. Undoubtedly he would be deprived of his post and fined in some enormous sum; if she was in that sort of a mood, the Highest One, in order to save her face, might have him tried for high treason. But he must just be content to feel that he had done the Highest One the greatest possible service, sacrificing himself for Her good and that of his country.

To the Catholic Powers, and to that young fool, James of Scotland, the same sort of explanation could be given, while, of course, stressing the fact that Mary had been convicted, after a trial conducted by a Commission of thirty-six peers of the realm, of plotting with Babington to take the Highest One's life. And Burghley would write with his own hand to all these personages, regretting that he had been absent from the Council when the warrant was actually dispatched; he had been ill; he had suffered from these little sicknesses from time to time during his political career.

There was little to be feared from public opinion at home. His admirable 'device' (for, having succeeded, it had ceased to be Mr Secretary's 'practice'), had cut the ground from under the Catholics' feet, and really discredited the Old Religion in the eyes of the majority of Protestants. The printing-presses were already busy upon a broadsheet which would be distributed everywhere once Mary was safely dead, and which had been given the title, A *Defence of the Honourable Sentence and Execution of the Queen of Scots*. The public would be able to read therein the two fatal letters (with Mr Phelippes' forged interpolations) together with the skilfully doctored confessions of Babington, Nau, and Curle.

There remained the Highest One herself, who just possibly might not be content with one scapegoat. He sighed. She really had been most difficult these last few months. The Commission of Peers had pronounced Mary guilty as long ago as October, and ever since then the Highest One had continued to shilly-shally. Burghley had worn himself out with the hours he had spent coaxing, explaining, persuading, frightening. But all he had managed to get out of her was one of those entirely meaningless answers which she reserved for occasions when he had cornered her:

"If I should say I would not do what you request, it might be peradventure more than you thought, and to say I would do it might perhaps breed peril of what you labour to preserve, being more than in your wisdom and discretion would seem convenient."

And then she had cocked her red-wigged head at him, as much as to say: Make what you can of that.

He began to write again. He would draw up a draft memorandum to be presented to the Highest One the moment he received the news that the axe had fallen at Fotheringay, explaining why the warrant had been sent off in defiance of Her orders. Her Council's extreme care for Her Safety and that of the realm, their desire to save Her from the consequences of Her extraordinary clemency and well-known reluctance to shed blood, etc. 'And yet we are now at this time most sorry to understand that your Majesty is so greatly grieved with our proceeding...' Something like that.

In a Paris seminary, Mr Gilbert Gifford petulantly tossed back his flaxen hair as he wrestled with the composition of a reply to a letter he had received from his old friend, Mr Thomas Phelippes.

It was a kind letter. Mr Secretary, wrote Phelippes, had accepted GG's explanation of his sudden and abrupt departure from England last July, though he had been a little vexed that GG had not obtained his permission first, especially at a moment when his service had been so vital. But Mr Secretary fully appreciated all that GG had done, and was sorry that during the Babington trials the Government had been forced to 'write and speak bitterly against you' as though GG had been a genuine conspirator.

Mr Secretary was delighted to hear that GG was certain of being able to continue to do useful service on the other side of the Channel, and asked for details. He was sending a special messenger over with a new kind of invisible ink and with instructions how to use it. And it gave Mr Phelippes himself great pleasure to be able to inform GG that the Highest One had been prevailed upon to give him some material reward, actually promising him a pension of one hundred pounds a year.

I wonder how many such empty promises she's made during her long reign, the parsimonious old hag, thought Gilbert bitterly. Never mind. Though he would never see a penny of her money, he had done very well for himself since his flight, telling so pitiful a tale to the Queen of Scots' agents in Paris that they had made a collection for him. And next week he was actually to be ordained priest, so well had he established his credit among the Catholics in France, and this would give him endless opportunities for the sowing of the discord which was his chief delight.

But in his reply to Mr Phelippes he would not mention that he was about to be ordained. For it might happen that in future he, Gilbert, would have occasion to cross over to England, and it *might* happen, by some ironic accident, that he would find himself condemned to death under the Statutes directed against priests.

In his bed at Barn Elms, Mr Secretary lay tortured by another boil; but his mind was filled with a deep satisfaction.

How skilfully had he piloted his great 'practice' through a perilous passage safe to port! What storms had he weathered, what rocks and quicksands avoided! The only thing that he did most sincerely regret was that he had not been able to punish that rogue Topcliffe for the death of the unfortunate boy, Bartholomew Bellamy.

Oh, Mr Secretary knew precisely what had happened. For years Topcliffe had been looking round for some nice little country estate, not too far from London and his odious work; Uxendon, near Harrow, would suit him admirably; and he had got it. And how had he got it? By prevailing upon Jerome Bellamy, the heir, to make it over to him in a deed of gift before Jerome went with the rest to the gallows. And how had he so prevailed on Jerome? By forcing that youth to witness the torturing of his younger brother, Bartholomew. And Topcliffe, making one of those rare mistakes which can happen to the most experienced of rack-masters, had gone too far with his torturing, and Bartholomew had died on the rack. It was impossible to bring it home to the man, reflected Mr Secretary, grinding his teeth; as an indispensable official in the service of the Government, Topcliffe had had to be protected, and it had been given out as usual in such cases that the lad had committed suicide.

Well, thought Walsingham, trying to be sensible, and thrusting a hand under the coverlet to seek the comfort of Dearlove and Knave, curled up there side by side, it was no good tormenting oneself with something that was over. It was better to keep his mind fixed on the knowledge that the great 'practice' had achieved its object, that within the next few days the Queen of Scots would be dead and all their troubles over, and that the general public had no suspicion that the Babington Plot had been instigated and nursed by the Government.

He had had little difficulty with the two secretaries, Nau and Curle. For they had always been on bad terms with one another, and they had been most thoroughly frightened before being examined. They had even been taken by Topcliffe on a tour of inspection of his torture-chamber in the bowels of the White Tower, and had emerged ashen-faced and shaking; though if they had had their wits about them they might have realized that, neither being an English subject, torture could not be used.

Nau had been examined first, and had succumbed fairly easily. Terrified by hearing of the criminal carelessness of Babington in not burning the fatal letter from Mary (it had been found, the Frenchman was told, in Babington's lodging after his arrest), his only desire had been to throw the blame of the writing of it on to Mary herself. He had urged her again and again, he cried, not to answer Babington's treasonable letter; Monsieur Curle could bear him witness that he had. But was this, they had demanded, an exact decipherment of the Queen of Scots' answer? and they had read out to him Phelippes' decipherment with the forged interpolations. He had hesitated; there were certain phrases in it which sounded unfamiliar; but it was a long while since it had been written, he had a little difficulty with the English tongue, and it was not he who had written the letter; all he had done was to take notes for it as dictated by his mistress.

Mr Babington, they had told him, had attested this letter as a true decipherment; and if Monsieur Nau would do the same, then he should have permission to return to his native France, with, possibly, a little something by way of reward. So that had been the end of Nau.

Curle had proved a trifle more difficult. He had been badly shaken when confronted by the original letter from his mistress, as enciphered by himself, for he could not deny it was his (and indeed it was; Burghley's foresight in preserving the original for just such an occasion had been rewarded; Curle *had* put a certain secret mark on the encipherment, by which he would know it again). But with Scots' obstinacy he had demanded that he be allowed to check the encipherment with this decipherment they had shown him; it was so long a letter, he insisted, two months had elapsed since he had written it, he could not swear that the decipherment was exact unless he checked it word for word with the original. They had shown him Babington's signed 'confessions' and Nau's attestation; but even then a certain amount of pressure had had to be brought upon Curle before grudgingly he had consented to attest that he had enciphered 'the like, or what I think to be the like'.

It was enough. Both secretaries had been given (really given on this occasion, Burghley had seen to that) pensions by her Majesty as a reward for 'their free and frank confessions' of their mistress' guilt, and the one bundled off to Scotland, the other to France. Nothing remained but to make a little bonfire of such of the original and forged letters, the drafts and the minutes found at Chartley, as had either served their turn or might prove embarrassing some day if retained, and to try the Queen of Scots, basing the charge against her upon the forged interpolations in her correspondence with Babington.

She had put up a spirited defence, thought Mr Secretary, forcing himself to be just. (Naturally she had not been allowed counsel.) She had persisted in her denial that she had ever plotted against the life of Elizabeth, or ever received a suggestion of it from Babington.

"If he or others affirm it," the clear, composed voice had cried, "I protest that it is false. Why was he put to death without being brought face to face with me, so that I might have been convicted by his testimony if I were guilty of what is laid to my charge?"

Walsingham could see her now, her frame so feeble that she had had to be carried into the Great Hall of Fotheringay, but regal in her black velvet and gossamer veil, her demeanour majestic, her worn face still beautiful and serene, her glance utterly fearless as it moved from one to another of the thirty-six hostile faces of the peers who had conducted this farce of a trial.

"Nay," she had cried, waving away Mr Phelippes' skilful forgeries, "what security have I that these are mine? Think you Mr Secretary," she had added, turning her large hazel eyes upon him, "that I am ignorant of your device used so craftily against me? How can I be assured that you have not counterfeited my ciphers to bring me to my death?"

It had been a shot in the dark, but a shot that had gone home. Furious, Walsingham had sprung to his feet and demanded that her words be stricken from the record; but the clear voice had interrupted, contemptuously sweeping him aside.

"I do not deny that I have longed for liberty, and earnestly laboured to procure it – nature impelled me so to do. But I call God to witness that I never conspired against the life of the Queen of England. I have written to my friends to assist me to escape from the miserable prisons in which, despite her pledge of love and protection she sent to me ere I came into England, she has kept me for nineteen years. But I never wrote the letter you pretend, nor would I have done it to purchase a crown."

Wincing with the pain of his boil, Mr Secretary turned over in bed, wishing to God he could erase from his mind the echo of that clear and fearless voice. For a monstrous and intolerable suspicion nagged at him that, for all the success of his great 'practice', his victim, the Queen of Scots, had had the last word.

In a room in Fotheringay Castle, Sir Amias Paulet was writing one of his long, rambling letters to Mr Secretary. He would be very grateful to hear when the execution of 'this lady' was to take place; every day's delay meant more expense for her Majesty in maintaining so large a household; and though there were no 'honest men' in the vicinity (he heavily underlined the word 'honest' to make it clear that he was being sarcastic), prices were high enough. Moreover he himself was in a continual state of uncertainty as to how much provision to order; and for how long wages must be paid.

Then he must tell Mr Secretary of his recent dealings with 'this lady'. He had many enemies; all sorts of false reports about his conduct might be circulated; it was only fair to himself to explain, in minutest detail, why he had just removed her cloth of estate. He had never approved of her being permitted these royal dignities, but he had bowed to authority in the matter. Now, however, when in a manner of speaking she was already a dead woman, in his simple opinion it had been his duty to take these trappings from her.

He had visited 'this lady' yesterday, he wrote, and in order to bring home to her her situation, he had remained covered in her presence. He had informed her that he had ordered the removal of her billiard-table, since she could have no further use for such pastimes. She had answered that she had never used it, and indeed had other occupations now.

> I told her likewise, Madam, your steward must no longer carry his white rod before you when you go to dinner, for it is a privilege sacred to royalty, and you are not now entitled to such honours. At which she smiled. Then I requested her, with moderation, that she order her servants to take down her cloth of estate beneath which she is used to sit both at dinner and at supper and at all times when I visit her. She told me that I might bid them do it if I pleased, but that she could not so betray her royal rights. Thereupon I called in her Yeomen of the Wardrobe and bid them take it down, and upon their insolent refusal I was forced to summon mine own servants to perform this duty.

Sir Amias paused, and sucked his large, square teeth. He was not by nature a spiteful man, but a secret humiliation filled him with venom now.

> She continueth in her former wicked and wilful disposition, no outward sign of repentance, no

acknowledgement of her fault, no craving of pardon, no mention of desire of life; so that it may be feared that as she has lived, so she will die, and I pray God that the ignorant Popish priest, her almoner, be not permitted to have access to her any more (though she wearies me with petitions that he might come at her), it being in my simple opinion very like that he would increase in her her stubbornness in her errors in matters of religion. She swears that if she perceives him in the crowd at her death, she will kneel before them all for his benediction.

"Pah!" exclaimed Sir Amias aloud, throwing down his quill.

And whether he would or no, he saw in his mind's eye that which he had seen earlier this morning when he had gone to gloat upon the apartments of the condemned woman, stripped of the outward signs of her regality. Where the cloth of estate with its quarterings, the Lion of Scotland, the Cross of Lorraine, the Lilies of France, had hung above the dais, he had seen her placing a crucifix, the Body stripped, the Head crowned with thorns. She had turned and looked him straight in the eyes, her own bright with quiet triumph.

"You have taken away the dignities bestowed upon me by God and man," said the Queen of Scots, "but you shall not deprive me of my crucified Saviour."

Jane Lane

A Call of Trumpets

Civil war rages in England, rendering it a minefield of corruption and conflict. Town and country are besieged. Through the complex interlocking of England's turmoil with that of a king, Jane Lane brings to life some amazing characters in the court of Charles I. This is the story both of Charles' adored wife whose indiscretions prove disastrous, and of the King's nephew, Rupert, a rash, arrogant soldier whose actions lead to tragedy and his uncle's final downfall.

His Fight Is Ours

His Fight Is Ours follows the traumatic trials of MacIain, a Highland Chieftain of the clan Donald, as he leads his people in the second Jacobite rising on behalf of James Stuart, the Old Pretender. The battle to restore the king to his rightful throne is portrayed here in this absorbing historical escapade, which highlights all the beauty and romance of Highland life. Jane Lane presents a dazzling, picaresque story of the problems facing MacIain as leader of a proud, ancient race, and his struggles against injustice and the violent infamy of oppression.

JANE LANE

SOW THE TEMPEST

Jane Lane gives a deft and masterful retelling of the volatile and tragic story surrounding Henry VIII, a handsome, passionate, arrogant king. England is abuzz with talk of a golden era when Henry VIII ascends to the throne. But possessed by an immature will, Henry will stop at nothing to get what he wants and when Ann Boleyn enters his life, Henry is determined to have her whatever the costs. Ultimately his wishes prove disastrous for a nation, its Faith, and all those who oppose the royal desire.

A SUMMER STORM

Conflict and destiny abound as King Richard II, a chivalrous, romantic and idealist monarch, courts his beloved Anne of Bohemia. In the background, the swirling rage of the Peasants' Revolt of 1381 threatens to topple London as the tides of farmers, labourers and charismatic rebel hearts flood the city. This tense, powerful historical romance leads the reader from bubbling discord to doomed love all at the turn of a page.

Jane Lane

Thunder on St Paul's Day

London is gripped by mass hysteria as Titus Oates uncovers the Popish Plot, and a gentle English family gets caught up in the terrors of trial and accusation when Oates points the finger of blame. The villainous Oates adds fuel to the fire of an angry mob with his sham plot, leaving innocence to face a bullying judge and an intimidated jury. Only one small boy may save the family in this moving tale of courage pitted against treachery.

A Wind Through the Heather

A Wind Through the Heather is a poignant, tragic story based on the Highland Clearances where thousands of farmers were driven from their homes by tyrannical and greedy landowners. Introducing the Macleods, Jane Lane recreates the shameful past suffered by an innocent family who lived to cross the Atlantic and find a new home. This wistful, historical novel focuses on the atrocities so many bravely faced and reveals how adversities were overcome.